Stop thinking of her. You must find out how much she knows and why she lied.

Dizzy, gasping for breath, Katrine stumbled, nearly falling into him. He reached for her, finding through the shapeless wool where the curve of her hip melted into her waist. Steadying her, he pulled her close, until the wool of her dress flowed over his legs.

Desire catapulted through him.

She swayed with him, gently as a banner in the breeze, so slight beneath her shapeless sack that she might blow away.

Deceiver. Her slender form sheaths a will of iron.

And yet, she made him yearn for things long forbidden.

* * *

Innocence Unveiled
Harlequin® Historical #902—June 2008

BLYTHE GIFFORD
Innocence Unveiled

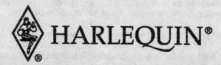

HARLEQUIN®

TORONTO • NEW YORK • LONDON
AMSTERDAM • PARIS • SYDNEY • HAMBURG
STOCKHOLM • ATHENS • TOKYO • MILAN • MADRID
PRAGUE • WARSAW • BUDAPEST • AUCKLAND

ISBN-13: 978-0-373-29502-9
ISBN-10:   0-373-29502-2

INNOCENCE UNVEILED

DON'T MISS THESE OTHER
NOVELS AVAILABLE NOW:

#899 THE LAST RAKE IN LONDON—Nicola Cornick

Dangerous Jack Kestrel was the most sinfully sensual rogue
she'd ever met, and the wicked glint in his eyes promised he'd
take care of satisfying Sally's *every* need....
Watch as the last rake in London meets his match!

#900 AN IMPETUOUS ABDUCTION—
Patricia Frances Rowell

Persephone had stumbled into danger and the only way to
protect her was to abduct her! But what would Leo's beautiful
prisoner do when he revealed his true identity?
*Don't miss Patricia Frances Rowell's unique blend of passion
spiced with danger!*

#901 KIDNAPPED BY THE COWBOY—Pam Crooks

TJ Grier was determined to clear his name, even if
his actions might cost him the woman he loved!
Fall in love with Pam Crooks's honorable cowboy!

Author Note

In the fourteenth century, before the great war between England and France that lasted one hundred years, an embassy was sent from England to the Low Countries to gain allies for the King. The chroniclers tell us the delegation included a group of knights who wore eye patches and refused to speak until they had performed some valiant deed of arms against the French.

I could see these fifty knights, riding their horses off the cogs and onto the beach, then gathering for their ceremonial entry into the city. But in my vision, one of them took off his eye patch and rode away alone.

This is his story.

For Phyllis, a woman who has never lacked passion or courage.

To C. Dx4

And with thanks to Linda Fildew, who shared my vision for the story and made it better, and Lindsay Longford, who has liked it every time I've rewritten it.

Chapter One

Flanders, The Low Countries—Spring 1337

Shadows hid the stranger's face, but over the pounding of her heart, Katrine heard the threat in his voice, as casual as a shrug.

'You decide,' he said. 'I can get you the wool you need, but if you let the opportunity pass…' the slight lift of his shoulders blocked the morning sun streaming into her weaving room '…there are many other willing buyers.'

'Every weaver in Ghent is willing.' Katrine fought the tremble in her tongue.

It was no secret. Deprived of the wool that was its life-blood, this city of clothmakers was starving. So when a stranger had claimed he could find fleece for her looms, she had recklessly agreed to listen. He didn't need her, but she needed his wool. Desperately.

Arms crossed, the smuggler leaned against the wall, filling the space as if he owned it. 'Decide, mistress. Deal with me or go hungry.'

Backed against the loom, she felt the wooden upright press against her spine like a martyr's stake. She stroked the taut warp threads for comfort. They quivered beneath her fingers. Looking up, she tried to read his eyes, but the sun cast him in darkness. She must not yield too easily, or she'd not be able to bargain at all.

'Your voice does not carry the accent of Ghent.' She knew nothing about the man. Not even his name. 'Where is your home?'

A shaft of sunlight picked up a reddish strand in his chestnut hair. He did not speak at first, and she wondered whether he had heard her. 'I was born in Brabant,' he said, finally.

His answer seemed safe enough. The neighbouring duchy was one of half-a-dozen fiefdoms clustered near the channel between England and France. She should at least discover what goods he offered.

Fingers hidden in the folds of her skirt, she pinched the fabric, taking comfort in the even weave. 'My mark appears on only the finest cloth. I buy with care. Is this wool of yours English or Spanish?'

'English.'

'Good.' Clasping her fingers in front of her, she paced as if considering her choices. Best not to ask how he would come by it. The English king had embargoed all shipments to Flanders for the last nine months. 'Where were the sheep raised? I prefer Cistercian-raised flocks from Tintern Abbey, though I will accept Yorkshire fleece.'

'Accept?' Amusement coloured his voice. 'You will accept whatever I bring you. You have no choice.'

Sweet Saint Catherine, what shall I do?

She had bargained with the larger cloth houses for any fleece they would spare. She had scrambled for the poor stuff grown on the backs of Flemish sheep. She had even directed her weavers to make a looser weave, hoping that the fullers, cleaning and beating the cloth to finish it, could thicken the final product.

She had no tricks left.

She had begged her unsympathetic uncle for help, but she feared, unless she trusted this mysterious stranger, there would be no business remaining if—no, *when*—her father returned.

At least the stranger's hands, large, with long, strong fingers, looked reliable, even familiar.

'How much can you get?' she asked.

'Maybe one sack.'

'A weaver will use that in a week,' Katrine scoffed, to cover her disappointment.

He did not move from his comfortable slouch. 'One sack is one sack more than you have at the moment.'

She squeezed prayerful fingers. 'What is your price? *If* I agree.'

'Twenty-five gold livres per sack. In advance.'

'Fifteen.' With good negotiation, the pouch of gold her father had left might pay for three sacks. 'On delivery.' She gritted her teeth behind a stone-saint smile.

'Twenty-eight.'

Her smile shattered. 'You said twenty-five before.'

'I'll say thirty tomorrow, if I please. Don't try to bargain with me, mistress. You have nothing to bargain with.'

The sunlight shifted and revealed his eyes for the first time, the dusky blue of indigo dyed over grey wool. One eye hovered on the edge of a wink.

'Or maybe,' he said, softly, 'you do.'

Something more than fear burned her cheeks and chilled her fingers. Something that had to do with him.

Stifling her body's betrayal, she folded her arms, mimicking his stance. 'I bargain only with gold. I want the wool, but I have another source.' She trusted her uncle little more than she trusted this stranger, but she would not give him the power of that knowledge. The man already had the advantage. 'If your offer is better, I will take three sacks and pay *twenty* each—ten in advance, the rest on delivery. If you want more…' she hesitated '…if you want more money than that, find one of your other willing buyers.'

'It does not matter what you say. It is your husband who will decide.'

Her hand flew to the wimple hiding her red hair. The married woman's headdress was one of the little lies of her life, so much a part of her she had forgotten it would signal a husband who ruled her every action. 'I have been given authority in this matter.'

In her father's absence, the drapers' guild had allowed her to conduct his affairs, but she was reaching the limits of their regulations. And their patience.

She waited for him to turn away, as had so many who refused to deal with a woman. Yet when the smuggler spoke, respect tinged his words. 'You bargain like a man, mistress. I suspect you run your business well.'

'I do.' She willed her tongue to silence, waiting for his answer. Outside, the sign painted with the trademark of the four-petalled Daisy creaked in the breeze.

He barely moved his chin to nod. 'We are agreed.'

Her sigh of relief slipped out without disguise. 'Agreed *if* my other source does not better your offer.' Now, she had an option if her uncle failed her. 'You will have my answer by the end of the day.'

'See that I do.' The respect, if she had heard it, had fled

his voice. 'I will not wait on your whim when there are others eager to buy.'

'If I tell you yes, when will I see my wool?'

He shrugged. 'I will stay here while I make arrangements.'

'Here?' She had been mad to deal with a stranger. Already he was changing the bargain.

'Unless you want our business on the Council's agenda. Any hosteller will be glad to collect their coin for reporting my every move.'

She could not argue. England and France were near war. The town was swarming with suspicion. An innkeeper would notice a tall, blue-eyed man speaking accented Flemish. 'I am paying you twenty livres for the wool. What will you pay me for the lodging?'

No shadow of surprise crossed the deep blue moat of his eyes. 'Are you re-opening negotiations?'

'You were the one who did that.' Her tart words made her feel in control again. 'If you stay, your room will cost you five pence a week and I'll provide no board. Take a pallet on the third floor,' she said, vaguely uneasy at the thought of him sleeping under her roof.

He frowned. 'With the apprentices?'

'They left months ago.' No need to lie. He'd learn that soon enough.

'No apprentices? How do you operate a draper business?' He spoke as though he already knew her answer.

She sighed. 'Without wool, there has been little business.' Instead of being stacked with red, green and blue woollen cloth bearing the Mark of the Daisy, Katrine's shelves were bare.

Leaning over, he lifted his sack and slung it across his shoulder without effort. Strong arms, then, and a light load. 'So, what will you make with this wool of yours?'

Anything would sell these days, but deep blue would fetch a good price. Indigo dyed over grey wool…

He watched her with a half-smile. The thread of her thoughts unravelled. His glance seemed to expose her secrets while sharing none of his own.

'Indigo-dyed worsted,' she said crisply. 'The market hasn't seen its like since before Christmas and it should fetch at least fifty florins. If, that is, you bring me wool worth weaving.'

'Whatever I bring, you'll pay for.'

She bridled. 'Of course. I'm an honest woman.'

'So you say.' Walking past her towards the stairs, he paused beside the loom. His fingers stumbled as he plucked the threads, the first awkward gesture he had made. 'This is important to you, isn't it?' he said, not looking up.

I leave it in your hands, daughter. Guard it well.

'It is my life.'

He scrutinised her wordlessly, as if gauging what kind of a life it was. She forced herself to remain still, hoping he saw a trustworthy guild wife. He must not suspect who she really was.

The midday bell tolled, breaking the stillness.

'I must go.' Her uncle would be home soon for the main meal. If he had spoken to the Count about her wool, she might be able to send this smuggler on his way. 'I'll be back before the mid-afternoon bell. Be here when I return.'

He raised his eyebrows and laughed. 'Do you order your weavers about so, mistress?'

'When they need it.' She gave him a final assessing glance as she opened the door, reluctant to leave him there alone. 'How do I know I can trust you?'

One corner of his mouth curved into a parody of a smile. 'You don't.'

Saint Catherine, save me from my foolishness. I know nothing about him, yet he called me by name when he entered the shop.

'At least tell me what you are called.'

'Renard.'

'Like the fox?' Everyone knew the tales of the irreverent trickster Renard the Fox. Their recitation was an evening's entertainment.

This time, he definitely winked. 'Exactly.'

As she closed the door, the words of the familiar tale echoed in her head. 'Renard knows many tricks and ruses. He cheats at any time he chooses.'

High Gate Street was quieter than usual as families gathered behind closed doors for the midday meal. Many avoided the streets these days. Without wool, there was no work. Journeymen, even proud master weavers, lurked on corners, begging, or threatening, for bread or coin.

She lifted the cloth swaddling her hair to let a breeze tickle the top of her head. Then, hair-hidden again, eyes down, she walked with controlled, deferential steps towards home.

You bargain like a man.

Even a stranger could see her failings.

She did not act as a woman should. Now that her father was gone, her uncle told her that often enough. Woman was born weak and sinful. Only by obedience and submission could she attain perfection—leaving home only to go to church, keeping her distance from all men except her kin—

Katrine sighed, suddenly aware that her steps had lengthened to a stride and she had looked the silversmith directly in the eye and said good day.

Starting again with a measured tread, she looked at the ground to avoid meeting any other man's eye.

It was the world outside her shop that confined her. Within the walls of the weaving room, she was free. But now, a man had invaded her sanctuary and created doubt in the only place she had ever felt certain.

Yet she prayed he would still be there when she returned.

Twenty gold livres, Renard thought, as he watched Katrine walk towards Fish Market Square. He should have forced her to thirty.

Her first steps were small and mincing, but before he lost sight of her, she was striding down the street so confidently that he wondered whether she really did have another source for the wool.

He kneaded the tight muscles between his neck and shoulders and shrugged off his chagrin at the bargain he had struck. What did he care about the price of wool he would never deliver? He could have bested her, had he chosen.

He was the expert negotiator. Always in control, he could hear the nearly indiscernible hesitation in his opponent's voice that meant he had pushed his rival to the edge, found his weakness, identified what he—or she—most feared to lose. With the power of that knowledge, Renard could complete any bargain on his own terms.

It was a talent the King had used freely over the years.

And she was no challenge at all. A wisp of a thing, breasts and hips, if any, disguised by a shapeless shroud of wool. Not the kind of woman to tempt a man.

If he were a man to be tempted.

Startled to find himself gazing down a street now empty of her, Renard turned from the window to climb the stairs, noting the creak in the third step so he could avoid it later. The house was as quiet as he had anticipated after watching it for three days. In fact, it seemed as if no one lived here at all.

He peered into a sleeping room at the top of the first flight, dusty with disuse, wondering idly where she slept. He would not be here long enough for that to matter.

On the third floor, he ducked as his shoulders threatened to brush the steeply sloping ceiling and dropped his small sack under the eaves. It held little. A fresh tunic. A cloak. A scrap of red silk and a well-worn piece of wool safely hidden at the bottom.

Cistercian wool. What the devil was the difference?

Taking care not be seen, he peered out of the small window overlooking the back garden and gauged the distance to the cherry tree. It was a slender escape route, but it was hidden from public view. He picked up his sack, grabbed a branch of the tree, and eased himself to the ground.

Be here, she had ordered, as if he would wait on a weaving woman's convenience.

She cared too much, almost burned with it. Soft brown eyes glowing with need, body rigid with fear he would refuse, she acted as if a few sacks of wool were the difference between life and death.

Such feelings led to dangerous mistakes. He should have had the advantage. He should have been able to get fifty livres.

Instead, he had let her win with a fabrication about another source. Well, he got what he wanted. Let her think she would be seeing wool at twenty livres a sack.

By the time she returned, he would be gone, leaving one little Flemish draper waiting a very long time for her wool.

The smell of fish stew greeted Katrine as she opened the door to the snug town house. Until her uncle had usurped her father's house and the income that paid for it, Katrine had loved its whitewashed walls and tiled fireplaces. Now, since the Baron preferred it to the dank stone corridors of his own castle, the house no longer felt like her home.

The servant girl, Merkin, looked up from laying the plates out on the high table and wiggled her fingers in greeting. 'Did you hear, milady? An English bishop is coming to make peace with the Count.'

Peace. The very word made her breathless with hope.

The English King and the French King were snarling over the throne of France like dogs over a bone. Each had spent months trying to force Flanders to his side. First, the English King stopped wool shipments. The Flemish Count had retaliated by jailing the English in Flanders. Then King Edward imprisoned all Flemings unfortunate enough to be in London.

Including her father.

Now, Count and commoners were at an impasse. The Count remained loyal to French Philip. The people, dependent on English wool, preferred English Edward.

An agreement with England would end the struggle and bring her father home. 'When does he arrive?'

'I don't know,' Merkin said, 'but I heard there's forty-nine English bachelor knights with him.'

'Forty-nine?' *An odd number.* 'Why not fifty?'

'I don't know, milady, but every blessed one is wearing a red silk eyepatch day and night.'

Katrine shook her head. 'How can a knight fight with only one eye?'

'Not only can't they see, but they don't talk.' Merkin's voice dropped to a conspiratorial whisper. 'I heard they vowed to their ladies that they would wear the eyepatches and speak to no one until they had performed some deeds of arms against the French.' A sigh escaped her grin. 'Isn't that romantic?'

'Romantic?' Katrine sank on to the bench, cradling her forehead in her hand. At sixteen, Merkin still had dreamy notions in her usually level head. 'My father is in prison, my coffers are empty, England and France are near war, and the English have nothing better to do than gallop the countryside wearing real eyepatches and imaginary gags?' Unseemly laughter spilled over her anger. 'And my uncle harps on the lunacy of women!'

'Ah, there you are.' Her aunt Matilda squinted in the direction of Katrine's laughter as she entered the room. Matilda's weak eyes could barely see what was before her nose. Her pale forehead was lined from years of trying to focus on things beyond her scope. 'We were worried. How many times have we told you not to be on the streets without an escort?'

Every day for nine months, Katrine thought, sending yet another silent prayer to Saint Catherine for forgiveness. At least her name saint had always listened to a motherless child. 'Without apprentices, it is all for me to do.'

Let her aunt think she left the house only from necessity. The woman would hear no ill spoken of her husband.

'Well, I'm glad you're back, Catherine.' Her aunt spoke the French of the nobility and always called her 'Catherine' instead of the Flemish 'Katrine'. 'I need you to tell the girl that the Baron did not like the wine she bought yesterday and she must always buy Gascon wine in the future.'

'The girl's name is Merkin,' Katrine said, before she translated, softening the rebuff as she did. Her aunt spoke the Flemish of the workers as little as possible, a blessing, since she did not speak it well. Merkin rolled her eyes heavenwards, muttering something that sounded like 'no wool means no wine'.

Katrine's lips twitched towards a smile. 'What was that, Merkin?'

The front door swung open and hit the wall with a dull thump. Katrine's smile died. Charles, Baron de Gravere, was home.

'English bastards think loyalty can be bought,' her uncle shouted as his men swarmed in behind him towards the watered wine set out for the main meal.

Her aunt scurried to help as the squire unbuckled the Baron's sword belt. Impatient at Matilda's slow fingers worrying the knot holding his cloak, he jerked it, breaking the tie for her to sew again, and let the garment drop on to the floor. Matilda stooped to pick it up.

'We leave for Gravere today,' he said, sitting at the table. 'The castle must be in readiness should the English actually have the stomach for a fight.'

Katrine's appetite fled. 'I thought they came to speak of peace.'

'Pah! This English Edward acts like a merchant, not a king.' Her uncle drained his goblet and slammed it down on the table for his wife to fill. The Baron's wine was never watered. 'He thinks the Count will break his God-given oath of fealty to King Philip for English gold.'

If the Count's belly were as empty as those of his subjects, he certainly would. She had heard her uncle admire the Count's loyalty to the French *fleur-de-lys* too often. The man cared more for fealty than his people's stomachs.

A king was necessary, of course. You gave allegiance; he gave protection. Such loyalty was a luxury of the nobility and, she was beginning to think, a foolish one. While the lords battled, the burghers suffered. What did it matter to the dyers who claimed France's crown? Why should the weavers care whether the throne passed through the daughter or the son? Cold winters grew thick wool all the same.

Her uncle waved his goblet. 'Here's to Philip of Valois. Now and for ever King of France.'

The men at arms, mouths full, echoed 'Valois' without looking up.

Katrine rested her head on cold hands. Deeds of arms, the English promised. Flanders's soil would be soaked with blood as red as their eyepatches.

And she might never see her father again.

'Is there word of my father? Do they want a ransom?'

'No one cares about him now,' he said.

Least of all you. 'Then what about my wool? Can the Count get some from France?' It would be poor stuff, but she could weave it.

He filled his spoon with fish and vegetables. 'I didn't ask.'

'You promised!' Her words exploded. The men at the closest table looked up. She lowered her voice. 'I cannot make cloth without wool,' Katrine said, angry at the Count, at the French, at the English, at all of them who cared for affairs of state instead of people's lives. 'The Count is bad for business.'

'Catherine, hush. If anyone heard you, you might be imprisoned.' Aunt Matilda peered anxiously at the knights breaking bread over their trenchers. 'We all might be imprisoned.'

'No one cares what she thinks,' her uncle said with a shrug. 'Her hair bears the mark of the Devil. She speaks French with a Flemish accent and has calluses on her fingers. No man of noble blood will soil himself with her.'

She winced at his words. He made her ashamed to be alive.

She pushed the pain away. 'All the more reason for me to tend to my weaving.' There, at least, she could do something of value.

'Bad enough that my brother violated the God-given order of things, wielding scissors instead of the sword he was born to.' At first, the family had tolerated her father's dabbling in the cloth trade. He was a younger son and gold was always welcome. But with the gold and her father gone, her uncle unleashed his true feelings. 'He let you grow up like the spawn of that weaver instead of a noblewoman.'

'That weaver had a name.' Giles de Vos, her father's partner, had died childless two years ago and left his share to her. She missed him almost as much as she missed her father. 'You welcomed Uncle Giles into your house as long as our looms turned wool into gold.'

Her uncle's temper flared like a poked fire, lifting him out of his seat. 'Don't call him that! He was a common burgher. *I* am your uncle.'

She stood to face him, no longer caring who heard. 'I wish I shared his blood instead of yours.'

'Enough!' He raised his fist.

Her aunt's hand blocked it. 'Mind your tongue, Catherine. Apologise.'

His hand wavered. No mealtime noises drifted up from the retainers' table.

'I'm sorry I offended,' she said, to buy time. If only she could be like the smuggler, who let no word pass his lips before considering it. 'I did not think before speaking.'

'Now gather your things,' her aunt said. 'You heard your uncle. We leave this afternoon.'

Ducking her head, she held her tongue, glad to escape the room. She must leave the house unseen and return to the shop and the secretive stranger who was her last hope.

She sent up a prayer to the saint that he was still there.

Chapter Two

Renard hurried along the towpath, easily passing an uncomplaining ass pulling a boat with lowered mast beneath one of the city's innumerable bridges. It was different, this city of weavers, with its stairstep rooflines and endless waterways. He missed the air of England.

The goldsmith who opened the door of the stone house facing the canal looked both ways before letting him in. 'You leave today?' he asked.

'Tomorrow,' Renard replied, as he mounted the stairs to the goldsmith's private solar.

He sympathised with the man's nervousness. It took courage to harbour an English merchant in disguise.

It would have taken more had he known he was hosting a king.

But as Renard looked at King Edward, standing at the window, he was amazed the goldsmith had not guessed. Touched by sunlight, his hair glowed like a golden halo painted on a saint. Edward Plantagenet had never needed to seek his place in the sun. The sun had sought him out. Straight, strong, vigorous—surely no man had ever looked more like a king.

Many whispered that Edward and Renard could pass for brothers, both tall, blue-eyed, energetic young warriors. But Edward's blond good looks and restless, expansive energy blazed like noonday while Renard's chestnut-brown hair, self-contained air and mysterious past suggested the shadows of sunset.

Renard inclined his neck, a pale imitation of a bow. 'Your Grace.'

'Ah, there you are. What have you found?' Edward looked as if he needed good news.

With the King's permission, Renard poured some wine for himself. 'There is no wool in the city, your Grace. Every weaver listened to my offer. I could empty our warehouse in Brussels.' Or could if he had taken any coin for his promises. 'The people support you. Only the nobles resist.'

Renard had opposed Edward's wild trip from the start, but the King had insisted on sneaking ashore with the official embassy to assess the situation personally. Renard had come in advance and in disguise to put his rusty Flemish to work on behalf of his king.

Edward tightened his grip on his goblet. 'Perhaps *I* should meet with the Count.'

Renard shook his head. 'Better if no one knows you are here.'

'Surely the Bishop can persuade him. He has brought three others to my side already. Only Brabant and Flanders remain.'

Renard wagered that the other duchies supported the King because they were related to Queen Philippa, not because of the Bishop's persuasive powers, but he held his tongue.

'I leave for Brabant tomorrow.' Renard had requested that assignment. It would force him to face his past.

Edward paced the room, tapping his finger against his wine goblet. 'I *must* have Flanders. Unless our trade resumes quickly, my wool growers will be just as unhappy as the Count's weavers.' He looked at Renard, narrowing his eyes. 'Brabant can wait. Stay here.'

'But you need the Duke's support, too.' Renard kept his voice calm, but he was weary of living at the King's whim. Edward knew full well that Renard's trip to Brabant was about more than diplomacy.

'Yes, and I trust you'll produce it, but if the Bishop fails here, I need an alternative. The citizens of Flanders have risen against the French before. If the Count refuses an alliance, you must create a revolt among the workers that will force him to my side.'

Renard swallowed his resentment. The King never controlled the quicksilver temperament they shared. Renard did. 'I'm not sure I could pass as a flat-footed wool stomper to rally the rabble.' Though living disguised among the artisans could hardly be more difficult than smuggling a king in and out of Flanders.

Edward sat down in a high-backed wooden chair near the fireplace. Suddenly, it looked like a throne. 'I don't expect you to rouse the ryffe and raffe personally. Find someone else who will.'

Renard bowed and sank into the chair opposite his liege, hiding a sigh. The King asked Renard to produce an uprising as if he were ordering a suit of chainmail. 'I serve, your Grace.'

'Just make sure the embargo holds. The longer they go without wool, the better for my cause. This should only take a few weeks, then Brabant and then you can come home.'

He longed for home, though he had nothing to return to:

no family, no land, nothing that the King did not give. There had been talk of marriage, but as an illegitimate son, Renard had little to bequeath to a legitimate one.

Edward clasped his shoulder. 'I need Flanders, whether you or the Bishop get it for me, but when you succeed, I'll reward you with something worthy of all you have done. Something like…' His face lit with a new idea. 'Bishop! That's it!' He slapped the arm of the chair. 'Bring me Flanders and I'll make you a bishop.'

Bishop.

Renard's heart beat in his ears and blood surged through his arms as if he had just been called to battle, but years of repressing his responses served him well. The reward was everything he could have hoped for. A secure position of power, safe from the temptations of the flesh. Once given, even a king could not take it away.

'You honour me, your Grace.'

The King smiled. 'Of course I do. Can't run the country without money from the Church. Too many of them think their pope is more important than their king. I need bishops I can depend on.'

But as a bishop, Renard's power and position would no longer depend on the King. 'It will not be easy, your Grace.' The King could propose a bishop, but the Pope must confirm him. 'I am not yet of an age to be a bishop.'

Edward waved away the protest. 'Ridiculous rule. I assumed the crown at fifteen. You can be bishop before thirty.'

'And I have not led a life of celibate contemplation.'

Edward rose, impatient, and paced again. 'Neither have any of the bishops I know, except perhaps Stoningham, and I've never quite trusted him.'

At the King's move, Renard rose, more slowly, and leaned against the wall. Even when they were alone, Renard did not sit while his sovereign stood.

'You are no lecher, Renard. In fact, I could use some of your self-control, but there's no need to take up celibacy when you embrace the vows.'

'Nevertheless, I will honour the vows I take.' Unlike some, who broke more than they kept.

Thoughtless lust had brought him into this world without name or position. Renard refused to make the same mistake. Over a lifetime, he had battled passion as if it were a well-mounted enemy. If he could not unhorse his opponent every time, he could usually force him to withdraw from the field. As a bishop, he would be safely removed from temptation.

'Then,' he continued, 'there is the matter of my station.'

The King stopped pacing and turned his piercing blue eyes on Renard. 'I am fully aware that a bastard needs dispensation from the Pope. A letter of recommendation from the Bishop of Clare will solve that.'

He fought the urge to refuse the support of a pompous hypocrite like Henry Billesh, Bishop of Clare. After refusing to support young Edward's ascension to the throne, the man had changed his tune only after the outcome became clear. Renard would never trust him. 'He may be reluctant to write on my behalf.'

The King drained the last of his wine. 'He is a man familiar with human transgression. He'll understand yours.'

This time, he could not hold back the words. 'But the transgression was not mine, your Grace.'

The temper they shared exploded. Edward hurled the goldsmith's best goblet into the fire. Clattering, it bounced on to the hearth, scattering ashes across the floor. 'You presume on our common blood! Do you forget that you possess only what I give you?'

'Never, your Grace.'

Had Renard been born the illegitimate son of a prince, he would have had a place in the shadow of the throne. But he was the son of a princess. So the truth of his birth, and her shame, was a secret only the King shared.

As quickly as clouds passed over the sun, a hearty laugh wiped out Edward's anger and he draped an arm around Renard's shoulders. The laugh meant he forgave Renard's insult. The gesture meant he forgave himself for insulting his cousin.

Smiling, the King reached for his wine goblet, surprised that it was not on the table.

Silently, Renard offered his own.

'You are harsh on those of us who are mere mortals, my friend.' An unusual moment of reflection stilled the King's energy. 'Just once, I would like to see you humbled by passion. You might find the kind of joy I've found with my queen.'

Renard shook his head. There was a reason lust was one of the seven deadly sins. Passion made you powerless as his mother had been when she could not resist—who? That secret, neither of them knew. 'I shall welcome the vows.'

'Be certain, my friend.' Edward clasped his shoulder. 'It is the highest honour I can give, but once bestowed, you will never be Renard again.'

Regret bit him. He had been so intent on controlling his joy, he had not even thanked his childhood friend. Power. Position. It would be everything the secret of his birth had denied him all his life. 'Forgive me, your Grace. There is nothing I want more.'

Nothing, at any rate, that the King had the power to give. The King could award him many things, but he could never acknowledge his royal birthright.

Edward inclined his head and returned to the window, gazing across the canal as if he could see all the way to Paris. 'There is something more I want, Renard, and you are going to make sure I get it.'

Renard silenced the growl of jealousy at the bottom of his heart. Edward already had a crown. Why did he need another?

Yet he knew the answer. Edward wanted his birthright, a birthright denied him because it came through the daughter of a king instead of through the son.

That, Renard could understand.

'Just think, Renard, you'll have a bishop's ring as big as Clare's.' He laughed. 'And you won't have to bow to me any longer!'

Renard smiled for the first time. 'A bishop bows only to the Pope—and to God.'

Now, unable to leave the city as he had planned, Renard knew he could prevail upon the goldsmith no longer. He needed a safe, inconspicuous haven. Perhaps the weaving woman's house would serve. In a crowded city, an empty house would be perfect for a man who wanted to hide his comings and goings. But if he were to stay there, he must learn more of the woman with the tart tongue than the name he'd overheard when he followed her from the Cloth Hall. Her house might prove a sanctuary.

Or a trap.

When Katrine returned to the wool house, no indigo-eyed stranger waited at the window. She searched the counting room, then, frantic, climbed the stairs.

'Renard?'

No one answered her unseemly shouts.

He had threatened to find another buyer. What if he had not waited? On the top floor, Katrine faced a row of straw pallets, long abandoned by apprentices. Had he left his sack here? If so, she could be certain he'd return.

She lifted the first pallet to find only bare wood.

Blinking back angry tears, she kicked aside the next pallet and the next, spewing straw across the planks until the room's disorder matched her mood.

She lifted the last pallet, ready to hurl it out of the window in frustration.

He was her last hope. What would she tell her father if she failed?

Her pounding heart slowed and she caught a breath, knowing straw littered the floor behind her, stable-deep. *Saint Catherine, will I ever master my temper?*

When she turned to clean the mess, she faced the stranger holding a dagger.

He loomed taller than she had remembered, his eyes a darker blue. She had expected to feel relief at his return, but the uncertainty in her stomach felt more like fear. Or excitement. 'So,' she said, lifting her chin, 'the prodigal returns.'

Renard set down his sack and sheathed his dagger, its silver handle catching a glint of the afternoon sun. 'You said I was to guard the house. I thought you were a thief.'

She groaned, looking at the floor, feeling the fool. Had he seen her display of temper? She had no excuse, so she would ignore it and treat him as if he were an errant apprentice. 'I told you to be here when I returned. Where were you?'

The straw crunched as he stepped closer. He towered over her even as he stooped to avoid the rafters.

'I do not recall, mistress, that reporting my whereabouts to you was part of our bargain,' he said, in a tone as sharp as his dagger. 'In fact, we don't yet have a bargain.'

'No,' she said. 'We do not yet have a bargain.'

He reached for her chin with cool, firm fingers, turning her face towards the window, as if to read her by the sun's light. She struggled for a breath.

'Did your other source make you a better offer?'

She blinked, betraying herself.

A lazy wink disguised his emotions. 'Then I take it we are agreed.'

'Yes.' She jerked her chin from his hand and started to put the room to rights.

He knelt beside her and shoved a handful of straw into the first pallet. Astounded that he would humble himself to help, she picked up another pallet and scooped the straw inside.

They worked in silence. She tried to study him, but his face was impassive. What manner of man would help clean up the mess she had created? He deserved some appreciation for that.

'You have my thanks,' she said, when they were done at last. 'Why did you help?'

'If I am to sleep here, I must keep it in order.'

She swallowed. Sleep. Suddenly it seemed much too intimate a word. 'I have changed my mind. It is not safe to harbour you here. You must find other lodging.'

He shook his head. His eyes were implacable. 'You cannot change the contract now. You want your wool, don't you?'

The air around her seemed to crackle like lightning. She was beginning to fear that this wool was going to cost much more than she had bargained for.

'Yes, of course.'

'Then let's break bread together to seal our agreement,' he said.

'I told you. I offer no board.' The cupboards were bare.

A smile flickered across his face. 'I bought my own. It seems only right to share.' He paused, holding her eyes with his. 'Please.'

Suspicious, her tongue curved around 'no', but her stomach growled. She had eaten nothing of the main meal. Maybe the tickle she felt was neither fear nor excitement, but hunger.

She nodded.

Finished with the pallets, she led the way downstairs. He settled in front of the fireplace, leaning on one elbow, long legs stretched across the floor, and set out a loaf of bread, a hunk of cheese, and some beer as if the hearth were his own. 'Join me.'

She sank to the floor, skirt flaring around her. She must put this man on the defensive or he would take over. 'Have you any oranges?' She smiled, waiting for his answer. Oranges were dear in good times. In bad, they would be precious as wool.

His lips twitched. 'There is an embargo, you know.'

Pulling out his eating knife, he cut a slice of the cheese and placed it carefully on the crust of bread. Not even that was done by chance.

'You disappoint me. I would expect an expert smuggler to supply whatever I want, no matter how costly.'

'Bread and cheese will have to serve.'

She reached for the bread and touched his fingers instead.

Her glance tangled in his. Neither moved. Neither spoke. Warmth from his fingers crept up her arm, weaving them together. Something sweet and weak happened inside her.

Flushed with shame, she snatched her hand back and popped the bread and cheese in her mouth. He took a swig of the beer, then handed it to her. She sipped it to wash down the cheese, then tried to hide her surprise. He might be a stranger, but he had found the best brewer in the quarter quickly enough.

What manner of man had she allowed under her roof? If she were not more careful, she might lose her coin and more.

'Tell me of yourself, Renard. You must share our Count's allegiance to King Philip to go to such lengths to overcome the English embargo.'

'Kings are nothing to me,' he said finally. An upraised eyebrow teased his face. 'What, mistress, are they to you?'

Her gaze travelled over the familiar room. A lonely grey cloud of coarse Flemish fleece floated on one woven basket handle. Hooks were bare instead of piled with hanks of carded wool ready to sell to the spinsters. Empty shelves should have been stacked with ells of cloth ready for market.

She had a sudden, fierce desire for him to see it as it was supposed to be—busy, bustling, shelves piled high with a rainbow of fine woven woollens.

'As you can see,' she said, finally, 'this shop has been one of their battlegrounds.'

'A battleground? With whose forces do you fight? Valois or Plantagenet? Philip's or Edward's?'

She ignored his question, as he had hers, steeling herself this time not to fear silence. The more she talked, the more lies she had to tell. Nibbling her cheese, she glanced at him from the corner of her eye. 'I cannot fight. I am only a woman, not a *chevalier.*'

'There are many ways to fight a war,' he answered.

His words gave her pause. How did he fight?

And for whom?

'This husband of yours, for example,' he continued. 'Where is he?'

Husband. Where is my husband? She took a bite of cheese, trying to think. Aunt Matilda was right. She should be mindful of her tongue. She was creating too many lies to count. She should never have left the man here alone. If he had prowled the house while she was away, he would know no man lived under this roof.

She took another sip of ale. 'I told you I am responsible. He is away.'

'Away.' He pulled at the word as if it were the thread that could unravel a whole cloth. 'And what is he doing…away?'

What lie is something like the truth? 'Buying…selling.'

'Buying and selling what?'

He leaned towards her. Too close. A shaft of late-afternoon sun sculpted his strong cheekbones, softened by an unruly curl of chestnut hair.

The silence grew so large that she had to fill it.

'He is trying to find more wool.' That at least was true. But it was her father, not her husband, who had travelled to England on a wool-buying trip.

'How pleased he will be when he returns to find you have succeeded.'

'Certainly he will be pleased when *you* succeed.'

He gave her a lazy smile. She let go of her breath. He was satisfied. There would be no more questions about her husband.

'Has he been away long?'

She had relaxed too soon. 'A while.'

'You must miss him.'

She felt her face melt. Too late, she wondered if her expression was appropriate to a wife. 'Yes.'

'And where is your husband looking for this wool?'

She reached for the ale again. Any answer she gave would be wrong.

If she said her husband was in England, Renard would know he was either jailed or a traitor to the Count of Flanders.

If she admitted she had no husband, she would be caught in her lie and exposed as a vulnerable woman at Renard's mercy.

If she admitted she was under her uncle's protection, Renard would demand to confer with him.

'I really don't know where he is this week, Monsieur Renard,' she said.

'You're unprotected?'

She bit the unguarded tongue that had revealed too much. Once again her impulsive words had led her to the brink of disaster. He must learn no more.

Yet his eyes would not let her turn away. They put her in mind of the things that men and women did. Alone. What would she do if he reached for her?

If he kissed her?

A sinful thought no decent woman would have. 'No,' she answered. '*You* will be my protector.'

Did she only imagine his eyes became a darker blue? 'More demands? You haven't even paid for the wool.'

'I said you would have an answer this afternoon, not your pay.' Her father's bag of coins lay hidden safe in her chest. 'I do not keep such sums lying about.'

His smile became a scowl. 'First you cannot decide, then you cannot pay.' He sat up, wrapping the last of the bread and cheese as if to leave. 'I have no more time to waste with you.'

'No. Please. Wait.' She grabbed his arm. She must not lose him now.

He paused. 'For how long?'

How long would it take to get to her uncle's house and back? ''Til curfew.'

The lazy smile was gone and she saw no pity in his eyes. But something shifted inside him.

'Curfew. No longer.'

She nodded and left the shop, closing the door with shaking fingers. She was still trembling as she crossed the bridge and hurried past the Count's castle, thrusting out at the junction of river and canal like a mountain looming over the city. But she had no time to think about Renard's eyes or the uncomfortable feelings he raised.

She must enter and leave the house without being seen or she would not be back before curfew. If her uncle forced her to go with him to Gravere, she would not be back at all.

Chapter Three

Katrine tiptoed up the stairs to her room unseen by her aunt, who was peering carefully at each fork before she wrapped it for travel. But as Katrine opened her trunk to grab the bag of coins hidden under her clothes, she heard the heavy thump of her uncle's steps.

Wood scraped on wood as he flung open the door. She stuffed the coins back to the bottom of the trunk, then smoothed the folds from her second-best kirtle, refolding the warm gold wool with damp palms.

'Don't turn your back on me.' He grabbed her right arm and swung her around him. The kirtle tumbled into a golden puddle.

A sour taste cut her tongue. 'I am facing you now,' she said, chin up, looking squarely into his eyes. There was a strangeness there that made her shiver. 'What do you want?'

'Hurry your packing. We must be well along before dark.'

Think before you speak. But there was only the truth. 'I am not going. I must tend my father's work.'

He tightened his grip and shook her. 'Your place is where I say it is.' He closed the open lid. 'With us. Your father indulged you too long. The shop is closed. Now. Today.'

'No.' She wrenched her arm away from his grip, rubbing the spot his fingers had bruised. It was too late to placate him and she had never been good at it.

'Wilful wench. You're a curse on the name of Gravere.'

Over and over, he had said so, until all she wanted to do was hide from a shame she didn't even understand. 'If you think so, then I'll free you from concern about me. I'll move to the shop.'

The thought alone brought blessed relief. How wonderful to be away from the reach of his fist.

'You think to live alone and play the whore?' His eyes turned hot, wild. She no longer tried to meet them. He looked frantically at her wimple, then at her surcoat, then at her skirts, as if searching for a way inside the layers of clothes concealing everything but her face and hands. 'You are an evil, red-haired daughter of Eve and the Devil,' he snarled, at last. 'A temptation to man.'

By the blessed saint, what have I done that leads him to these thoughts?

'I am the daughter of Lady Mary and Sir Denys de Gravere,' she said, wishing again she had told her father what went on when he was away from the house. It had not seemed important when he was gone only a few days. 'Your brother is no devil.'

His breath came faster. He flexed his fingers as if they itched to move over her body and glared directly at her mouth. 'You are your mother's daughter. You have her face. Her body. Her sins.'

'There was no sin in her.' She barely remembered her mother, but she knew that.

'Enough.' He laid his hands on her and pushed. Unprepared, her knees buckled, hitting the plank floor with bruising force. 'You will obey me.'

Saint Catherine, give me courage. She swallowed her fear, then stared back, pinching the wool of her skirt so tightly the weave carved its pattern on her thumb. 'No.'

His fingers hovered close to her throat. Then, his thumbs choked her breath until she could no longer swallow, could barely see, could only claw at his massive arms, desperate to break his hold.

Suddenly, he let go, pulling back as if her hands had burned him.

'Just like her.' He threw the words behind him and stomped out of the room.

Katrine sank back on to her heels, coughing, gagging, fighting the nausea rising from her stomach. She was no longer safe in this house. Leaving was no longer a choice. Leaving was a necessity.

At the clink of a sword in the hall, she looked up. Her uncle stood at the door with one of his retainers.

'Since you want to stay, you will. Here. In this room.' Her uncle pulled out a key and reached for the door handle, nodding at the man. 'Watch her here until I return.'

The door shut and the key rattled in the iron lock.

'No!' She struggled to her feet, tripping over her gown as she ran to the door.

Her palms were red and stinging before she stopped beating against the unyielding oak.

By the time the vesper bells rang, the household was long gone. Katrine had paced from bed to door to window too many times to count. She had winnowed the pieces of her life to a sack she could carry. A few clothes. A comb. A small round mirror of German silver from Uncle Giles, engraved with a four-petalled daisy. Her mother's ivory triptych, blessed at the shrine of Saint Catherine.

So few things. What mattered most was in the weaving room.

She weighed her father's parting gift in her palm. The bag of gold livres carried none of the sentiment of the mirror or the triptych, but it must pay the smuggler's price and more. It must support her until she sold cloth again.

If she could escape.

She paced back to the window. The roofs glowed orange in the setting sun. She smacked the sill in frustration. She had told him by curfew. It was near that now.

Merkin's cheery voice emerged through the door. 'Good evening. I've brought her supper.'

The guard mumbled a grunt. The lock rattled and the door swung open.

Merkin, her back to him, winked at Katrine and raised her eyebrows. 'Go eat, Ranf. I'll watch her.'

He closed the door. Footsteps descended the stairs.

Merkin rolled her eyes. 'The man's as dimwitted as he is ugly.' She put down the tray and stuffed the bread and cheese in her pouch. 'Hurry, milady.'

Katrine grabbed her small sack of treasures and her cloak, fingers shaking. 'How can I thank you? He'll beat you when he finds me gone.'

A grin split Merkin's face. 'He'll have to catch me first, milady. I'm coming with you.'

There was no time to debate. Katrine gave her a grateful hug and they slipped down the stairs and out of the garden door.

Shadows rippled on the river beneath the bridge and the leftover aroma of the day's catch followed them through the square. A man in rags crouched on the corner, hand outstretched, muttering a plea or a threat. She pushed Merkin ahead and ran past him, quickly.

As they hurried through the darkening streets, she prayed war preparations would keep her uncle away for a long time. Ranf wouldn't know what to do without orders.

Katrine drew a full breath only after she had safely closed the shop's door.

'Renard?' she called. Again, there was no answer.

She raced up the stairs, only slightly relieved when she saw his sack still there. Nothing about the man was certain.

'Why are you calling for a fox?' Merkin asked, as Katrine came downstairs.

She paused, giving her mind time to catch up with her tongue. 'I hired a guard. Since the house has been empty, I thought there should be someone here to watch it.'

Merkin rolled her eyes and muttered something about a fox guarding the chickens, but softly enough that Katrine could ignore her. 'He must be watching from the top of the bell tower, then, milady.'

Katrine smiled, though she knew she shouldn't. Merkin's tongue was as forthright as her own. '"Mistress," Merkin, not "milady". If we are to be safe here, he must think me a simple tradeswoman.' If he discovered she had run away from a noble family, he might turn her in for an imagined reward.

Merkin sighed just a little too loudly. 'Yes, mistress.'

'I'm sure he'll be here soon.' She looked at the gathering shadows as Merkin prepared a bed for herself in the kitchen. Truly, she was sure of only one thing: she had come home.

Katrine woke to see a tall, motionless shadow on the wall of the weaving room holding a dagger.

Renard had returned.

She didn't lift her head, cradled in her arm over the inventory book where she'd fallen asleep, her wimple pillowing her cheek.

Full darkness had fallen, she thought, sure she could hear the echo of the compline bell. The fire's remaining coals glowed red as the pits of hell.

Slowly, she stretched and yawned, raising her arms towards the rafters, closing her eyes, pretending she had not seen him. Pretending she did not care if she saw him. Yet with this man in it, her shop seemed no safer than the streets.

Her loose-fitting wool dress brushed her breasts through her chemise. She fought the urge to drop her arms and shield herself from his eyes, thankful for once that her breasts were so small.

Surely he could not see them.

As he sheathed his dagger, his shadow fell across her like a caress. 'I was not expecting to see you when most are abed.'

'And I was expecting to see you long before now.'

'Did you meet your money lender?'

She counted out the heavy coins, then handed them across the table without answering. No need to add another lie. 'Here. Though you've yet to earn it. I hire you to guard the house, yet you are never here. Then you persist in showing *me* your blade.'

Silent, he poured the money into the pouch tied to his girdle without counting. Coins she had recounted ten times. How could a smuggler be so careless with money?

She closed her inventory book. 'Tell me, Monsieur Renard, what has brought you to this life? Are you a weaver, trying to bring work to your fellow craftsmen?' The idea seemed absurd. He had the strong arms and chest needed to beat the weft with the reed, but his long legs had obviously guided a horse into battle, not atrophied beneath a loom.

He threw a stray twig of kindling into the coals. A blue-hearted flame flared up to devour it.

She waited for an answer, but neither of them feared silence now. She glowed with a moment's triumph. 'Monsieur Renard, your namesake, the fox, is never at a loss for words. Has Tibert the Cat taken your tongue?'

He looked at her then, though the shadows hid his expression. 'Renard the Fox always has a clever word. Usually, it is a lie.'

'Does that mean your words are lies?'

'Are yours the truth?'

She blinked, betraying herself again. *Is he a priest to know the truths of the confessional?* 'What is *your* truth, Renard? What do you tell the wife who wonders at your absence?'

She thought a cloud of anger shadowed his face, but his unreadable eyes protected his secrets as fully as a suit of chain-mail.

Yet a well-aimed arrow could penetrate even chainmail.

She aimed. 'Or perhaps the ladies refuse to wed a smuggler?'

There was the slightest hesitation before he answered. 'I see no need to marry.'

Her lips curved up before she realised she had cared what his answer would be. Reckless with small success, she pushed ahead. 'Your parents, then? Are they proud of their son?'

His left eyelid slipped into a wink and she sensed the muscles harden to sculpted stone beneath his skin. Though he never moved, the narrow, guarded drawbridge that linked him to the world clanged shut.

'The less we know of each other, the safer we both will

be. It is late.' In one fluid motion, he bowed and held his hand to help her rise. 'Since I am to be your protector, I will protect you between here and your bedchamber.'

She held out her hand.

With a stance anything but humble, he pulled her to her feet so swiftly that she had to clutch his solid arms for balance.

Nose pressed against his chest, she inhaled the lingering, smoky-sweet fragrance of the lichens that had dyed his tunic. His chin pressed the top of her head through her wimple.

Surrounded by him, she felt safe. Strange, to feel safe with such a menacing man. More than his arms held her. She was enveloped by his scent. Sharp. Rich. Mysterious. Did all men smell this way?

There was a catch in the steady rise and fall of his chest, or maybe it was a flutter in her own breathing. Then the fleeting feeling of safety was gone, replaced with something altogether different. Dangerous.

She looked up. His blue eyes looked intense now, not at all cold. Her chest tightened around an inheld breath as his steady finger hovered close enough to her lips to catch the sigh she refused to release.

Then, slowly, he traced her eyebrows, leaving a trail on her temple and her cheeks, gradually coming back to her lips, outlining them with a touch as soft as a feather. Finally, his finger slipped over the curve of her chin before tangling in the barrier of the wimple swaddling her neck. His hand encircled her throat, heat burning through the cloth.

He could have caressed or choked her, yet somehow, she knew this man would do neither.

Even if she wanted the caress.

'And who, my little weaving woman, will protect me from you?'

She ripped herself away from his arms, ashamed. He knew her sinful thoughts, had read her desire for his touch. Men, her uncle told her, always knew. 'You will need no protection from me. There's only one thing I want from you.'

She headed for the stairs, not waiting as he lit a candle from the embers and followed. At the top of the flight, she opened the door to the master's room. Her mother's ivory triptych sat, comforting, by the bedside.

He was close behind her. 'This your room, mistress?'

No. It is Giles's room. She had unpacked her small sack and put on new bed linens in Renard's absence. 'Of course.'

'Strange. It looked different earlier today.'

He did not wait for a response before he mounted the stairs to the third floor. A dismissal. As if she were a servant and he the master.

She closed the door and leaned against it, eyes shut. Above her, his boots hit the floor with a thunk. She listened for the whoosh of his tunic. As the straw rustled with his weight, she envisioned him lying on his pallet, the breeze from the window playing across his naked chest.

Who will protect me from you? Renard had read her secret feelings, feelings that must be sinful, even if she could not quite understand.

But she did not feel sinful. Sin should make you feel full of toads and maggots and bile. Fetid. Festering. Worse than a toothache and a stomachache and her monthly time all on the same day.

Instead, she felt as if it were the first of the twelve days of Christmas.

I must truly be a sinner if I feel no guilt.

Opening her eyes, she jerked away from the door, ashamed of her thoughts. They only proved that her uncle was right.

She tugged at her surcoat, glad she had not rousted Merkin from her kitchen pallet to help her undress. Surely his eyes would not look midnight blue in the sunshine. She had only felt hot and breathless at his touch because she had needed a good night's sleep. Only felt weak because she needed food.

Surely in daylight, he would look, and she would feel, quite ordinary.

She went to pull the shutters against the night. Glimpsing a man across the street, she blinked. Who was skulking in the shadows so late?

When she recognised the form, she shivered.

Ranf. Her uncle's man.

With damp palms and a dry throat, she swung the shutters closed, watching through the crack until he was out of sight.

Surely he would not take her by force without a direct order from her uncle.

She shuddered. Perhaps she needed a guard more than she knew.

Chapter Four

Renard rolled from his back to his side, seeking a corner of the thin pallet where straw would not prick his skin. The hum of voices drifted in the window on the cool night air. A neighbouring burgher and his wife arguing in their bed? Or the Count's men, searching for him? He'd seen someone lurking outside the house. An innocent man-at-arms or a threat?

God's blood, I make a poor spy.

Every sentence was a trap. Every word could mean his death. But he must play the part. Must convince her he was a rogue smuggler, interested only in money.

Eyes closed, he concentrated on his mission. And on the way the sapphire consecration ring would feel on his right hand when it was over.

Instead, he felt Katrine, small and delicate, in his arms again. He had held her longer than he should have, long enough that her scent, warm and spicy, filled his nose and teased his loins. Somewhere beneath the fabric that covered all but her hands and face, the rhythm of her heartbeat matched his. He knew it.

So with the instinct of a lifetime of practice, he suppressed passion's pull before he realised that this time, he had not really wanted to.

All the better that his control was second nature.

Who will protect me from you? The words had slipped past the barrier that let nothing escape. An experienced woman would realise what a weapon he had just put in her hands, but this woman seemed anything but experienced. Far from knowing a man's body, she was not even at ease with her own.

She responded to him awkwardly, as if she were a squire holding her first sword with barely enough strength to control the weapon. The blade wobbled, but it was still sharp, and perhaps even more deadly, because her blow would not be skilful and deft, but accidental. Painful.

Fatal.

As the sky lightened to butter yellow, Renard rose, ready to escape the house unseen. Danger filled the streets, but even these quarters held no safety. Below him was a slip of a weaving woman who wanted nothing more than to break Edward's embargo.

The tremble in her voice told him she was hiding something. This husband of hers was not searching for wool.

And he had been gone a long, long time.

The mid-afternoon bell was ringing by the time Renard returned to the city after spiriting Edward out and into the hands of the knights who would deliver him to his waiting ship.

Now, instead of moving on to Brabant, he was trapped in hiding. Some of the English knights had arrived, waiting for the Bishop before formal negotiations could begin. He must risk contact to assess the diplomatic situation.

He slipped unnoticed into a house near the Friday Market where Jack de Beauchance had rented rooms.

'Renard!' Jack said, clapping him on the shoulder.

'Keep your voice down,' he said, though his friend's cheery words eased his mood. Curly-haired Jack had been knighted beside him on the field in Scotland.

'Where have you been hiding since we came ashore, you fox? Are you on the King's business again?'

'If I were, would I tell you?'

'Whatever you're doing, you don't look as if it's going well,' Jack said.

Renard forced a smile, disturbed that his concerns had shown on his face. Such a careless display was dangerous. 'Look at you wearing that silly red eyepatch when you are alone in your rooms,' he said, to change the subject. 'Do you even sleep in that scrap of silk?'

Jack crossed his arms and arched his eyebrows. 'Handsome, don't you think? I promise you, the ladies like it.'

'The ladies like *you*, with or without it.' Everyone liked Jack. It couldn't be helped. A younger son, Jack's birthright was secure, if not his expectations. 'Why were you sent ahead while the Bishop tarries elsewhere?'

Jack rolled his eyes to heaven in mock agony. 'He found me with one of the junior ladies-in-waiting in a very dark corner of the garden.'

'Let me guess. A lady the Bishop himself wanted?'

'I don't think she'll have him, even with me gone.' Jack sighed, then the momentary cloud passed and his sunny expression returned. 'Watch this,' he said, holding up three cloth balls.

He tossed and caught the first and second, but he stretched so far for the third that he tripped over a stool and crashed to the floor. Three soft balls plopped on his back.

Renard laughed for the first time in a week and reached out to help him up. 'Is this part of the negotiation strategy? Get the Count to laugh so hard he will switch his allegiance?'

Jack rubbed his right knee and winced. 'The Count hasn't even agreed to meet with us. That may be as much of a reason as my lovely lady-in-waiting that the Bishop tarries with the Queen's relatives.' King Edward's wife was related to nobility throughout the Low Countries. 'He doesn't want the blame for failure.'

Renard frowned. 'That bodes ill.' If official negotiations failed, Edward's throne *would* depend on Renard's success in fomenting a revolt.

'He sent a few of us ahead to arrange his lodgings.' Jack winked. 'And to make friends among the people.'

'By flinging gold into the streets and stealing a kiss?' The antics of the English knights were already the stuff of legend. 'You even managed to enjoy the Scottish Wars. This is much more pleasant duty.'

'These women have the fairest hair and the bluest eyes I've ever seen.'

Katrine's eyes were brown, he thought, suddenly, wondering what colour hair her wimple hid. Her eyebrows had a reddish cast.

He turned the hardness in his loins into a hardness of soul. This time, no muscle flinched in his face. 'I hadn't noticed.'

'You used to enjoy the women as much as I do.'

'I was younger then.' And too foolish to truly understand that his lust could get a bastard who would live in the same earthly purgatory his life had been. He would not wish that on any man.

'It's a shame you can so easily resist the pleasures of feminine comfort.'

'Easily?' he scoffed. 'You know better. But I did not come to the Low Countries on a mission of pleasure.'

'Neither did the rest of us, but the Bishop of Clare doesn't let business, or his vows, interfere with his pleasures.'

'The Bishop is a hypocrite.' Renard spat out the words as if he could not bear the taste. He laughed then, so Jack would not think much of it.

'You need a lady to change your mood. I met a lovely one at the bath house.' He wiggled his eyebrows with a grin.

Renard laughed again, meaning it this time. 'If you met her at the bath house, she is no lady.'

Jack pressed a hand to his chest in mock indignation. 'It's a very strict establishment. She has such red lips, such smooth skin, such blonde hair, and if you don't like her,' he cajoled, 'I'm sure you could find another who would please. Come with me.'

'I cannot risk being seen with you.' He rose. 'After I leave, forget I was here.'

'If you change your mind about the bath house, it's on the fork of the river beyond the Count's castle.'

After he left Jack, Renard pondered the idea. A bath house was a hotbed of gossip. If he kept his ears open, he would hear the city's mood and perhaps a name or two that might be sympathetic to Edward's cause. But instead of Jack's respectable house, he'd visit one hidden among the taverns near the Square of Forbidden Attractions…

Where no one would ask any questions.

Renard returned to the shop after the compline bell, his jaw aching from a day of framing harsh Flemish syllables. Even a lumpy straw pallet sounded inviting.

In the markets, taverns and public baths, his height and blue eyes were remarkable, but his Flemish, though rusty, was convincing enough for him to pass as a visitor from Brussels.

And fomenting revolt might not be as difficult as he had feared. Angry about the dispute that had snatched the thread from their looms and the bread from their tables, the people were like dry kindling. The right spark might ignite a rebellion favourable to Edward and England.

Unwelcome moonlight chased him into the shadows. The man he'd seen outside the house was missing tonight, but he could not afford to be questioned by the watch. He had taken the risk of staying out past curfew, hoping she would be abed when he returned. He must avoid her questions. And her temptation.

Wrinkling his nose at the lingering scent of cabbage soup, he slipped into the kitchen, the familiar weight of his dagger moulded to his palm. The glow of uncovered embers drew him, cautiously, into the front room.

Katrine slept over her account books again. Her wimple askew, a lock of hair, reflecting red from the dying coals, escaped to caress her cheek. An ink blot stained the middle finger of her right hand, protectively stretched on top of the ledger.

He sheathed his dagger and stepped into the room quietly so she would not wake. The fire's glow left deep shadows in the narrow room's corners. The house did not stretch far beyond the firelight. Such a small place. King Edward needed more room than this just to pace.

Yet this was all she had. No fields, no vast estates, no serfs toiling for her outside these walls. Only a cherry tree and a bolt of cloth shielded her from starvation.

No wonder she needs the wool. Couldn't this husband of her take care of the woman?

He knelt before her, his face dangerously close to hers. Before he could stop them, his fingers slipped past his self-control to touch the lock of hair on her cheek. When he tried to tuck it beneath her wimple, the strands slipped through his fingers like silk.

At his touch, she woke, brown eyes weighed down by a thicket of lashes and a sleepy smile touching her lips.

A matching smile tugged at the corner of his mouth. He spoke softly, the Flemish rough in his throat. 'Do you fall asleep over your accounts every night, mistress?'

She blinked, suddenly awake, and drew away, leaving his fingers empty. 'The business is all I have. I will do anything I must to keep it.'

He rose, abruptly, wondering what passion she had left for her husband. If she had one.

Suddenly, it seemed important to know. He had negotiated with kings. He could certainly force the truth from a simple weaving woman. 'And your husband, will he, too, do anything he must?'

Her dark eyes looked huge in her pale face, framed by the rumpled wimple. 'Of course.' She hesitated over the words.

He was certain in that moment she had no husband.

The rush of blood throbbed in his loins before he could summon his control. *No man possesses her.*

Denial struggled with hot, sweet desire.

He clenched his jaw and felt his eyelid flinch, but he refused to break his gaze, glad to be safely towering over her again. He would resist her, but she mustn't know that. 'If you will do anything you must, mistress, will you do anything I ask?' He must keep her off balance, wondering about his intentions.

A delicate flush—anger or shame?—spread beyond her cheek. She bit her lower lip with small white teeth, inflicting enough pain to steady her resolve. He had seen a knight in battle try the same trick, slashing his forearm to create a new, superficial wound to distract him from the mortal blow.

Staring back at him, her defiant eyes did not waver, but he heard the whisper of inheld breath, as if she had recognised the fire in his eyes and was burned by it. 'What do you ask?'

Longing rushed through his blood like poison. What he would ask had no words, only the vision of wild joining.

He fought the image. Even if he permitted himself careless pleasures of the flesh, he was hiding in the belly of a country that might soon be at war with his. One unmeasured word uttered in passion could be his death. He gritted his teeth against the feeling. 'I ask for the truth.'

She rose and slipped into the shadows surrounding the loom. Hiding.

He would not let her. 'And the truth is, you have no husband.'

She whirled to face him, the wool of her skirt crushed in her fist. 'I have no husband.' Angry words. 'Would you have dealt with me, had you known?'

Yes, but he would not tell her that. He shrugged. 'Then why wear the wimple?'

Her slender arms crossed her chest like a shield. 'There is little safety on the streets these days. People are more respectful of a married woman.'

'But you are not on the streets now.'

'I still need protection.'

'I thought I was to protect you.'

She smiled. 'Who will protect me from you?'

She had turned his words back on him. He had thought to keep her off balance, yet he was the one who felt dizzy. He donned a mask of disdain to blot out all traces of attraction. She must not know his weakness for her. 'What makes you think you need protection from me?'

Her eyes widened and narrowed in an instant, but he saw his insult had hit its mark. For a moment, he was sorry for it.

'I am glad to hear I do not.' She patted the wrinkles from her skirt, now all brisk business. 'When will I see my wool?'

Uneasiness rippled through him. She had recovered faster than he expected. He had thought her a simple burgher mistress but, so far, this woman was nothing that he had expected. 'I cannot order contraband wool at the market. If it were easy, you would not need me.'

'How long must I wait?'

'As long as it takes.' As long as it would take to turn the people of Flanders to Edward's side. 'Weeks, not days, mistress.'

'I've waited months already.' Urgency shook her voice.

'Patience is a virtue you don't possess.'

'Patience is *no* virtue when dealing with spinsters and weavers. I have no patience for sloppy work or I will have nothing fit to sell.'

Her words intrigued him. What would it be like to be so pleased with who you were and what you did? 'You are proud of your work, aren't you?'

The smile that transformed her face would have, for most women, come at the mention of a paramour. 'The Mark of the Daisy is known throughout the Low Countries.'

She sounded lovesick, he thought, irritably. 'And what makes your cloth so special?'

'I can recognise the best wool by touch. My spinsters

deliver seven skeins a day instead of five. When my dyers are finished, the colour is fast. My weavers' work is so tight we rarely need the fullers' craft.'

'Fullers?' He followed most Flemish words, but sometimes missed the meaning. 'What do they do?'

She cocked a suspicious eyebrow. 'How can you deal in wool and know so little of it?'

'Do I need to know how to grow wheat in order to trade it? Or how to take salt from the mines in order to sell it?'

'Well, if you knew wool, you would recognise our mark. Even before I was born, we made a special fabric for the Duchess of Brabant.'

A burning numbness filled him, like a blow from a broadside sword. Duchess cloth. A scrap of indigo-dyed wool carefully wrapped around a dagger of German silver. An orphaned bastard's only inheritance from the princess who had married a duke.

What terrible fate had drawn him to the very shop that had made the cloth his mother had worn? 'Duchess cloth? You made that?'

'You know it?'

He clenched his fist behind his back. 'I've heard of it.'

'I'm surprised. It was so long ago.'

'I was born in Brabant, remember?' His throat tightened around the words that jarred against each other. 'Those who have seen it claim only a miracle of God or the Devil's witchcraft could produce such an intricate design.'

She laughed. 'Neither God, nor the Devil. Just Giles de Vos.'

He lowered his voice, afraid that he would shout to make himself heard over the blood pounding in his ears. He must ask the question as if the answer made no difference. 'So he knew the Duchess?'

He was suddenly hungry to hear of her. No one had spoken of his mother since she had died.

'The Duchess was a great patroness of his,' Katrine said. 'He wove a special length and sent it to her every year until she died twenty years ago.'

'Nineteen.'

She looked puzzled, but did not ask him how he knew. 'He never wove it again after that.'

'Why?'

'He said there is a craft and an art to weaving, and the art must come from the heart. I think he lost heart for it after she died.'

A woman's romantic notion. The truth was certainly simpler. De Vos was a merchant. The money had stopped. 'He didn't even make some for your mother?'

'My...my mother?'

'You say your father only made this cloth for the Duchess. Surely he wove some for his wife.'

She shook her head, flinching as if in pain. 'My mother's not...'

Her voice cracked again. He wondered whether she had lost a mother, too.

Chapter Five

Thank you, Saint Catherine, for stopping my flapping tongue.

Renard thought Giles was her father. When he said 'your mother,' he meant Giles's wife. She had almost told him that her mother was dead and her father was a Flemish noble.

In an English jail.

She poked a stick into the fading fire, releasing a flame. Better he think Giles was her father. A dead man would not mind the untruth and he had never had a wife who would be wronged by the tale.

Forgive my sin of omission.

'No, not even for my mother,' she repeated. 'Many asked for it, but Duchess cloth was made only for the Duchess.'

When she turned back, his midnight-blue eyes looked as if they had just stared into the pits of hell. She blinked against the agony, but when she opened her eyes, the pain had been swept clean.

She shook her head to clear her muddled vision. She must have been mistaken. This man had no feelings. And no reason to mourn a dead duchess.

'Tell me,' he said, with an expression more serious than the question, 'about your father.'

She sighed with relief. It would be easy to pretend a daughter's affection for Giles. 'He taught me everything he could and left me everything he had.'

'When did he die?'

'Two years ago Michaelmas.'

'You miss him very much.' His voice felt like an arm draped over her shoulder.

'Yes, I do.'

'It cannot be easy for a woman to be a draper.'

She resisted the temptation to rest in his sympathy. Better he not know how difficult it was. He must see her as a business owner, not a woman who might be prey for his passions.

She donned again the voice she used with strangers. 'The workers respect me. I know my business.'

'How many times every day must you prove it?'

He heard too much. 'As many times as I must.'

Renard walked over to the loom, squatting just beyond the firelight.

'That loom was his,' she said, watching Renard stroke the uprights, the threads and the batten, as if he were searching for a secret lock. His hands, strong and graceful in all things, seemed awkward only when they neared the loom. 'He was a weaver before he started dealing in cloth.'

'But he kept weaving, you said. He wove the Duchess cloth.'

'He was always experimenting, trying new things, until the stiffness took his hands.' Joining him by the loom, she rubbed her thumb over wood worn smooth for more than fifty years. 'He taught me on this loom. He said I must know how to weave in order to supervise weavers.'

'Show me.'

She stilled her fingers and tried to read his face. A strange request. 'Why would you want to learn?'

He never moved his gaze from the threads. 'When you are finished, you have something to show.'

His whispered words seemed a confession. A smuggler's very life was secret.

'Perhaps tomorrow.' In daylight. When the intimacy of the night had passed.

'Now.'

'In the dark?'

His silence, thick and heavy, touched her as his fingers had touched the threads. 'You were the one,' he said, finally, 'who told me I needed to know my trade.'

No harm in teaching, she supposed. Good weavers worked by touch anyway, so the dark should not matter. And she could prove to herself that she felt nothing unusual when she shared his space.

Taking a seat on the end of the bench, she patted the wood to her left. 'Sit.'

He did, his legs so long they nearly overshot the treadles that she could barely reach with a pointed toe. Through the layers of his chausses and her skirt, she felt his leg muscles flex at the unfamiliar movement.

'These,' she said, struggling to keep her voice even, 'are the treadles. Think of them as your stirrups. Your feet ride there to control the loom.'

He placed one foot on each, his knees within a whisper of the cloth on the loom. 'Are all weavers such small men?'

She smiled. 'You are a very tall man. And this is an old loom that I've adjusted to my size. The newer ones must be worked by two men.'

'How tall was Giles de Vos?'

He asked the question without looking at her, his fingers running ceaselessly over the loom, stroking the batten, reaching for the heddles, smoothing the warp threads.

The sight of his fingers caressing the loom made her skin tingle. She rubbed her sleeve as if she could scrub away the feeling. 'Giles was shorter than you. By at least a head.'

He spread his arms to span the loom, easily reaching the width of the cloth. She caught a whiff of soap and skin. He must have visited the bath house today. His scent, the pressure of his leg against hers hidden in the darkness, made her heart trip.

Sweet Saint Catherine, is this what they mean by temptation?

If so, it felt good—warm, cosy, exciting, perhaps a little dangerous and very, very alive.

She felt no answering surge from him. His concentration was all on the wood and the wool.

He said I did not need protection from him. I must indeed be an immodest woman, if I feel like this while he feels nothing.

She slipped off the bench, smoothed her skirt and stood at the corner of the loom, where his scent was fainter and it was easier to fight her shameful urges. 'I can show you better from here.'

She ran her hands over the loom, checking the tautness of the threads, trying to concentrate. Where could she start? She had learned as a baby to recognise the right-spun threads that must constitute the warp, the left-spun ones that must be used as the weft, to string the threads evenly, not too tight, not too loose.

'Let me show you how to throw the shuttle.' She picked

up a boat-shaped wooden shuttle, empty of the bobbin thread, but worn smooth by Giles's fingers. 'Practise first with an empty one to get the feel of it so you don't ruin my cloth.'

He watched her, silent and intent. She forced herself to inhale, letting the air fill her chest and calm her fluttering heart. 'Hold the shuttle in the palm of your hand, then insert the tip between the threads, flick your wrist, and catch it on the other side. Let me show you first.'

Reaching over his shoulder, she felt a chestnut curl tickle her cheek. She flicked her right wrist with the expertise of long practice. The shuttle went skimming across the warp threads and flew out the other side, the pointed prow nearly denting the wooden floor.

'Why didn't you catch it?' she grumbled. Kneeling, she searched under the loom in the darkness.

'You did not say "catch", mistress.' The imperial tone had returned to his voice. 'Your words were "Let me show you first".'

Fleece dust clung to her fingers before she found the shuttle. She rubbed her thumb over both pointed ends. Neither was damaged. 'You might have broken the point or caused a splinter,' she said, crawling out from under the loom and losing her dignity with a sneeze. 'Then it would catch on the warp threads. Now you try. Flick your wrist to throw it and catch it with your other hand. Neither your fingers nor the shuttle should touch the threads. Then throw it back the other way. A master weaver can work equally well left to right or right to left.'

He took the shuttle, grasping it like a sword.

'No, here.' She cradled her small hand around his large one, placing his index finger on the well-worn wood. A hot flush crept up her arm at his touch, but she refused to let go.

'Now, flick like this…' She guided his wrist in the familiar gesture. 'Let go next time…and catch.'

The shuttle skimmed partway over the threads and stopped in the middle. She sighed, and reached in to pull it out.

His fingers locked around her wrist. 'I'll get it,' he said.

She pulled her arm away. A bracelet of fire circled her wrist where his hand had been.

She stepped away and watched as he rescued the empty bark. Then, after flexing both wrists, he sent the shuttle skimming through the threads. Again it stopped like an arrow short of the target.

Without a word, he retrieved it. Instead of cursing at the shuttle, or at her, as her uncle did when something went wrong, or at himself, as her father would have, this man calmly threw again.

And again.

On his next try, the little boat shot safely through the threads and into his waiting hand.

Grinning, he waved it in triumph and she clapped with delight, belatedly realising the racket might wake Merkin. 'You handle the shuttle as if you had weaver's blood.'

A look of fierce warning wiped out his first genuine smile. He stood, the lesson over. 'My blood is none of your concern.'

She ignored her hurt and turned to light a candle from the embers. 'I meant it as a compliment. Particularly since you seem to know nothing of the trade.' She touched another candle to the flame and handed it to him.

'It is more important that I know my buyers.'

'I thought you said the less we know of each other, the better off we both will be,' she said, surprised to remember his exact words.

He winked again, conveniently hiding his feelings. 'I should have said the less you know of me. You are my buyer. I must know what you need.'

His words were as tempting as his body. She was tired of lies, tired of being alone, so tired that, for a moment, she wanted to tell him everything.

She took a breath and bit her tongue. Impossible. She had lied about too much. And he was a man to fear, not to trust.

She covered the embers and let darkness hide her. 'You know what I need. Three sacks of your best wool.'

As she mounted the stairs, leaving him to follow, she remembered the advice of the titmouse wise enough to avoid the jaws of Renard the Fox: 'I trust none of the lies you tell. If I did, I'd surely burn in Hell.'

The Bishop of Clare, Henry Billesh, arrived in the city with full pomp and settled into a three-storey stone house near the Friday Market. Renard mingled with the foodsellers and tradesmen, arriving in the Bishop's solar unnoticed and unannounced. For Edward's sake, he would put aside his distaste to co-operate with the man.

It would not be easy.

'Ah, it's the King's messenger boy.' The Bishop extended his ring to be kissed.

The sapphire was bitter on Renard's lips. 'I have a report to share. I expect you've the same.'

In the midst of a starving city, the Bishop plucked a plump, golden orange from an overflowing basket and picked at the skin with a scrupulously clean, trimmed nail. 'I can't think of anything you might know that would interest me.'

'You can't be sure until you hear it. And it is the interest of the King that should concern us both.'

'The King's interest *is* mine, Renard. It is you, I understand, who have been given another motive. A bishop's seat
in exchange for Flanders, is it?'

It was Edward's way to pit the two against each other.
Edward would win either way. 'I would have served my king
regardless.'

'You may be disappointed. When I gain the Count's allegiance, there will be no need for your devious tricks.'

Renard bowed. 'So we all hope, your Excellency. But the
King is wise to prepare for many possibilities, including
your failure.'

The Bishop frowned at the insult. 'Just remember, even a
king cannot turn a bastard into a bishop without help.' He
plucked a section of orange, turned it into the light, found it
not to his liking, and discarded the rest of the bitter fruit. '*My*
help.'

Renard looked at the glowing sapphire on the Bishop's
hand and wondered how high the price would be for his own.
'I am aware of my special circumstances.'

The Bishop picked over the fruit in the basket. With the
palate of a glutton, he kept the scrawny neck and sunken
stomach of a hermit at the end of a forty-day fast by select-
ing only the choicest morsels. The rest was left for scrap.

'Well,' he began, 'if anything goes wrong with these negotiations, it would be…' the Bishop paused to examine a
date before looking back at Renard '…difficult for me to
write such a letter.' He decided the date was worthy and
popped it into his mouth.

'I trust it will not be difficult for us to work together on
the King's behalf.'

He waited.

The silence was punctuated by the mulching sound of the

Bishop chewing. 'Your report then,' he said, with a weary wave of his hand. 'Though I don't know what you could say about the artisans that would be useful. It is not as if they hold any power.'

'In this city, they do. Direct negotiation with the Count will be less fruitful here than elsewhere.'

The Bishop licked his sticky fingers. 'Why would that be?'

Renard smiled. 'Well, first of all, he's not related to the King by marriage.'

'The Queen's many relatives have made my mission more difficult, not less.'

'That may be, but here, the Count does not have the final say. The guilds have rights even the Count cannot ignore.'

Renard summarised the rest of his findings. The working folk bore no love for the Count and his Francophile ways. They still spoke fervently of the day their grandfathers, on foot and carrying only spears, had defeated French knights on horseback and stolen their spurs as trophies. Their loyalties lay with England, their partner in trade.

And he had already identified a potential ally who might sway Flanders's support officially to Edward.

He knew better, however, than to share the man's name and station.

When he was done, the Bishop shrugged. 'Play among the peasants if you like. I'll handle the diplomacy.'

'Has the Count agreed to support Edward's claim?' Renard knew the answer. He only wanted to watch the man squirm.

'He will, in time. There's no obstacle in Flanders or anywhere else that money won't melt. Should you sit in a bishop's chair as long as I have, you'll learn that gold and a woman are the two temptations no man can resist.'

Especially you. 'May the victory be the King's,' he answered, and took his leave before he lost his temper.

He'd learned more than he wanted to know. The Bishop's blunt instrument was more likely to fail than succeed. And if it did, any hope that he could escape this assignment was gone.

Renard would have to risk approaching the man who might lead a revolt.

He was said to frequent Jack's reputable bath house.

The bath house, in the wealthy area west of the Count's castle, *was* reputable. While he was there, Renard planned to make a calculated visit to a private room with one of the working 'ladies' to rid his thoughts of a certain weaving woman.

Jack's 'lady' looked no different from all the others. She was pretty in the conventional Flemish way—fair haired and well rounded, excessively so, compared to Katrine's slender shape. But she did not rouse his feelings, so he left her with a coin and a smile.

Strange, when he'd been fighting physical urges all week.

He surveyed the public room quickly before he entered. Enough of a crowd that they would not be noticed. Few enough that they would not be overheard.

He closed his eyes to let the damp air invade his pores. Instead, Katrine invaded his mind. It was as if he sat beside her again—her small fingers holding his around the shuttle, her breath teasing his ear, her thigh pressing against his through layers of finely woven wool.

He shook off the feeling, eyeing the room again. Daydreams were dangerous.

He recognised the man as soon as he walked in. He had

the lean stomach and straight bearing of a military man, coupled with an aristocratic air. Renard ducked into the water, emerging to sit on the wooden bench beside him as if by chance. Each nodded.

'I am a visitor from Brussels,' Renard said, casually.

'What brings you to Ghent?' Was the question innocent or suspicious?

'The wool trade.'

The man looked away. 'There is little of that now. Hasn't the embargo affected your city?'

'Badly. That is why I have come.' No one was within earshot. Now he would drop a hint. 'But I hear the English have come with gold. Mayhap it will mean an end to these troubles.'

The man looked at him sharply. 'You are a stranger. There are many who support Philip of Valois no matter what the English do.'

Was that gaze assessing or hostile? He must take the risk. 'And some who don't.'

'Yes. Some who don't.'

Renard let go the breath he had been holding and waited. The man did not leave. A good sign.

He must take the next step. 'In my city, there are those who say an alliance with the English would be better than loyalty to Philip.'

An angry denial would mean the man was loyal to Philip and France.

It did not come.

'Some say that here, too.' His eyes never left Renard's.

'I come to the bath house on Tuesdays.' He held his breath, listening to the splash of another bather, waiting for the answer.

They looked at each other for a long minute, each taking the other's measure.

His companion finally nodded. 'Perhaps I will see you here again.'

Chapter Six

Back still damp beneath his tunic, Renard quickened his steps as the last strokes of the vesper bells faded. Across the street, the baker's wife lowered her shutters, cutting off the faint aroma of the morning's leftover bread.

His spirits soared as tall as the unfinished bell tower. He had not been followed. The assignation was safe for the moment, but he must remain vigilant.

Still, the day was flush with satisfaction. His earlier worry about Katrine now seemed foolish. If the buxom beauty at the bath house couldn't stir him, there was no need to avoid a tiny woman with breasts little bigger than his fist.

The man he'd seen in the street was there again, so he bypassed the front door to the shop and circled around to slip in unseen through the yard, nodding to Merkin as she left for a late-day errand. The girl had accepted Katrine's pretence that he was a guard.

At least, she seemed to.

Katrine was sitting alone on the bench they had shared, tossing the shuttle smoothly from side to side, then slamming the heddle against the weave. Absorbed in her work, she did not hear him enter.

Silent, he let his eyes rest on her again. Short, slender, no higher than his heart. Rough fingers unlike a lady's. Brown eyes revealing her every thought.

She clasped her hands behind her neck and rolled her head back. Her shoulders must be tired. In his small time at the loom, he had learned that much.

'Here,' he said, stepping across the room. 'Let me make the ache go away.'

His hands were on her shoulders before she could protest, before he could remind himself that touching her was dangerous.

She stretched, then sagged against him and closed her eyes, as if she had been waiting for him to come home.

He told himself his touch was impersonal, even when his fingers longed to linger. The soft curve of her breast was just out of reach. He rubbed the graceful arch between her neck and shoulders through the fine wool of the ever-present wimple, hiding…what?

Slowly, trying not to startle her, he slid the wimple from her head and let her braids fall free.

He felt his first sight of her hair deep in his loins. Glowing red-gold, it summoned the vision he had strugged to deny. Warm, wild, waiting.

He crumpled the crisp wimple as if crushing his feelings. *Deny. Control.*

Katrine turned, eyes wide, frightened, and grabbed the head covering. 'Please, give it back.'

'Why? I know you have no husband. You are not on the street.'

She tugged at the cloth now firmly in his fist. 'I don't

like people to see my hair.' Her words were ragged, her eyes anguished.

He tightened his grip. What had happened to the woman with the tart tongue? Suddenly, she was cowering before him.

'Why? Your hair is beautiful.'

'You make mock. You can clearly see it is red.'

It was true that fair-haired, blue-eyed beauties like Jack's were considered ideal, but looking at Katrine's mane of fire, he could barely restrain himself from unravelling the braids and running his fingers through her hair.

'Some would call it so.' Red was too poor a word. It was sunset fire. Breathtaking, just as he had feared it would be.

She lowered her eyes and shook her head, pressing her fingers against her skirt over and over as if trying to rub out a spot. The fiery, fearless woman who had badgered him had become a mouse who would not raise her eyes to his. 'It is one of the marks of the Devil.'

He had heard some priests prattle about red hair and Satan, a part of the canon he had no interest in preaching. Women were lustful creatures. He knew that better than most, but to see her transformed by misery because her hair was red instead of brown stirred his anger. 'Who told you that?'

She shook her head, then turned to stare at the loom. He knelt beside the bench and seized her arms, shaking her. 'Tell me.'

She faced him, tears tangled in her lashes. 'Everyone knows. Mary Magdalene the whore was so marked.'

A deep ache for her, stronger than his anger or his censure, roused a sense of chivalry that no lady of the court had ever sparked. Katrine needed more than physical protection. She needed protection from her feelings.

That was something he could teach her.

He knelt beside the bench, gently stroking the curve of her chin with his finger, coaxing her to look at him. 'I am not everyone. I do not know that and I do not believe it.'

A small, gratifying smile flickered across her lips. 'Perhaps that is because you are the Devil.'

'Perhaps that means you belong to me.' The words slipped out and, for a moment, he did not care whether he meant them.

Wimple forgotten, she swayed towards him, eyes closed, as if her body knew the truth of the statement. He slipped his fingers through the silken rope of her braid, wanting to unlace every strand, drowning in the scent of her.

He wiped one of her tears away, then the other. His lips hovered so close to hers he could fill his chest with her breath. He inhaled, bringing her lips closer to his...

She stood, shattering the moment.

He slumped in relief. He had almost lost himself. Almost kissed her and more. No matter his intentions, with this woman, he had no control. Something in her passion called to his, as if her weakness matched his own.

Safely beyond his reach, she cleared her throat. 'No, you are not one of Satan's devils, but you do give a passable imitation. That must be a useful trait in your profession.' She plucked the headcloth from the floor and pulled it over her hair with fingers that shook as much as her voice. With the wimple as armour, she lifted her head, again the strong woman he knew. 'So, have you brought my wool?'

'I told you. It may take weeks.' Leaning on the bench, he rose on unsteady legs, grateful for her strength. His body was a weapon that had turned against him. In an unthinking moment, he had nearly succumbed. His secrets had become burdens. He had almost told her who he was. That what he was doing would be good for her.

But to do so would jeopardise his mission, his king, and his life. Even in the grip of passion, how had he forgotten? 'I will come and go at my pleasure, not yours.'

'Nothing you do is a pleasure to me except bringing me wool and staying away from me.'

'Liar,' he said, desperate to rebuild the wall between them. He took no satisfaction from the shock on her face, but he needed her to be angry with him. It was the only thing that could save him from his own weakness. 'But it will be my pleasure to stay away from you.'

He braced himself against the pain in her face.

He was the liar, he thought as he climbed the stairs. Thinking he could resist her, he lied to himself. Now he knew better.

He must not stand in temptation's path again.

Days passed. Katrine saw Renard no more. Merkin, who had taken a liking to the man, asked embarrassing questions that Katrine ignored. The floorboards above her groaned softly under his weight just after curfew, but she never glimpsed him, nor, more importantly, she told herself, any English fleece.

He had said she could not trust him. For that moment at the loom, she had forgotten. Instead, resting in his sheltering strength, she had believed everything he had said when he touched her. Believed she might be lovable just as she was.

But as soon as he saw her hair, he knew. Despite what he said, he despised her so much he had not even entered the same room since then.

Her unthinking trust was gone. She had let her yearnings

blind her to the truth, foolish enough to believe without proof that he would bring her the wool she had paid for.

She must be sure.

Even if it meant spying on him.

Only because she was concerned for her business, of course. She cared not where he came and went, but if he was not going to honour their bargain, she must find another way to string the looms.

Since he had taken to going before she awakened and returning after she was abed, she spent the next night in the weaving room. She had slept over her books before. He would not be suspicious. Just after the prime bell woke her, she felt him enter the room. He made no sound, but the air changed. She kept her eyes closed and forced herself to breathe evenly.

He stopped.

One breath in, one breath out. Don't let your eyelids flicker.

He passed so close that her skirt moved.

She kept her breath even.

The door closed. Still she didn't move.

Three more breaths and she jumped up, ran into the street and followed him.

Trailing his long-legged stride was harder than she had expected. Trying to keep up, she trotted past the Town Hall, then had to duck behind the herring seller's stand in the Fish Market when he threw an aimless glance behind him.

No. Not aimless. This man did nothing by chance. It was almost as if he expected to be followed.

Fortunately, he was tall and easy to spot and she was short and easy to overlook.

She bit her lip when he crossed the bridge leading towards the castle. Was he the Count's man?

But instead of entering, he crossed the placid canal and turned down the street where her father's town house stood.

And where Katrine saw her aunt directing the servants to unload the horses.

Her uncle had returned.

Pulling her wimple closer, she turned away, pretending interest in the glassmaker's wares, thanking the saint for her aunt's poor sight. It would not be long before her uncle discovered she had gone. After he punished Ranf, then what? Would he drag her away from the shop and force her home?

She hurried after Renard, keeping her face hidden. The wool was more urgent than ever. Only money would sway her uncle. If she could get new wool, if she could weave new cloth...

Renard's steps slowed as he came towards the end of the street. If he kept going, he would reach the tranquil house of the Béguine Sisters, an unlikely destination for a smuggler.

But as the rich odour of the shoemaker's leather filled her nose, he paused before the Van Der Hoon bath house, then disappeared inside.

She watched from across the street, cheeks burning, unsure what to do.

She had never been in a public bath, although this one was reputable. But she had smelled soap on him only a few days ago. This trip to the bath house must be for something more than cleanliness.

Squaring her shoulders, she walked up to the entrance.

A beefy matron guarded the door. 'Tomorrow's women's day.'

Katrine's blush was real. 'I...I know.' She fingered a coin she could ill afford to spend. 'But I'm here for a private room.'

The attendant looked at her with milky-blue eyes. 'You aren't one of the regular girls. You can't ply your trade here.'

Katrine touched her wimple and stared back at the sceptical attendant with the same expression she used on the spinsters late in delivering her allotment of yarn. 'Do I look like a strumpet? I am a married woman and I am here for a bath. This *is* a bath house, isn't it?'

The woman reared back. 'It is. My pardon, mistress.'

Katrine followed her bulk down the lattice-lined corridor, which echoed with men's voices drifting up from the public pool below. She strained to hear Renard's, but the woman did not allow her to tarry.

She was given a small room with a tub, a fireplace and a bench. The attendant padded the tub carefully with linens to shield against splinters, then stood, as if waiting for her to disrobe.

'I need no help. Just hot water and a winding cloth.'

'Rosemary or sage?'

'Excuse me?'

'In your bath. Rosemary or sage leaves?'

She selected rosemary and tapped her foot as the woman stoked the fire and filled the tub. 'That's enough. Thank you.'

'Until the next bell. If you want more time, it will cost you.'

The woman slammed the door behind her, not waiting for an answer. Fully clothed, Katrine looked longingly at the luxury of the fire and the tub, then opened the door a crack.

The hall was empty. The doors to the other private rooms stood open. So, he was not here for that. She smiled as she tiptoed to the other side of the corridor. She heard tantalising voices, but the lattice screen open to the floor below started beyond the top of her head. She could see nothing.

Evidently, Van Der Hoon's bath house deserved its spotless reputation.

Katrine went back into her room, moved the linen sheets from the bench and dragged it to the door. Oak scraped on stone, deafening. She stopped, listening for footsteps, afraid the noise would draw the attendant.

Splashes and an occasional masculine chuckle drifted up from the large room below. The hall remained safely empty.

She wrestled the heavy bench to the wall, breaking the clunk with her foot. Stepping up and standing on her toes, she was just tall enough to see to the room below.

At the sight, she nearly fell off.

Intent on finding Renard, it had not occurred to her that the bath would be crowded with other men.

And that they would all be naked.

Tall and short, fat and thin, hairy and smooth, they filled the tubs and the benches like an overpopulated Garden of Eden.

She gripped the latticework with icy fingers. In that collection of Adams, she saw only one.

Though she saw only his back, she recognized that easy grace she had come to know. He ducked down into the water and dipped his head back, chestnut hair straight and dark, then stood. As he emerged, water flowed over his muscles, shaping his shoulders and back.

She had never seen a naked man, but somehow she knew she would never need to see any other.

Water streamed down his back to the cleft just before the strong strokes of his thighs. Her eyes touched him everywhere the water ran.

The fire she had only played with before started in her breasts, moved lower...

He turned around and her heart stopped beating.

Desire washed through her, starting at her shoulders, where his hands had been, and ending in the centre of her being. Her palm ached to feel his damp skin, to follow her eyes up the curve of his calf, to trace the sculpted muscles of his thigh. She closed her eyes and grabbed the lattice to stand steady, welcoming the jab from a splinter.

Her uncle was right. Eve's sin must live in her. This wicked heat, this giddy hunger must be it. And now she could see its danger, for it tempted her to trust a man who had no truth in him.

Katrine squeezed her eyes shut, willing the dizzy, disgraceful hum to go away. There was nothing special about this man. No reason to think this feeling was one to honour instead of disdain.

When she opened them, she sighed with relief. Renard, now sitting on one of the benches lining the room, had a winding sheet wrapped loosely around him. Even without clothes, he seemed perfectly at ease.

She devoured the sight of his chest, decorated with a shield of wet, dark curls, and his long muscled legs, disappearing beneath the cloth to meet where she blushed to imagine.

Forcing herself to look away, she glanced at the man next to him. Shorter, he had the unbending carriage of a soldier. As she saw his face, she gripped the wooden lattice, plunging the splinter deeper into her palm.

It was Sohier de Courtrai, Lord of Dronghen, the city's militia commander.

And he was speaking to Renard.

Chapter Seven

⌒⌒⌒⌒⌒⌒

Draped in a winding linen, Sohier de Courtrai sat stiffly on the wet wooden bench beside Renard. Neither man looked at the other, but Katrine, scrutinising both, knew the pursing and stretching of their mouths formed words, lost quickly among damp echoes.

A chance meeting? No. The Lord of Dronghen was trying too hard not to be noticed.

He sat rigidly, as if he surveyed his troops instead of a bath house full of naked men. His face was calm, as Katrine remembered it from military displays, but every muscle was in place, battle ready.

Ghent's militia commander was one of the most respected men in the city. He had the wealth and power of one nobly born, although his money had come from trade. He was a confidant of the Count, held a pension from King Philip himself, and yet was also beloved by the common people. His daughter was wife to a powerful member of the burgher city council. He had everything. He was trusted by everyone. There was nothing he could need from a smuggler.

She watched their lips, trying in vain to make out the words.

Renard's lazy eyelid hid the fact that he was scanning the room, as he had scanned the streets behind him. She ducked, afraid he might glance up.

Footsteps thumped up the stairs. Scrambling for safety, she jumped off the bench and tripped over her skirt, catching herself on the heels of her hands. The steps paused, as if someone had stopped to listen, then resumed, faster.

Katrine dragged the bench back into the bathing room, the groan of wood across stone so loud, that she was sure the woman could hear it.

She closed the door and shoved the bench before it, terrified the attendant would fling it open to find her still dressed. Fingers clumsy with fear and the sharp burn of the splinter, she fumbled with her surcoat laces.

The footsteps approached her door.

Flinging her surcoat, tunic and shift to the floor, she sank into the tepid water, gasping at the chill. Submerged, she felt the rosemary leaves tickle her collarbone. Her chest rose and fell, rippling the water.

The attendant banged on the door and, without waiting for leave, pushed it open.

It hit the bench, which rocked on its legs like a crazed cradle and then tipped over with a clatter.

The woman's mouth opened and closed like a fish's. She looked from the bench blocking the door to the clothes scattered on the floor to Katrine—sitting naked in the tub with a full wimple still swaddling her head.

Katrine fixed an indignant eye on the woman, flaring her nostrils. 'What excuse have you for bursting into my private bath?'

'I thought I heard…' She stared at the bench and then at Katrine, wimple sailing above the water, and shook her head.

'I see your marriage vows are genuine.' Not bothering to right the bench, she paused. 'Till the next bell.'

The door slammed behind her.

Leaning her head on the cloth cushioning the edge of the tub, Katrine tried to think. Instead she saw Renard rising from the pool, water cascading down his back and over thighs sculpted by days on a war-horse.

Her breath quickened and her breasts puckered, teased by the rosemary leaves.

Lead me not into temptation, she began, then paused. It was too late for that. Saint Catherine already knew her shame.

She tried a different prayer. *Let me not be misled by temptation to trust him.*

When his hands had cradled her and his scent had surrounded her, she had wanted to believe he cared about her. She had wanted to trust him with everything she was.

The bath water was cold, but reality was colder.

Renard was having clandestine meetings with the city's chief military officer. Whatever he was, he was no simple smuggler. Perhaps no smuggler at all.

Yet now that her uncle had returned, she could not simply toss him out and his temptation with him. He had taken her money and, even if he did not bring her wool, his presence might at least prevent her uncle from seizing her by force.

She shivered as she climbed out of the tub. Drying and dressing quickly, she escaped the bath house without being seen. She could brook no more evasions. She must make him confess who he really was.

She should have remembered the words from the fox's tale: 'Renard's promise was mere invention. He said the words without intention.'

* * *

That night, Katrine sent Merkin to her kitchen pallet and lay on her bed, still dressed, listening for the soft creak of his step on the third floor.

A soft thump above. He was back.

She started up the narrow stairway, rubbing the wool of her skirt between finger and thumb. 'Renard,' she called, trying to make her voice stronger than her fear. 'I must speak with you.'

When she reached the third floor he was waiting for her, wearing only chausses, his chest bare.

Her defiant words evaporated.

If she reached out her hand, she could touch the lush curls covering his chest.

She shut her eyes, but then she saw him rising out of the water, just before he reached for the winding sheet—

'It seems,' he said, coldly, 'that I really do need protection from you.'

She opened her eyes and crossed her arms, trying to calm her racing heart. She must not let him dissuade her. 'Where do you go every day?'

'It is none of your concern.'

A hint of rosemary clung to her nose. Her scent or his? 'You smell like the bath house. Is that where you go?'

He raised his eyebrows. 'You take an inordinant interest in me, mistress.'

'Not in you,' she lied. 'But you have my money and I have nothing to show for it.' His gaze unnerved her. She wanted to be free of the feelings he raised. 'If I cannot have my wool by tomorrow, I want you gone. Now, tonight.'

'With your money? What a generous offer.' He smiled, and reached for his sack.

Her thoughtless tongue. Being near him stole her sense. 'No. Give me my money first.'

'It's already been put to work. But don't worry. Someone else will want your wool.' He stood, silent, as if knowing she would change her mind and beg him to stay.

'Tell me,' she said, finally, ready to risk it all. 'Are you really a smuggler?'

She watched for a shift in his expression, anything to tell her she had hit the mark.

'I thought,' he said, all smile and temptation, 'you had decided I was the Devil.'

'I don't know who or what you are.'

'Ask all the questions you like. You have all the answers you will get.'

His tone was cold, but his eyes were warm and she wanted to believe all over again. Maybe you belong to me, he had said. Then he had held her as if...as if she were worthy of love.

She stretched out her hand, all other thoughts gone.

He grabbed her wrist and wrenched her arm away before she could touch him. But that only brought her closer until she was pressed against his naked chest.

No longer able to think or speak, she leaned into him. He bent towards her, lips close enough for her to taste. Just a little more...

She pressed her lips to his. And for a moment, she could not separate her breath from his.

Perhaps you belong to me.

He stiffened and thrust her away. Chest heaving, she gulped for air.

So did he. For the first time he looked as ruffled as she felt.

'It seems you want something more from me than the wool. Is that why you chase me to my bed?'

She closed her eyes and shook her head, crossing her arms against his accusation. Shame, shame to throw herself into his arms. The man had made his hatred clear. No man could love a woman with such wanton thoughts.

'Now return to your bed before we do something we will both regret.'

He turned his back and she fled.

He lay in the darkness, taming his breath, struggling for control. His lust would get him killed if he weren't careful.

Are you really a smuggler? How much did she know? Suspect? Would she tell anyone of her suspicions? If so, he could find the Count's sword at his back on the morrow.

He should leave, leave her money behind and disappear. There must be other, safer places to find shelter.

Even had he not desired her, this woman was a worthier opponent than he had bargained for. He thought he would be safe here. He thought he could intimidate her.

But she would not be cowed except with the threat of lovemaking. The one thing he must avoid was the one weapon he had. And even that was no longer certain. Tonight, she had reached for him. If he had not pushed her away, if he had let himself go…

So he must dance on this dagger's edge, keeping her off balance while keeping his own.

A dangerous game.

The next morning, she rose and broke fast as if nothing had changed.

But everything had.

She could not face him again, in daylight or dark. She had reached for him, asked for his kiss, done all those things her uncle had always said she would do—made her shame public.

Now, she must find someone else to get her wool. She might not know the truth, but she knew she couldn't trust him. If there was one smuggler, there must be others. Surely someone at the docks, someone who travelled the trade routes, could help her.

She shuttered the shop and tied the leather pouch with her father's remaining livres securely under her tunic, patting the surcoat to make sure it was well hidden. Men had been killed for far lighter purses.

The heavy bag banged her leg with each stride as she crossed the bustling Corn Market Square. The streets were crowded as the fishmongers gathered for their annual guild parade. The procession would begin after midday, but the revelry would not end until after midnight.

If revelry it was. Complaints were voiced on the street now, loud enough for her to hear. So angry at the Count, they no longer bothered to conceal their hate.

Something moved behind her and she walked faster, glancing back. Was it a beggar with a knife or a stray dog? Or was it Ranf? Her uncle's silence was more ominous than his bluster.

All she saw looked ordinary. People going in and out of the massive guild halls facing the river. Sellers of wood and water calling out their wares. She turned back, keeping her eyes straight ahead, and ignored the prickle at the back of her neck.

By the quay, a purple sheen castoff from the boats smudged the reflection of the stairstep roofs. Ship by ship, she was met with suspicion, disbelief and comments in languages she was grateful she didn't understand.

Renard was right. It was not easy to find wool.

She heard only one suggestion. Black Pieter. Outside the city walls beyond the Muide Gate where the lepers lived.

By the time she started for the gate, the sun was high. The parade had begun, snaking through the city, blocking her way. She stood at the edge of the street while the sun crawled across the sky, trying to dart across, but each time forced back by the revellers, drunk already.

Then, beside her, a squire cried out, announcing his master, a knight on horseback.

Forgetting that a woman should not look overlong at strange men, she stared. The curly-haired knight looked out on the world with an amused smile, as if everything had been assembled expressly for his delight. He wore a red silk eyepatch.

English, then.

Riding into the street, he parted the parade as if it were the Red Sea, then waved her across, following to see her safely through.

'My thanks to you.' She gave him her first smile of the day. 'What may I call you, sir?'

The knight clutched at his heart with one hand, shaking his head. He looked towards heaven with the eye not covered and then traced an 'X' over his lips with his finger.

They vowed to their ladies to wear them and speak to no one until they had done some deeds of arms in France, Merkin had said.

She sighed, regretting her boldness of speech. He would never have been so chivalrous if he had seen her last night.

The lady of such a knight would have fair hair and soft fingers and downcast eyes and she would never, never chase a man to his bedchamber.

Hand still clutching his heart, the curly-haired one sighed in agony worthy of a miracle play. He pressed his fingers to his lips and blew her a kiss, then tossed a handful of coins into the street. The paraders and the crowd dropped to their knees, scrambling in the dirt to grab one.

She ran on. At least the English had some pity for the wreckage their embargo had created, unlike their own count.

She hurried across the final bridge in the lengthening shadows. She must be home before dark. Passing through the city gate gave her pause. Who would live beyond the protection of the walls by choice?

The tinkling of a leper's bell followed her to the last shack. The smell of rotting apples seeped through the wooden shutters, closed against the late-afternoon sun. Taking a deep breath, she asked Saint Catherine for courage, and knocked.

'Come.'

She pushed the door open, covering her nose against the smell.

A man with matted black hair and torn braises sat in the room's only chair, fondling a tankard of ale. His eyes widened as Katrine stumbled across his threshold, but he spoke as he might to a passing hound. 'What brings ye here?'

At the shock of him, she was equally direct. 'Wool.'

He looked her up and down with watery eyes. 'Ye having or wanting?'

She stared at the large mole on the left side of his nose instead of meeting his eyes. 'Wanting,' she said.

'Ah…' He shook his head. 'That's a hard one.'

'If you are Black Pieter, I've been told you can get it. Can you?'

He looked at her for a long time before he answered, 'Maybe.'

'How much can you get for me?' The question she had asked Renard echoed like the memory of a bad dream. This man looked even less trustworthy.

'Depends. How much is it worth?'

She had learned something about negotiation since the last time. 'Fifteen gold livres a sack. On delivery.'

He shook his head. 'Twenty-five. In advance.' His eyes crawled over her. 'And maybe something else.'

Katrine fought the urge to run. This shack was the end of her road, too. 'Twenty. On delivery.' Her last words came through clenched teeth. 'Nothing else.'

He shrugged. 'If you don't want it, there's others that do.'

'None that can pay in gold, I wager.'

His eyes gleamed. She had made the right appeal.

'I'll give you five now and a total of twenty per sack on delivery for two sacks.' Renard's first payment had depleted her precious hoard.

He gave a gap-toothed grin. 'Show me the five.'

Her face burned. 'Turn around while I retrieve it.'

The mole on his nose seemed to twitch with anticipation. 'Oh, I think I'll watch. Can't be too careful, you know.'

She turned her back, hoping she would know if he moved too close. Pulling up her surcoat and tunic, she reached the purse, trying to muffle the clinking of coins. If he knew she had fifty livres with her, he might kill her for the money.

Rearranging her skirts, she turned back and held out the gold piece as she would a piece of meat to a rabid dog. He snatched it away, mercifully without brushing her fingers.

'When will you have it?' she said.

'I'll let you know. Where's yer home?'

'Leave word at the Gheilaert sisters' booth at the Cloth Market.' She did not want him to know where she lived. She did not even want him to know who she was. 'Tell them you have a message for Katrine.'

He swilled his ale and then wiped his mouth with a grimy sleeve. 'Did your husband leave you with an empty bed as well as an empty loom?'

'It's only the loom that needs to be filled.' She summoned a glare that would have chastened a master weaver and backed out of the shack, not willing to turn her back on him again.

The setting sun cast golden light on the city wall as she hurried through the gate. The parade was over, but leftover revellers gathered outside the taverns, laughing and quarrelling over their beer.

Even her wimple did not protect her from the catcalls and whistles. No respectable woman would be out alone at this time of day. One of them grabbed for her, but she pulled her skirt back and he stumbled away, too drunk to hold on.

To avoid further trouble, she left the crowded places for the narrower, emptier streets, lengthening her walk home. As the night wore on, even the watch would not be able to prevent drunken, armed men from committing sins they would have to confess on the morrow.

Daylight had nearly disappeared by the time she reached High Gate Street. She had walked this street so many times with her father, eyes on the heavens to see who could spot the first star of evening. She smiled, looking up to find the first star, wishing for her father's safe return.

She saw nothing before a shadow jerked her arms back and dragged her, stumbling, into the alley in the shadow of St John's Church. Her pouch bumped wildly as she kicked him. A drunken guild member, no doubt, thinking to force a kiss. Or more.

She took a breath to scream, but a familiar voice in her ear snarled, 'Don't.' The cold, dull edge of a dagger invaded her wimple, pressing against the edge of her jaw beneath her left ear. 'I have a message from your uncle.'

She stilled every part of her body and tried to hide the bulge of her pouch of coins.

'What a strange way to deliver it,' she said, heart pounding in her throat. 'He could have come to visit.'

'He doesn't want this to be public.' Ranf's words and his fist hit at the same time. 'Come back to his house—' a blow battered her ribs '—or the next warning will be more painful.'

She doubled over, clutching her right side. Another blow snapped her head back. Dizzy, she saw only moving darkness.

She focused hard on a rough, round ball, swinging from the shadow's hand until it took shape as a linen sack with a creeping red stain. 'And anyone else you ask to help will come to the same end.'

He opened the sack, spilling something into the street, where it rolled crazily, splattering blood and mud like a grisly witch's brew. She stared, shaking, unable to look away, unwilling to recognise what she saw.

It was Black Pieter's head.

And her last thought, before everything went black, was a prayer of thanks that it was not Renard.

Chapter Eight

Renard slipped into the back garden, glad to be done with the loose-lipped fishmongers. Revelry and ale beneath a full moon made a dangerous brew, but one that served his purpose.

Even the sellers of carp held no love for the Count and respected Courtrai. His plan might work.

Closing the gate, he looked over his shoulder one more time to be certain no one had followed him. He ached to be done with spying. Every moment posed a threat as he guarded his speech, guarded his back and struggled to decipher hidden meanings buried in public words.

Eyes ever mindful, he was no longer certain what he saw. He had even imagined Katrine behind him yesterday.

As he opened the door to the house, a wooden shoe whacked his shin, nearly bringing him to his knees before an awkward blow missed his stomach.

He grabbed and found his arms full of Merkin, flailing at him with a rolling pin as if fighting for her life.

'Merkin. Stop. It's Renard.' He twisted the weapon out of her fingers, straining to hear some noise of Katrine in the house.

Merkin stopped kicking and sagged against him, panting. 'Finally. Fine guard you are.'

Renard's dagger found his hand before he was aware of the thought. Silence, ominous, hovered where he should have heard Katrine's step. 'What happened? Where is she?'

Merkin's freckles blossomed on a face paler than usual. 'She was attacked not two houses away. They carried her here and I put her to bed, but now I can't wake her.'

He vaulted the stairs, two at a time. Muscles coiled, dagger still drawn, he flung open Katrine's door.

Burrowed under wimple, dress and covers, she lay curled within a cloth cocoon as if it could shield her from another attack. Blood—hers?—smeared the linens. A large, purple bruise spread around her left eye.

A bedraggled braid had escaped the wimple that had proven no protection on the street. It trailed, uncombed, across dirty bed linens. What was Merkin thinking to leave her like this?

Renard lowered his dagger slowly. Only the pounding in his palm convinced him his heart still beat. 'Katrine,' he said softly. 'Katrine, it is me. Are you all right?'

She did not stir.

He stepped closer, fumbling to sheath his dagger. Her fingers lay curled and stiff, as if she still clawed her attacker. Candlelight wavered over her torn left sleeve, making it hard to separate shadow from bruise. God knows what injuries he could not see.

His muddled thoughts felt like a prayer.

'It's all right now. I am here.' As if he could make everything right by being there. As he had made things wrong by being away.

She did not answer.

'Do you know me?' He barely recognised his own voice. Nothing.

He knelt beside the bed and shook her shoulder, careful to avoid the bruise. Her eyes, weighed down by that thicket of eyelashes, stayed closed, as if she were asleep.

Or dead.

He leaned closer and saw the shallow rise and fall of her chest. The smell of blood took him back to Scotland. When the battlefield turned red, sometimes a warrior would retreat behind his eyes to another, safer world.

Sometimes, he would never come back.

'Rest, then. Wake when you are ready. I will not leave you, I promise.' Promise. He had become such a smooth-tongued liar. He would promise anything to bring her back from the blackness.

He pulled up a wooden stool and sat, eyes fixed on her face. Words had not worked, so he tried touches, rubbing her frigid fingers, cradling her hand in two of his, stroking her arm. The candle flame trembled beside him, as futile against the blackness as a torch flung into the sea.

I still need protection, she had said.

I thought I was to protect you, he had answered, not truly understanding. A thought, the worst, grabbed his gut. Had this been not robbery, but rape?

The clatter of clogs at the door made him turn. Merkin, wide eyes wild with distress, paused on the threshold. 'Sir, you must leave. You mustn't—'

'What happened? Who did this?'

She worried her lip before she answered. 'I don't know. The watch found her near the church and carried her home.'

'When?'

'After dark. And, sir, there was something else.' She

looked at Katrine, then whispered, 'They said there was this man's head, next to her.' She crossed herself, as if it were on the floor before her. 'Cut off.'

He shuddered at the image, hoping it explained the blood on the sheets. 'Whose?' He had nursed a hope that the attack was random, but this was vicious. Personal.

'No one knows, sir.' Merkin was near tears.

'Did he—?' He could not finish the question. The girl did not need the burden of thinking that her mistress had been violated.

'I wanted to fetch the doctor,' she said, not noticing his silence, 'but I was afraid to go. Maybe he's waiting out there.'

Sympathy for the girl softened his tongue. 'Has she eaten?'

'She refused the spoon and just lay there like she wasn't really here at all.' Merkin stared at the bed. 'Did demons do it? Do they possess her now?'

'No, Merkin.' He spoke slowly, each Flemish syllable carefully formed. 'The demon who did this walks on two legs.'

And I will not let him walk for long.

He shook off the thought. How was he to punish a wraith?

'I know your mistress appreciates everything you have done. Now we need to bathe her and check for injuries. Heat water. Find a tub and soap. Let me know when it is ready.'

'Sir?' Her eyes widened in horror. 'I can't let you.' Mouth agape, she looked to her sleeping mistress for help.

Eyes closed, Katrine lay in her own world.

'You want to help her, Merkin. So do I. Do as I say. Now.' He lapsed into the tone of command he shared with his king.

The girl turned to leave, seeming glad to relinquish responsibility too big for shoulders even smaller than Katrine's.

Renard let silence reclaim the air as the clump of Merkin's shoes faded down the stairs.

'Katrine, I want you to open your eyes and look at me.' He spoke in a low, coaxing voice, personal, intimate, hardly aware of what words he spoke. 'Can you do that for me? Try, won't you?'

She lay still, silent.

'All right, *ma petite*, if you are too tired yet to open your eyes, *ce n'est rien*.' Her warm, slightly cinnamon scent floated up from the sheets, more alive than the smell of stale blood. 'Merkin will bring water so we can wash you. A clean, fresh start and then you will feel better, *n'est pas*?' Mindless in the stream of words, he hardly noticed that he had lapsed into French.

She nodded.

She had heard and understood his French.

Well, that was not unusual. Many patricians understood the language of the noble class. If she knew French, so much the better. It would be a relief not having to concentrate on his Flemish every minute.

'So you will like a clean start, *oui*? Would you like me to speak French for a while?'

Another nod, her eyes still closed.

Something tight within him let go. 'Then I will tell a story to amuse you.'

Eyes still closed, she rolled on to her back. Her lips tightened when she moved, but her fingers had lost their stiffness.

'In olden times,' Renard began, 'when animals could still talk and were much smarter than humans, there lived a fox they called Renard, which means "strong in counsel" because he was wise and cunning.'

He could recite every one of the dozens of stories about

Renard the Fox. By the end of each, Renard was no longer wise and cunning. He was exposed as a liar, a cheat and a faithless friend.

How his mother must have hated him to saddle him with such a name.

'On the tenth anniversary of the Queen's ascension,' he continued, 'all the land sent token and tribute, a gift from each to celebrate their happiness in her reign.'

Relaxed, her lips seemed fuller, tempting his finger to trace their outlines as he had that first night.

He cleared his throat. 'Gifts came from across the land. From the sheep came wondrous bolts of cloth of gold.

'From the lion came a crown of diamonds, each large as a goose egg, each reflecting thousands of tiny rainbows when the sun struck them.

'So the gifts streamed in, tribute to her beauty, wisdom and wise rule. But as the Queen surveyed her treasures, she saw nothing from Renard the Fox, and she wondered at it.'

His lips moved over the familiar story, but his eyes never moved from her. Lying on her back, eyes closed, she shifted easily, her body no longer rigid. Her calloused fingers lay loosely on top of the coverlet. He fought the urge to lace them with his and continued the tale.

'"What have you sent me, Renard, in tribute to my wisdom and beauty?"' the Queen asked the fox.'

'Pardon, sir.' Merkin's Flemish startled him.

Katrine flinched at the new voice. Delight at her reaction warred with irritation at the girl's interruption. 'What is it?'

'I… You said…you wanted… The water is ready.'

He looked at Katrine. 'I will be right back. I promise.' He brushed the back of his hand along her cheek and she turned towards it, eyes still closed. He didn't bother to deny his delight.

Relieved, he followed Merkin down the stairs. 'Doesn't she have family? You could have sent for someone.'

'Curfew had rung,' Merkin shot back. 'And what if *he* was still out there? Why weren't you here?'

His stomach twisted with guilt and he lashed back. 'Didn't anyone ask questions? Try to find the man?'

'On a night when the guild rules the streets?' She slumped with exhaustion. 'God looks after justice.'

He did not want to frighten Merkin any more than she already was, but no drunken seller of fish was to blame for this. The attack on Katrine was a message.

But from whom? Had the man he'd seen watching the house attacked her as a warning? Would Renard's turn come next?

'What was you telling her, sir?' Merkin said.

'Telling her?'

'In French. It sounded like a story.'

'It was the story of Renard and the Queen's gift.'

'Please, would you tell me, too?'

So he repeated the tale in Flemish while they gathered cloths and soap and he carried the small kettle with water that sloshed on to his feet as he mounted the stairs.

At Katrine's door, Merkin paused, whispering, 'Just hang it on the hook over the fire before you leave.'

'I'm not leaving. You can't change her clothes alone and I know more about injuries than you do.'

'But—'

'Merkin. Do as I say.'

As she stepped into the room, she rolled her eyes and gave him a glance that said she would be watching his every move.

Chapter Nine

Katrine lay as they had left her, her pale face and dark bruises clashing with her bright red braid. No fresh blood stained the sheets.

Good. Maybe none of it is hers.

'Come, Merkin. Build up the fire so she will not take cold.'

The bed sagged as he sat. The curve of her slim hip, padded by wool and bedclothes, pressed against his thigh and the scent of her skin, warmed beneath the covers, rose through the layers of fabric.

He wished Merkin would disappear and leave Katrine to him. Surely his voice and his hands could heal her. Her breathing was even now, and her eyes closed, but he did not know whether it was because she dozed or was trying to shut out the world.

'Now, *mon petit lapin*, Merkin will wash you and you will feel like yourself again.'

At his words, she curled in on herself, burrowing into the bedclothes as if to turn her back on a world in which she could be beaten on the street and left lying, helpless, next to a bloody head.

Firmly, but gently, he forced her on to her back, her eyes still shut tight. No wonder she tried to deny a world full of such horror. Horror he should have been able to spare her.

'We will not hurt you, *chérie*, but we must see if you are injured. Be a good girl and I will finish the story.'

She stopped straining against him and he slid his hands from her wrists to her shoulders, gently stroking, soothing her nervousness, feeling her flinch when he touched the bruised shoulder.

He motioned to Merkin. 'Get these clothes off. Let's see where else she is injured.'

He started to remove her wimple and Katrine reached for his hands, trying to stop him, eyes still tightly closed, unaware that an errant braid had already spilled out of the crooked headdress, revealing her silken secret. Her hands closed around his wrists, not strong enough to stop him, but strong as iron because he knew the agony it would cause her.

'Never mind, *ma petite*.' He tucked the stray braid back into hiding. 'We will leave your protection in place.'

One on each side of the bed, he and Merkin turned down the bedclothes. Merkin, keeping a suspicious eye on him, worked with brisk efficiency, pulling the front lacing free on the brown surcoat and pulling the sideless tunic off her body.

With the surcoat removed, he could see a lump beneath the inner tunic. 'What is this?'

Not waiting for Merkin's answer, he pinched the lump through the wool of her tunic. It clinked.

A pouch of coins. Heavy. More than enough to kill her for. Had the assailant wanted this instead of her?

Fear ricocheted to anger. 'Is it her practice to walk about the streets carrying all her worldly wealth?'

Merkin opened her mouth to argue and then closed it. 'No, sir.'

'Where was she going?'

'She didn't say.' Her eyes, normally so merry, filled with tears. 'Please, sir, don't take it. It's all we have.'

Her pleading face startled him. Did the child think he was heartless? Well, no wonder that she did. It was the role he played. He had given them no reason to trust him.

He mustn't start now.

He summoned his best fox's smile. 'I'll have it soon enough. I'm just glad to know she can pay me.'

'For protecting her?'

Her question stung. Certainly he deserved no pay for that. He rose abruptly and turned his back. 'Make her comfortable. I won't look.'

The coins clinked as Merkin placed the pouch on the trunk. From the sound, it was enough to pay for the wool she expected him to bring her. An honest woman, then, as she had said.

'Please, sir, can you help me?' Merkin's tone was grudging. 'I can't get the tunic and kirtle off by myself.'

The sight of Katrine, limp against the linens, chilled him. But he saw no new blood. And she had nodded at him.

Merkin tugged the gold tunic up and Renard slipped one arm under Katrine's knees, the other under her waist, and lifted her away from the sheets.

Katrine cried out.

He eased her hips back on to the bed, watching to see when she winced, trying to determine where she was injured. Merkin pulled the tunic over Katrine's head.

Now, only a thin linen chemise separated him from her skin and he could feel the reassuring warmth of life through the fine weave. The roaring in his ears, like the moment before battle, was a signal that he was ready to fight. But the only enemy here was his own weakness. A weakness that, despite all he had tried, seemed to be in his veins, beyond his control, like a separate soul inside him.

He wanted to close his eyes against temptation, but he forced himself to look at her impersonally, as if she were a knight felled in battle. No blood. No broken bones that he could see. Just the dark marks on her face, arms and side.

Picking up the cloth, Merkin dipped it in warm water and started washing Katrine's face. The warm water and the gentle strokes seemed to soothe her.

'I don't see anything else, sir. Maybe there's nothing but the bruises.'

He didn't believe it. Her breaths were too shallow. He leaned over, arms on either side of her. 'Katrine? Try to take a big breath,' he coaxed. 'Come on. One big one.'

He knew she heard. She took a couple of small breaths, but when she inhaled deeply, she doubled over to her right side. Her small cry stabbed his heart.

He exhaled in painful parallel. 'It's her ribs. We must bind her so she doesn't hurt them further. It's all right, *ma petite*,' he said, talking now to Katrine. 'I've seen these injuries before in…' Damn. He was losing concentration. He'd almost said Scotland. If he wasn't careful, he'd have no secrets left. 'We'll wrap them. They will heal.'

As Merkin stroked Katrine, he felt each touch as if her skin were his own. The bruise on her shoulder went deep. Loom-sculpted muscles rolled gently across her upper arms. The skin on her inner elbow was delicate, sensitive.

He breathed in shallow pants, not sure if the rhythm was his or hers.

Merkin arched her brows. 'Why don't you sit over there and finish your story while I wash her?'

Renard backed away from the bed, stumbling on the stool before he sat, uncertain he was capable of speech. He began too loudly and in French, he realised, when he saw Merkin's disappointed face. Flemish, then. Just as well. It would force him to concentrate on something other than Katrine.

'The Queen received tribute from all her subjects, for she was brave and beautiful and good and they loved her. She had hair the colour of a red-gold sunset sky. Her eyes had lashes as thick as a forest thicket. Her skin was white as the May blossom.'

'This queen looks like someone we know, doesn't she?' Merkin spoke cheerily to an unresponsive Katrine, but she looked at Renard.

He could hide his emotions from kings. How had he become so transparent that even this child could see through him?

Merkin's cloth stroked Katrine's left leg. The pale skin had taken on a slight flush. Instead of lying still, she shifted her leg beneath Merkin's hand as it disappeared beneath the tangled chemise.

Renard swallowed, struggling to continue. 'But the Queen still saw nothing from Renard. "Do you not honor me?" she asked.

'"Oh, most perfect Queen, I have sent a gift beyond price. One that will put all the wonders of the world in your hand and give you power beyond measure," he answered.'

Merkin placed the sheet carefully back over Katrine's left side and moved around to Renard's side of the bed. She folded the sheet away from Katrine's right arm and shoulder. The heat of the fire washed over him.

He kept talking. '"Where is this wonder?" the Queen asked. "I find no gift from thee among the treasures."

'And Renard told the Queen, "I sent you a globe of glass from beyond the seven seas. Look deep within it. Whatever truth you seek, whether knowledge of present or past or what is to come, you will see it there."'

Merkin re-covered Katrine's arm and shoulder with the sheet and uncovered her leg from hip to ankle, blocking Renard's view as she sat, but he knew the cloth would disappear to the valley between her legs…

He forced each Flemish word now through a stiff jaw and clenched teeth. '"But I have received no such gift," cried the Queen. "We must search the kingdom, for the treasure you sent is lost."'

His voice trailed off. Katrine was breathing easily now, asleep. Merkin pulled the covers over her.

Relieved, he drew a clear breath and motioned Merkin towards the door. 'Fetch the physician at first light. I'll stay with her.'

Merkin slipped off her shoes and tiptoed to the door. 'Tell me first, sir— What happened to Renard's globe of glass?'

Deceit tasted sour on his tongue. 'There was no magic globe. Renard's gift was a lie. The Queen's last words were, "Trust not a word that Renard says. Each is a lie, that's all it is."'

Katrine closed her eyes against the light, but she could not close out the vision. Black Pieter, lifeless, staring at her from a pool of red mud. Ranf's fists a bludgeon.

Day and night, dream and reality blurred. She was afraid to open her eyes. When she felt a scream bubble in her throat, she concentrated on each breath, clutching the bed linens while she fought the fear.

She remembered little of what came after. Cold slick

stones of the street chilling her cheek. Urgent, babbling voices. The thump, thump of being carried by some well-meaning Samaritan, each bounce a violation of her ribs.

The soft cocoon of feather pillows. Retreating and ashamed of herself for retreating, but so tired and so alone. Her uncle's silence had been broken. She had been brave for nothing. There would be no salvation from the stinking house at the end of the road. Nothing more to hope for. No reason to face the world again.

So her mind took her away to a netherworld where she would not have to face the truth.

Yet against her will, she followed Renard's foolish tale of a fox and a queen and a magical globe of glass. Gently, he pulled her back until she could sleep without the visions.

She remembered, too, his voice drifting like a caress across her skin, making her body quiver like a taut warp thread about to snap. His voice created a restlessness and a sweet, moist weakness deep inside.

And hope. Enough hope to keep the fear at bay.

Now, as the morning light washed her room clean of nightmares, she wished for Renard's globe of glass to tell her the truth of him.

He came from Brussels, but spoke Norman French. He was a smuggler, outside the law, yet he met with Ghent's militia captain. His tunic was ragged, yet he never hesitated to command. He showed no emotion, but she sensed tenderness in his voice.

Everything about him said she should not trust him. Everything about him made her want to.

Sweet Saint Catherine, lead me...

The prayer died on her lips. She no longer knew where she wanted to go.

Chapter Ten

'Did you spread out the alder leaves to catch fleas, Katrine?'

Snug in her bed, Katrine watched Aunt Matilda lean heavily on one knee and squint at the floor to see whether the requisite leaves had drifted into the corners.

'No, Aunt Matilda…' Katrine sighed '…but I did hang the honey-cords to catch flies.' While she slept, Merkin had secretly summoned the physician and then her aunt. Now, while it was comforting to have Aunt Matilda poke the fire, feed her soup and plump up the pillows, she must mind her words.

Her aunt, she hoped, knew no more than Merkin had told her. Surely she didn't know her husband had ordered Katrine beaten. But Katrine wanted her to bear no tales back to him, either.

About her or about Renard.

'Humph.' Her aunt lifted her bulk off her knees and hit her head on the dangling cord. 'You haven't changed them in weeks, I'll vow.' She untied the cord, now so dry that even a fly would not be tempted. 'You never have been able to look after a house, child. It is no wonder your uncle despairs of you. How can you marry if you cannot keep your husband's home?'

'I'm not going to marry.' *No one would have me.*

'Of course you will, though perhaps not to as fine a man as your uncle. We can't help your looks and many will frown on what you do here, but, given a large enough dowry, someone will overlook all that.' She waved the dried honey-cord helplessly. 'Where is that worthless servant girl? I should take her home and beat her for running away.'

Only half the words her aunt spoke were her own. The others came from her husband's mouth.

Katrine clutched her wrapped ribs and fell back against the pillows, moaning in only a slight exaggeration of her pain. 'You wouldn't want me here without Merkin, would you? I can't get up and down the stairs.'

Aunt Matilda shook her head, grudgingly. 'I don't want you here at all. You ran away from us to stay here with nothing but a servant girl, you wander the streets alone. Now look what has happened.'

No mention of Renard. But it was unlikely her uncle had told his wife all he knew. 'Does my uncle know you're here?'

'He's with the Count again. But when I tell him, he'll be furious. The first thing he will say is that you should return to us.'

Come back to his house.

Katrine had told no one of Ranf's message. Better for them to think her a victim of chance. 'The streets are safe for no one. It could have happened no matter where I lived.'

'Why should you run away just because your uncle has a man's temper? He's been so patient with you. Every night since we've been back he says he should bring you home to protect you. When he finds out what's happened now, he'll be beside himself. I'm sure he'll come to bring you back himself.'

Katrine gripped her aunt's arm and shook it. 'Finds out? Don't you know he's—?' She bit her tongue. God had blessed her aunt with nearsightedness so she could not see what happened under her own nose. For some reason, her uncle wanted her return to seem her choice instead of his force. Or maybe he just wanted her to fear him enough to come back begging for mercy. It had almost worked. 'He worries too much.'

'He has always worried about you. He was the same way about your mother.'

'My mother?'

'Oh, yes. She was such a sweet, gay thing at the beginning and he was the kindest brother-in-law, with your father gone so much and all. She was so delicate. Always some bruise or another. Charles would find her, no matter what room she was in, and make sure she was comfortable.'

Katrine closed her eyes and felt again the rat's claw prickle of his fingers on her arms. *You are your mother's daughter. Sinful.* There was something there, some wisp of an idea she couldn't quite grasp. Had her mother lived in fear, too?

Aunt Matilda's cheerful chatter seemed to be coming from a great distance. 'And then when she died so suddenly one night, not even ill, no one but God could ever explain it. I don't know who grieved more, Charles or Denys.' Her aunt shook her head and patted Katrine's hand. 'Maybe that is why he worries about you so much. Because he knows how frail she was.'

Katrine gripped Matilda's loose-skinned hand and leaned forward. 'I am not frail. You must not tell him.'

A cloud of understanding drifted across the sky of Matilda's blue eyes. She blinked and it was gone. 'But you've been beaten. You are bedridden.'

'Aren't there things it is better he not know?' Katrine said in a conspirator's whisper. 'Remember the time we went to the fair after he forbade us to go without him? A very handsome cloth merchant smiled at you, I recall.'

A garish blush stained her aunt's pale cheeks. 'Well, yes, but that was different…'

Katrine continued, reckless. 'There are secrets women keep for each other. Like what you told me about the potion you take immediately after a night with your husband if you don't want to—'

'Shush, child.' Matilda blinked and stammered, looking towards the door. 'If the priests hear you, we'll all be sent to Hell.'

A smile of triumph escaped. 'Just tell my uncle I am well.' If her aunt did not mention the attack, perhaps he would be unable to act without revealing how he knew of it.

Matilda lifted her blue-swathed bulk off the bed, shaking her head. 'No matter what I say or don't, he'll soon come himself. If the Count didn't need him at war council night and day, he would have come before now.' She hugged Katrine and gave her fingers an extra squeeze. 'I must be home when he returns. If you need anything, send that lazy servant girl.'

After her aunt left, Katrine opened the lid of the box with the mirror Giles had given her and traced the silver four-petalled daisy on the back. Then, she lifted it out of the box and turned it over, repeating the childish game he had played with her so many times. Like peek-a-boo, he would turn the mirror to her face to show her 'how special Katrine is.'

Now, she gasped at the truth in the glass. A large, purple bruise surrounded her left eye. A rough scab crusted over the raw scrape on her cheek.

What had Renard thought, to see her like this? She poked at the bruise and cringed. Yet he had seen even more. Her arms, her legs. She remembered being beneath his eyes as if in a dream.

But a dream, not a nightmare. She had sensed neither disgust nor dishonour in him, but only steadfast caring. Could it be like that for her with a man?

You could marry still, her aunt had said.

Could she? Carry the keys. Supervise the household. Stitch sloppy needlework. It would be so much easier. Surely when her father certified her to the guild as his agent, he did not expect her to endure all this for some hanks of cloth. When, pray God, he returned at last, would he care if the shop was empty of what he and Giles had spent twenty years creating?

The eyes in the mirror reflected a different truth.

It was not *his* loss that she feared. It was not *his* sorrow that pricked her tears. It was not his dream she clung to.

It was her own.

She could tell the guild she was doing this only at her father's behest, but she could no longer tell herself.

Her hands ached for the wool. For the rough, oiled feel of it before it was tamed. For the Joseph's coat-of-colours of it. For the comfortable rhythm of the loom. For the joy of creating something from nothing. For the one place on earth where she could feel alive and her sins, real or imagined, didn't matter.

Strangely peaceful, she put the mirror back in its box. Close the shop? She might as well die.

Now, Renard was her only path. She must stop this foolish wish that he might care for her and hide her shameful feelings for him. If he was more than a smuggler, so be it. As long as he brought her wool, she would ignore the rest.

Otherwise, there would be no reason to stay here when her uncle came calling.

The house was still being watched.

On his way to meet the Bishop a few days later, Renard gave the slip to the lazy guard. Was he connected to Katrine's attack? The man never followed him away from the house and he had seen no others, so his discussions with Courtrai seemed safe for the moment, but time was running out. The Bishop and Courtrai must meet as soon as possible and he must leave Katrine. Far from protecting her, he had put her in harm's way. Yet finding a new base would take precious days away from his mission.

Surely a few more days wouldn't matter, a few more days to see her every day. Until she was well enough to answer his questions.

As Renard entered the Bishop's solar, Clare did not look up from his parchment. His frown suggested his report to Edward would not be rosy.

Renard's knees refused to bend as he touched his lips to the ring on Clare's outstretched hand. 'I have done as my king asked and identified a potential ally to counterbalance the Count.' He explained the Lord of Dronghen's position and influence.

'Not a noble?' The Bishop's voice arched with disdain. 'Then how can he sway the Count?'

Renard felt his eyelid twitch. The Bishop stubbornly refused to understand that Flanders was different from other duchies. 'It is not only the Count who must be swayed. The people's rights are guaranteed by charter. If the Council declares for neutrality, the Count cannot compel them to change. And Courtrai is the one man held in the highest regard by the Count *and* the Council.'

The Bishop's nostrils flared as if at a stench. He tore off both ends of a loaf of bread and discarded them, then gouged a hole in the heart of a soft, pungent cheese with a knife and spread it on the slice. 'Well, you are so much more well equipped to deal with common people.' He took a bite. *You bastard*, hung unspoken in the air. 'What makes you think he will support the King?'

'He is prepared to entertain you for dinner at midday tomorrow.'

The Bishop brightened considerably, looking for the first time at Renard instead of the bread. 'Has he a good wine cellar?'

Renard wondered how much of the King's gold had gone into buying alliances and how much on to the Bishop's table. 'He is so popular that the town charges him no tax on the wine consumed in his house. I presume that means he can stock that much better quality.'

The Bishop smiled. 'Come 'round tomorrow. I'll tell you how it went.'

'It would be in the King's best interest for me to be there. Dronghen trusts me. He has no reason to trust you.'

And neither do I.

'Then you are coming out of hiding to join the official delegation?'

Renard hesitated. Hadn't he just considered leaving the house on High Gate Street? Once Courtrai and the Bishop had met, there would be no reason to stay in disguise and at risk of discovery.

No reason but one. Katrine was healing, but she still could not manage the stairs alone. Yesterday, she would have built her own fire if he had not stopped her. The day before she had insisted on chopping onions. He kept her from weaving only by teasing her into giving him more lessons.

And there was one more thing he must know and one more thing he must do for her before he left.

'The situation is unstable,' he said, finally. 'I can best serve by remaining invisible.'

The Bishop's attention had turned from the bread to the morsel of a flaxen-haired serving girl standing outside the door. 'As you wish.'

'There is one other thing.' Renard waited, forcing the Bishop's attention back to him. 'If I am to continue to play a smuggler, I must produce some wool or risk exposing my real mission.'

The King had given Renard free rein, but the Bishop's signature was required to withdraw wool from the guarded warehouse in Brussels.

'You wish to bring in the very wool we have been trying to keep out?'

'To operate in secret, I must play my role believably.'

'Who will receive this precious wool,' Clare said, '*if* I authorise it?'

The bravest little lady in Christendom. 'A draper who has been helpful and who knows nothing of who I am or why I am here.'

Eyes on the serving girl, the Bishop picked up his quill and reached for clean parchment. 'Very well. One sack.'

'I need three.'

'Three?'

Renard nodded. 'Three sacks.'

Clare threw down the quill. 'Whose side are you on?'

'*My* loyalty to the King has never been questioned.'

The man gritted his teeth and scrawled the authorisation in writing as spare and gaunt as his form. Then he imprinted his seal and handed the parchment to Renard. 'How do I find you if I need you?'

His safe house, Katrine's, was already violated. Until he knew why, he would take no more chances. 'It would be safer if I kept my whereabouts secret. I will relay messages through Jack de Beauchance.'

'De Beauchance? Nearly committed a mortal sin with one of the ladies-in-waiting in Valenciennes.' The Bishop turned his back on Renard to gaze at the corridor where the serving girl had stood.

Renard plucked a juicy orange from the top of the bowl, tucked it inside his shirt, bowed to the Bishop's back and walked out.

When he returned to the shop, he shut the door, took the stairs two at a time and gave Katrine the golden orange.

As soon as she saw it, she laughed in delight, bouncing on the bed until she had to clutch her ribs. She had Merkin cook the bitter fruit with honey, savoured every bite, then had the peel candied with hoarded ginger, saving it for later.

She left not a scrap.

Chapter Eleven

⎯⎯⎯✦⎯⎯⎯

He awoke that morning, as he had every morning, and told himself he would leave tomorrow.

The meeting between the Bishop and Courtrai had gone well and his next mission had been too long postponed. It was time to secure the support of the Duke of Brabant for Edward's cause.

No need to say, of course, that Renard would be negotiating with his half-brother.

Still, Edward's task and the Bishop's letter of release burned in his pouch. The attack on Katrine had been a warning to him, he was convinced. She refused to speak of it, though he had asked. Surely she would be safer with him gone, but he could not leave without being sure. Had she only been beaten, or was there something worse?

Thankfully, Katrine no longer came close enough to touch him, though she seemed to enjoy teaching him to weave. He warmed to her grudging praise at his progress. He was beginning to feel comfortable, riding the loom. The nut-brown piece grew rapidly beneath his strong arms. Tangible, measurable, it was a daily and direct result of his efforts, independent of the whims of kings or bishops.

But judging from the few skeins left in the basket, there was not enough wool to restring the warp.

He sat up, looked out the third-floor window, and vowed to leave tomorrow. Which meant today, he must know. She could refuse his questions no longer.

Katrine's voice drifted up the stairs, tickling his ear like a wisp of smoke. Rolling away from a sharp piece of straw, he welcomed her into his half-dream.

Until he heard her words.

'Merkin, can you help me down the stairs?'

Stairs.

He grabbed his chausses, controlling shaking fingers by battle-won habit. Why was the servant girl always out when she was needed? Only a few days after a savage beating, brave, foolish, barely able to stand, Katrine would never be able to walk downstairs alone. She would fall. This time, her ribs would break…

'Merkin, are you there?'

The wooden floor groaned, softly, accepting Katrine's weight. He left the last holes unlaced and ran.

At the top of the stairs, he could see her on the lower landing, swaying towards the first step. She hesitated, then, as if realising she was unsteady, reached for the wall, balancing herself with a flat palm.

'Merkin? Where are you? I need you.'

Silence.

Her legs trembled and she braced herself, arms spread wall to wall.

He choked back the warning in his throat, not daring to startle her into falling.

She leaned forwards, linen stroking the curve of her slender hip, and stretched her foot over the void of the first step.

His heart stopped.

Leaping down the stairs, he pulled her back from the step just as she was about to topple headlong.

Cradling her in crossed arms, touching his lips to the top of her head, he locked her against the rise and fall of his chest, his heart racing.

The silk of her hair was smooth on his lips and the sleeping-tinged scent of her rushed to his head. He held his breath as tightly as he held her.

'Let me go.' She wiggled against him.

All the denial he could summon could not control his body's swelling to nestle in the sweet curves pressing against him.

Her linen-covered breasts rested softly on top of his forearm and he loosened his arms, mortified to find them wrapped directly around her bruised ribs. As he did, her left breast slipped and the nipple grazed his inner wrist through the fabric.

The swelling became a throbbing. Strong enough for her to feel. Too strong for him to deny.

Making sure she was steadied on the landing, he unwrapped his arms and stepped away from her and from the feelings she created.

'You should not take the stairs alone,' he said.

'That's…' She closed her eyes, hiding her feelings, but the rise and fall of her breasts quickened. 'That's why I was calling Merkin.'

Daylight outlined her figure beneath the chemise, the binding linen a white shadow across her ribs. Her hair flowed like red silk across the fine woven linen, as it would across the sheets she would share with a lover some day.

The imaged pained him.

'You called her, but you did not wait.' He assessed her healing, as he had every day. Yellow patches now broke through the bruise shadowing her eye.

'I'm hungry,' she said, her chin lifted in the stubborn gesture that touched him.

Chagrined, he realised he had not thought of her need for food this morning. 'Go back to bed. Then I'll find Merkin.'

She accepted his arm this time, her legs shaking with the unfamiliar weight they had not borne in days, but her voice was tart. 'Thank you, but I hired you to get fleece. I would rather you find that.'

The wool. For her, it was always about the wool. 'Mistress, I will bring you wool when the time is right.' He pulled back the bedcovers to let her sit, then scooped her into the bed. 'Please keep yourself from further injury,' he said, in tones as harsh as he could muster, 'until I receive my final payment.'

She winced at his words. 'I don't need your help to get into bed.'

He covered her with the sheet. 'You need someone's help.'

'I can take care of myself,' she said, sitting up, clutching the linen shielding her.

'No, you can't. I can't go until I am sure you are all right.'

'I am. Go.' Yet she pursed her lips against the pain.

'You can't even go downstairs without help.'

'Is this another of your excuses? I've sheltered you for days and I have yet to see a scrap of wool for my pains.' He heard unshed tears in her voice. 'You've spent enough time in this house and I've spent enough time in this bed.' She kicked off the sheets he had just placed over her, struggling to rise again.

He captured both her hands in his. 'Katrine, we must talk.'

She pulled away, waving her hands as wildly as she flung her words. 'Talk about what? You owe me wool. I will owe you twenty livres per sack. Did you only say you'd bring it so you could use my house as an inn?'

He looked down at his empty hands, to hide the truth she might have glimpsed in his eyes. Holding her hand in his, he rubbed his thumb gently over the callous at the top of her palm. 'Katrine, I need to know what happened that night.'

She pulled away, turning her back and curling inwards on herself. 'No.'

Hands on her shoulders, he felt a knot, coiled like a skein of snarled yarn. He rubbed slowly and deeply, as he had that day he had told her her hair was beautiful. Despite her resistance, her body seemed to melt.

He whispered, this time in French, 'Who attacked you?'

She raised her shoulders, but he did not let her shrug off his hands. 'There was a parade. People are angry and starving. It might have been anyone.'

The night of the parade when the festivities descended into debauchery while the watch looked the other way. It was the perfect cover. For whom?

Hands never pausing, Renard worked on the new knot. 'Yet he did not take your purse.'

She paused for more than a breath. 'I concealed it well.'

'Did you see what was beside you in the street?'

She squeezed her eyes shut, and nodded her head *yes*.

'Do you know who he was?'

Her whole body knotted now, as if trying to deny the vision. Then she shook her head, back and forth until the gesture lost all meaning.

He slipped his hands down her arms, holding them to her

sides so she could not twist away, and whispered into her ear. 'Would you recognise your attacker if you saw him again?'

She kept shaking her head as if she could not stop.

'Did he...take you?'

She went very still. Then, she hurled her elbow behind her, digging into his ribs. 'You think I invited his attack?' She waved her fists at him as if he were her attacker. 'Am I, like Eve, to be blamed for the man's sins? Or do you think that if I am no longer a maiden then you are free to exercise your lusts?'

Ignoring her blows, he hugged her to his chest, as he had on the stairs, rocking her like a child. 'None of those things. I just need to know how painful to make his death.'

She stopped struggling.

'No,' she whispered, finally. 'He did not take me.'

Still mine.

He battled the idea, but the desire it brought raced through him, so alive it would not be silenced.

Abruptly, he let her go and stood, moving to the window, safely away from her touch. 'Well, then, I shall forgo the vengeance. If he had stolen your gold, I *would* have had cause to kill him.'

She sat tall, as if gathering her pride for a fight. 'I suppose I am fortunate *you* did not rob me of it.'

Keep fighting, he thought, wanting her to hear his thoughts. *If you do not fight, I will take you in my arms and we will both be lost.*

And he felt a moment's anger at her for showing him how much of his mother's weakness lived in him. 'I will get my share, but only if you stop behaving so foolishly. How am I to be paid for my troubles if you are attacked again before I return?'

'Return? How can you return if you do not go? I want to see my wool and see the last of you.'

Renard leaned against the window, sounds of a foreign city teasing his ears. The call of 'kindling for sale'. The tolling bell, opening the day's market. The whine of the midges, swarming where the river was slow.

See the last of her. That was why he did not go.

There would be no excuse to stay once the wool was delivered. No chance of sparring glances with her stubborn brown eyes. No hope of a glimpse of her flame-coloured hair. No more satisfaction in coaxing a smile from a face too often serious.

It was too late to deny his desire to protect and avenge her. He must leave before control left him utterly. Just now, again, he had almost kissed her. Worse, almost vowed to avenge her as if he had been a brother.

Or a husband. That was why he had to know. He had come to think of her as *his*.

He folded his arms. 'You will see the last of me immediately, mistress. I leave tomorrow morning.'

The spark left her eyes. 'How long will you be gone?'

'A week. Maybe more.'

She lifted her chin and, more slowly, raised her eyes to find his. 'And then?'

Her face was full of feelings she did not know enough to hide. Might not even know enough to recognise. Longing. Hope.

He must not let her hope.

'Then, you will reward me handsomely with gold, and I'll be gone.' He spoke lightly, as if in jest, tracing her chin with his finger, trying to think of how to wound her and protect himself. 'Unless you have a more personal reward in mind.'

He was not aware that he was going to kiss her until his lips met hers.

And by the time he *was* aware, she lay beneath him on the bed. Desire, like a living being, controlled a body no longer under his command. He pressed against her, wanting the kiss, and so much more…

The slap of her hand against his cheek brought him to himself.

'Get out of my sight,' she said, each word a blow. 'I don't want to see you again unless your hands are full of wool. I am not here for you to exercise your lust. You disgust me.'

He pulled away, hiding the trembling in his knees with a bold smile. A lifetime of denial and control had always worked before. But not with her. In another moment, if she had not been the strong one—

The downstairs door opened and closed and he heard the clump of Merkin's shoes.

He bowed, gravely. 'I will send Merkin so that you may break fast.' Then, he forced his feet, step by step, to carry him too far away to touch her again.

His words, his kiss, had ripped the fabric of feeling woven between them. He had made her glad to see him go. Afterwards, she would not miss him, not hope for something he could not give.

And he? He would deliver her wool, request absolution for his lustful thoughts, and never think of her again.

Oh, yes, God had taught him the humility he would need to be a bishop. He had learned too much about himself that he did not want to know. It would be easier to forgive the sins of others since he had discovered so many of his own.

Chapter Twelve

It was better this way, Katrine reminded herself with each toss of the shuttle, as the afternoon sun cast sharp, hot shadows on to the street outside her weaving room.

He had been gone six days. No. Only five.

The days had been uneventful. Afraid to venture out, she had not left the shop. Her aunt had visited.

Her uncle remained omimously silent.

She slammed the heddle, jarring her ribs. Her body was healing. Her soul still ached.

You disgust me, she had told him, as if saying it could make it true. She disgusted *herself*. She had behaved like a strumpet. He had done no more than take the kiss she had offered. Why was she angry?

The truth was, her anger was not for Renard. It was for herself. She had not only invited his kiss. She had enjoyed it. Wrapped in his arms, she forgot his intentions were no more honourable than Black Pieter's. Because she had thought, just for a moment, that he might care for more than her body.

That was easy to do when he swore to avenge her and

cradled her in his arms as carefully as if she were a piece of Venetian glass. In those moments, the whole world seemed to live inside her. It was a feeling she'd never had before, even on her most joyous days in the shop.

A feeling so wonderful she had almost told him all.

Thank the Saint, she had not, or all her lies would have been for naught. She had convinced him that she was responsible for the business, even though she was a woman. If he discovered that she had an uncle who opposed her work, her precious fleece would disappear into someone else's hands.

Merkin's broom hissed in rhythm with the loom. 'He's more than just a guard, isn't he, milady?'

'Mistress,' she corrected without thinking. What Merkin didn't know, she probably suspected. 'Yes, Merkin, he is.'

'He's gone to get wool, hasn't he?'

Katrine stopped weaving and looked at the girl. 'What makes you say that?'

'And you miss him, don't you?'

'Merkin, that's enough,' she snapped.

Merkin leaned on her broom, cheerily undisturbed by Katrine's temper. 'He's a clever fox, milady. He'll bring back the wool.' Merkin, and the broom, were quiet for a moment. 'And some oranges, too. I would put a wager on it.'

Just bring him back safe, Katrine prayed, clasping the shuttle as if it were a saint's relic. *Just bring him back.*

As the day faded, Katrine watched for him from her bedroom as long as there was enough daylight to see. She had let her hair free and it floated in the evening air, rippling across her breasts. She trembled, stretching her fingers with unanswerable longing.

She found no salvation in sleep so she prowled the house, as if she might find his leftover essence lurking in a corner, finally climbing the narrow stairs to the third floor. She kneeled on his empty pallet, stroking the rough wool, caressing the hills and hollows his form had left in the straw.

This was his space, his air. This was what he saw, night after night, in darkness and at dawn.

Did he ever think of her?

She welcomed the bite of the straw poking through the wool. *If I sit where he sits, see what he sees, will I know what he thinks of me?*

Katrine never needed to confess the sin of vanity. She knew she was not beautiful. Ugly hair, short legs, blunt fingers, slim hips and breasts that refused to round into a woman's fullness. Thin like a peasant, her uncle had said. But what did it matter? The flesh was deceptive and sinful and even an ugly woman was a temptation to man. Best to hide beneath woollen swaddling.

But Renard had called her hair beautiful.

Pinching the slippery locks in the long, blue light of the midsummer eve, she tried to see it through his eyes. Straight. Not so much red as copper coloured. She let the strands fall through her fingers, like Parisian silk.

Through her tunic, she cupped her breasts in her hands, trying to assess their size and shape. If his hands replaced hers, would he find them beautiful?

She waved at her toes, surprised at the way the loom had shaped her arms. When she lay beneath his eyes, had he found their form pleasing? She let the fingers of her left hand explore her right arm, but the touch she felt was not her own. As she tickled her inner elbow, she gasped at the rush of feeling and dropped her hands to her lap, where they followed the curve of her leg from her knees, higher, and her legs parted involuntarily with wanting.

Sweet Saint Catherine, deliver me from the sin of Eve.

But the saint was silent.

No woman could escape Eve's stain.

But tonight, she longed to know what married women knew, what put secret, catlike smiles on their faces when they thought only their husbands could see.

What would it be like, to smile that way at Renard?

Groaning, she rolled over, hiding her face in her arms, welcoming the painful prickle of straw against her stomach and breasts. A bunched piece of cloth, wedged into the corner where the roof met the floor, brushed her fingertips and her heart surged with happiness.

He had left something. He *would* return.

Limp with relief, she pulled it free and sat up, trying to gauge from its weight and shape what he had left behind. It looked like a bundled, lumpy cape.

She wanted to wrap herself in it, in something he had touched. There was no harm. He would never know. She would put it back, she told herself, as she shook the cape free.

Long, dark, warmer than he needed now. A few other things, wrapped inside, fell out. An extra tunic.

A scrap of red.

She held her breath, suddenly jealous it might be a scarf, some lady's favour. Then, she saw it was something much, much worse.

A red silk eyepatch.

Chapter Thirteen

She stared at the scarlet silk, deadly as a drop of blood on the rough grey pallet, her fingers cold and shaking despite the summer heat.

English. He is English.

She could not think beyond those words at first, because her next thought was even more terrible.

Worse than a smuggler. A spy.

Not for him a public parade into the city with forty-nine other knights. He had slipped in among the shadows. Met with the Lord of Dronghen secretly.

And since then, the man had become a vocal supporter of the English alliance. That must have been why Renard had come. To find allies for England.

It made terrible sense, now. He had come to her, a naïve woman alone, speaking Flemish just well enough to deceive her. Staying with her, coming and going for weeks without explanation.

Not for wool.

For war.

He had told her he was a deceiver, a Renard. The name

was no doubt as false as its bearer. Just like the fox in the story, he had lied. Every time she pressed him, he had touched her gently or kissed her boldly.

How he must have laughed at her folly for thinking he might care for her.

Just like the poem said, 'Believing him I was the fool. The truth, now learned, is doubly cruel.'

A breeze wafted over her numb hands. The eyepatch fluttered, alive. Warily, as if it could wound her, she reached for the scrap of red silk.

Smooth and slippery, it danced away. She grabbed it this time, crushing it in her fist. Gulping in air to fight her wrenching sobs, Katrine doubled over with a cry of pain that came from much deeper than her ribs.

The week Renard had promised to be gone became two. Katrine carried the scarlet scrap with her, hidden like a secret sin.

One night, as the day's heat pooled upstairs in the solar, she sat with Merkin in the weaving room and opened the ledger book.

She made no entries.

Instead, out of Merkin's sight, Katrine played with the eyepatch as she had a dozen times that day. She flattened the crumpled silk, as if she could wipe out her unwanted knowledge along with the wrinkles.

But she knew. And she must choose.

She could put it back. When Renard returned—she smiled at her foolishness in still hoping he would—she could pretend she had never seen it and let him conduct his secret war.

Or, she could tell her uncle. If Renard returned, he would be arrested and taken to the Count.

He would die.

That thought left an ache so deep she wanted to scream, but no sound would come.

Sitting by the empty hearth, Merkin played with a tuft of Flemish wool, pulling, turning, and twisting it around her finger as if she were trying to turn it into yarn. 'How do you spin the wool, milady?'

Startled, Katrine dropped the eyepatch, hidden from Merkin by the ledger book, then smiled at the welcome distraction.

'First you need to know whether it is to be used for wool or worsted, and whether for warp or weft—'

A blunt rattle on the wooden door cut her off. No one welcome would pound that way.

Merkin bit her lip.

With shaking fingers, Katrine closed the book on the guilty evidence. Lifting her chin, she put on a brave face and walked to the door, then peered through a gap between the boards.

Pounding the door with a fist that looked even bigger than she remembered, stood Ranf.

And beside him, her uncle had come at last.

She clenched the wool of her skirt, wishing she could slow her galloping heartbeat. She might not be able to protect herself, but she could protect Merkin. 'Merkin, run. Hide in the shed.'

'Open the door, Katrine,' her uncle shouted.

The girl shifted from one foot to the other, looking at the door, then at Katrine. 'If I leave you—'

'You will only raise his wrath. Go.' Pounding drowned the clunk of Merkin's shoes as she disappeared.

Katrine braced herself against the door and reached for the latch. Renard, whatever he was, could not help her now.

She opened the door a crack and her uncle pushed into the room. 'Don't ever lock me out.' His wine-soaked breath soiled her cheek.

By all the saints, how did my mother endure?

Katrine clasped her hands, shielding her roiling stomach. 'I did not know it was you. I must be cautious.'

Her uncle pushed past her and jerked his head at Ranf, who circled the room, searching for something.

Or someone.

'No decent woman lives alone. I know you've had men here. How many?'

She had seen Ranf watching the house, but all she had thought about was herself. Why had she never realised he might see Renard and wonder?

'You are mistaken. No one else is here.'

Finding the room empty, Ranf mounted the stairs. Katrine held her breath. Surely he wouldn't search the top floor.

Her uncle's voice brought her back. 'Pack your things. You are coming home.'

Fingers hidden in the folds of her skirt, Katrine pinched the smooth, gold wool for comfort. 'Thank you for your concern, but my place is here.'

He slammed his palm against the wall. 'There'll be no more arguments. You've already been attacked, wandering the streets like a strumpet.'

Her fingers flew to the forgotten yellow bruise around her eye. His blunt finger followed hers, stroking the tender skin with just enough pressure to hurt.

Katrine jerked away. 'Dangers lurk everywhere. I'm sure you know that.' Anger surged, overcoming her fear. She dared him with her gaze to confess what—and who—had bruised her eye.

His fingers fell to her shoulder and lingered. 'That's why you need to be with me, where I can protect you.'

She bit her tongue. It was protection *from* this man that she needed. There was something wrong in his gaze. Something wild and inhuman. 'I prefer the roof Giles left to me.'

He shook her. 'Witless girl. You've no money and nothing to weave.'

Above her, Ranf rummaged through her sleeping chamber. She prayed he would not find the money.

'I cannot abandon my father's work.' She turned her back on him, but before she could walk away, something on the floor caught her eye.

The red silk eyepatch fluttered gaily as a tournament flag beneath the table.

Heat drained from her face. She stared, unable to look away, praying that it would lie still and not call attention to itself.

'I've indulged you too long,' her uncle said, behind her. 'Willing or not, you will come tonight. Now.'

She closed her eyes to keep from looking at the scrap of silk beneath her bench. He had not seen it. If he did, Renard's fate would no longer be hers to choose.

A gust of warm air ruffled her skirt and sent the eyepatch skipping towards the fireplace.

Katrine turned, blocking his view. 'I need to be here,' she said. Nonsensical words in a tone more measured than her heartbeat.

He pulled his dagger and waved it in the air. The threat left her strangely numb. All her fear gathered around the scrap of silk. 'You are coming with me.' He grabbed her arm and pushed her towards the stair. 'Bring the serving wench, too. Where is she?'

The eyepatch, caught by her swirling skirt, danced merrily beside her and landed on top of his scuffed, brown-booted toe.

She swallowed a gasp.

He leaned down and lifted it by the string. 'Are you trading in silk now?'

'Yes. No. I'm… It's just…' Renard lied so easily. She couldn't think of words.

He started to let the scrap of silk slip from his fingers and she held her breath.

Then he held it up again, his brows meeting across his nose. 'It's one of those patches that the cursed English wear.' He waved it in front of her face until it was a red blur. 'Where did you get this?'

She bit her lip, hard. Fear tied her tongue for a moment. 'The wind must have blown it in.'

Another lie to forgive, Saint Catherine. But when the time came to choose, she had not hesitated.

'There *was* an Englishman here. Why? Were you trying to get your father released?'

'I did not know the man was English.' That, at least, was no lie.

'Don't take me for a fool.' He shook the red scrap at her. 'Even you know what this means. Why did you shelter him?'

She wanted to lie, but it was too late. And she knew no more lies. 'For this place. For the wool.'

'You shame our name for a mound of fleece?' Revulsion curled his voice.

Thankful he did not know all she had done, she met his eyes. 'He was wearing no eyepatch when I made the bargain. The Count should be pleased I tried to breach the embargo.'

'It's the English who want the embargo. Why would he break it for you?'

'I don't know,' she answered. She had wondered that, too, but, of course, he had brought no wool. Only promises.

'You had no coin. Did you pay him with your body?'

She nearly laughed, remembering how carefully she had bargained with her few livres, but if she told him about the gold he would take it and she'd have nothing left.

Seeing her hesitate, he grabbed and shook her until she was dizzy, clutching at his arms to stay upright. 'Tell me. Have you lain with him?'

Always, men were so desperate to know this. But there was none of Renard's calm conviction in his voice, only frantic desperation.

'No,' she answered, finally. But she had lain beneath his eyes. Her body warmed at the memory.

Ranf ducked his head as he came down the stairs. 'Look!' He dangled her precious pouch of coins. 'There's a king's ransom in here.'

'No! Give me that.'

She reached, but her uncle grabbed the purse. 'Where did you get this?' He opened it and pawed through the coins. The sound sickened her.

'My father left it for me.'

'He should never have trusted you with such a sum. You knew no better than to give it to an Englishman.' Her uncle balanced her heavy pouch in one hand and the feather-light red silk in the other, then turned to Ranf. 'Check the garden.'

As Ranf left, her uncle started pacing. 'The Lord of Droghen has been pressuring the Council to support Edward. We suspected someone was behind it, paying for all his fine, public pronouncements. This must be the man. Where is he?'

'He said he was going to get the wool.'

'When does he come back?'

She shrugged, trying to pretend it didn't matter. 'If he's the spy you think, why should he come back at all?'

He looked at her up and down with a knowing gaze. 'He'll come back.' He pocketed the pouch of coins. 'Stay until he does.'

In her relief, she didn't question why he had relented. 'I'll need the coin to pay for the wool.'

'You think I'll let you give the English anything? Tell him you must send the girl for the money. When she comes to me, I'll see he ends up in the Count's dungeon.' He stroked the eyepatch in his left palm with a rough finger until the silk snagged.

Think before you speak. Renard's life depends on you. 'If I do not pay him, he will be angry and leave. I can't force him to stay.'

The menace in his eyes chilled her. 'He'll tarry long enough. And if not, use your body to hold him. At least you will sin for a righteous cause.'

Shame prickled her skin even as desire curled in the pit of her stomach. 'How can you suggest that?' Yet he suggested no more than she had dreamed. 'I won't do it.'

'Won't?' He leaned against the loom, strung with the mix of her work, Giles's and Renard's. 'It seems you learned nothing from your first lesson and need another.' He crushed the eyepatch in his fist, then pulled out his dagger and stabbed two holes in the walnut-dyed fabric.

'No,' she shrieked, running.

But before she could reach him, he had slashed the warp threads, leaving them trailing in the dust.

Pain split her chest, as if he had cut her instead of the wool. The cloth sprawled like a dismembered body, threads running over the floor like life's blood.

'Do as I say, Katrine, and I will catch the spy with gold in one hand and a lady in the other. Then you can confess all the details of your sin to the priest. Maybe he'll absolve you.'

He dropped the crumpled eyepatch on the floor and crushed it beneath his boot.

Chapter Fourteen

Despite his vow to forget, Renard thought of Katrine every day for a fortnight.

With the help of the King's gold, he had pursuaded John, Duke of Brabant, to support Edward's cause, but as he took his leave, Renard doubted that the man's loyalty ran very deep.

'We'll send word when the King is ready,' Renard said, as they crossed the ward together. Reaching the two-wheeled cart, part of the disguise that had brought him safely to Brabant, Renard paused.

He and John had shared much over bottles of Burgundy, but he was no closer to understanding the truth about his mother than when he arrived. Still, one more question burned in his chest, next to the cloth he had stuffed in his tunic.

Reckless with passion, his mother had left him without a father, a station in life, without even a name. What man could have been worth the risk of ruining two lives?

Or three.

He pulled out his scrap of Duchess cloth and thrust it towards the Duke. 'Does this look familiar?'

His half-brother took a step back, staring at the fabric. 'Should it?'

'Did you ever see her wear it?'

The Duke raised bleak eyes to Renard. 'She was buried in it.'

Wearing the weaver's touch through eternity. The thought stunned him. Could Giles de Vos have been more than a tradesman to her? Was that why she had left a length for her son?

'What do you know of the man who wove it?' John was older than Renard. Old enough to remember.

'Nothing.'

His denial was too quick.

Renard shrugged. 'I came across his shop. Apparently he stopped making the cloth after she died.'

'Probably no one else would pay his prices. Plantagenets have a way of spending more than they have.'

It was the same explanation Renard had given himself. How could he have thought a king's daughter would couple with an artisan's son? He sighed, relieved it had not been true.

It would have made Katrine his sister.

The Duke spoke again. 'Mother was ruled by her passions. For things and for people.'

It was a condemnation he knew too well.

Renard threw the cloth on to the seat of the cart and climbed up. There was nothing more to be learned here. Beneath his half-brother's icy stare, Renard shook off the re-membered pain he had felt as a powerless child. John would never call him brother. He had faced too many bastard brothers.

Renard was the only one who wasn't the old Duke's.

He left the castle, drove to the wool house, and loaded his

cart at the warehouse, hiding the wool under mounds of straw, studded with onions. Then, lulled by clopping hooves, he swayed in the driver's seat as the cart lurched slowly over rutted roads.

The flat fields looked as he remembered them when, as a four-year-old child, he was torn from everything he knew. The low sky still clung oppressively close to marshy, river-riddled ground that faded to a blurred horizon, then rolled into a cold, grey sea.

The Duchess had died and nothing in his world was stable. They had put him on a ship and with a roiling stomach, he had clung to his nurse's hand on a wildly shifting deck, staring at the heaving water, terrified that he would slip overboard and be lost beneath black waves.

At the end of that voyage, on solid English soil, he had never faced his history again.

Until now.

Confronted with his mother's past, he wondered whether he knew her secret after all. For the first time, he wondered why she hadn't cast him out the minute he left her womb. Instead, he had been raised as the son of her favourite lady-in-waiting. She had seen him every day. Why would she want a reminder of her terrible mistake?

Unless it had been something more.

He shook off the thought. Fantasy. Just like the feelings he had had about Katrine. Only a passing rumble, as fleeting as the sound of the cart's wheels.

Sunset flamed over the city by the time he reached the gate. Ready for his evening meal, the guard waved him through without inspection. Tired, dusty, hot and determined to unload as quickly as possible, Renard only glanced at the lengthening shadows as he pulled up beside the garden shed, smiling to think of Katrine's face when she saw the wool.

Merkin answered his knock, peeking out with narrowed eyes. She threw open the door when she recognised him.

'Look lively, girl,' he said. He felt foolishly happy. Throwing and catching an orange in each hand in a poor imitation of Jack's juggling, he tossed one to a squealing Merkin. 'Not only do I come bearing oranges, I've brought all the wool that your mistress and her father, God rest his soul, could ever have wanted.'

Merkin crossed herself quickly, her happy squeal severed. 'Her father? They killed him in that English prison?'

'English prison?' A terrible, still clarity gripped him. The weaver Giles de Vos had been dead for years. If Katrine's father was in an English prison, he was not Giles de Vos.

'Nine months of prayers for her father's safe return all for naught.' Merkin's words wobbled and her eyes filled with tears. 'Oh, I don't want to be the one to tell her.' She scrubbed her damp cheeks with her sleeve.

A bolt of lightning cracked him open.

She had told him she had a husband who was alive, then a father who was dead. All lies. Whoever her father was, he was not a dead weaver. He was a live enemy.

Renard felt his eyelid slip dangerously low. 'Tell her nothing. I misspoke,' he said, he who only spoke after measuring each word to fit. 'How would I know anything of her father? I was thinking of Giles de Vos.'

Merkin wiped her nose on her sleeve. Her curly hair bobbed with her nod. 'Ah, God rest his soul. But he's no blood kin to her, although they were closer than many who are.' Merkin's sniff was a commentary. 'I ain't naming any names, you understand.'

No blood kin.

The man who had deceived kings had been fooled by a simple weaving woman he had been careless enough to trust. So who was her father? And why had she lied?

'Merkin, who is it?'

Framed by the doorway, Katrine stepped into the kitchen, swathed in her shapeless brown wool and creamy wimple. He stared, hungrily, unable to stop himself. She seemed thinner than when he left, tired eyes barely shadowed by a faded yellow bruise.

He denied his desire, but he was helpless against the tenderness.

But the tenderness was edged with fear. He could trust nothing about this woman. Not even who she was.

She had not moved from the doorway, and he swept a mocking bow. 'Mistress, as promised, your wool awaits.' Rising, he balanced the orange on his fingertips and held it out to her, absurdly hoping it would make her smile. 'And your orange.'

'I didn't think you would come back,' she whispered, reaching for the fruit, but looking at him. He stretched his arm out and rolled the orange into her palm, careful to stay at arm's length. 'I thought I would never see you again.'

She spoke as if it mattered.

Remember her lies. He conveniently forgot his own.

The mocking reply he intended came out as a husky murmur. 'Just because you cannot trust me doesn't mean that I never keep my word.'

She swayed, dropping one hand to press the smooth wool of her skirt. The gesture pinched his heart. It was the one she used when she needed courage.

Her next, tart words proved she had found it. 'Just

because you sometimes keep your word does not mean I should trust you.'

Her words brought him back to himself. 'Do you doubt I have brought the wool? Come, look. I've had a weary, four-day drive to get it here.' He made the mistake of touching her, tugging her hand to lead her to the spoils of his hunt.

She snatched her fingers back, clutching the orange with both hands. Relieved, he let go, trying not to breathe, fearing her scent would rush to his head. For despite everything he knew, even now, his body seemed helpless against her.

She faced him with eyes too big, too brown. 'Well then, let's see if this wool I have paid so dearly for is worth the price.'

He crossed his arms to keep from reaching for her. *I, too, have paid dearly for this wool in ways I never intended.* 'No matter what you think of the wool, the price is the same, but you'll find it good Cistercian fleece.'

Her smile was worth the staple master's grumbles after he insisted the man search the warehouse for it.

She dropped the orange on the table. 'Where is it? Let me see.'

'In the cart. I split each sack into twenty bags.'

'Each sack?'

'Each of the three.'

She clasped her hands over her mouth to hide a cry of delight.

Outside, the warm air smelled of coming rain and squashed cabbage leaves. His borrowed bay neighed rest-lessly and he soothed the horse with a pat and few soft words, unhitching him, before leading him to the shed.

The three of them set up a line. Renard lifted a straw-covered sack from the wagon and handed it to Merkin, who passed it to Katrine, who stacked it just inside the door to the workroom. Katrine soon fell behind, for she stopped to open each one, plunging her hands into the greasy fleece, exclaiming over the colour or fineness, laughing at the sight of sixty little bundles that meant the Mark of the Daisy would have another chance at life.

Jealous of the fleece, he watched her.

She told me from the beginning, she will do anything she must for the wool.

He cursed himself for forgetting. He thought he was using her, but it was she who had neatly tricked him into getting exactly what she wanted. How many lies had she woven? Was her innocence, too, feigned?

When the last bundle was on the floor, Katrine grabbed Merkin and spun her into an awkward dance. Then, releasing the girl, Katrine whirled in joy, as Merkin clapped time. He had never seen her truly merry and, despite everything, he revelled in her giddy laughter, glad it was because of something he had done.

Stop thinking of her. Protect yourself. You must find out how much she knows and why she lied.

Dizzy, gasping for breath, Katrine stumbled, nearly falling into him. He reached for her, finding, through the shapeless wool, where the curve of her hip melted into her waist. Steadying her, he pulled her close, until the wool of her dress flowed against his groin and over his legs.

Desire catapulted through him.

She swayed with him, gently as a banner in the breeze, so slight beneath her shapeless sack that she might blow away.

Deceiver. Her slender form sheaths a will of iron.

And yet, she made him long for things long forbidden.

He traced the edge of her wimple with his finger, from her jaw across her forehead, lingering on the fading bruise in a touch gentle enough to be a caress. 'Is it…all right now?'

She closed her eyes, her lashes shadowing her cheek. Her fingers plucked the fabric of his sleeve. 'My eye? Yes, it's all right.'

He stroked her bruised ribs gently through the folds of wool, glad she had kept a linen wrap in place to protect them. The touch brought his fingers within a breath of her breasts. 'And here?'

His hand rode the breath swelling her ribs. Her eyes, huge, full of questions, searched his. Before, he would have sworn her innocence was real. Now, he had no doubt she could have feigned that as well as everything else.

She covered his hand with hers, and her calluses grazed his knuckles until he ached, not knowing whether it was with anger or longing. 'It only hurts if I move too suddenly.'

'Then, *ma petite*, we should move very slowly.'

Hands gently, but firmly, on her hips, he resumed the dance. He filled his eyes with her face, surrounded by wisps of auburn hair escaping recklessly from her wimple. He imagined her beneath him. Flushed. Breathless.

Merkin's Flemish syllables jarred him. 'Mil—mistress, do you want me to run that errand before I go to bed?'

'No—' Katrine never looked away '—tomorrow will be soon enough. Goodnight, Merkin.' She didn't turn to watch the girl leave the room.

Renard's hands still rode gently on her hips. The heavy scent of raw fleece permeated the night air.

When she realised they were alone, Katrine pulled away.

Relieved, he paced before the empty hearth, wondering how far he must move to escape her lure. She was dangerous. Not only her lies, but the temptation she presented. He had fought and fought and still he could not best it.

She swayed towards him as he walked from corner to corner, as if she were a flower following the sun.

'Give me my money and I'll be gone,' he said abruptly. It was the only way to escape the danger she presented.

'You are weary from your travels. You need food and drink.' Fingers lightly on his back, she guided him to the wooden table where the forgotten orange lay. 'Sit. Let me bring you cheese and ale.'

His back tingled where her fingers had touched. Was it a sign of desire or danger? 'You have your wool. Keep your bargain.' He wanted to leave without the coin, but that would only prove, if she had any doubts, that he was not what he seemed.

Her fingers curved around his back, but he refused to let his knees bend to sit. 'Where would you go tonight? Curfew has rung. The watch would wonder why you are about.'

He let her push him on to the bench, uncertain whether the greater danger lay in the house or in the street. Yet if he didn't discover why she lied and what she knew, he would leave her free, perhaps to destroy his entire plan.

Pouring him a tankard, she overfilled it. Foam cascaded over her hands and into the rushes. She set the brew before him.

'Let me prepare a bath for you. I owe you that simple hospitality.' She rushed, as if she might forget the words if she did not say them quickly enough. 'For just this night, you are my honoured guest.'

Not waiting for him to say no, she picked up a pouch of herbs and climbed the stairs.

A bath for a weary guest is common courtesy. Surely my control extends so far.

No fire lit the room's dark corners and he spared only a glance for the shadowed loom. He sipped his beer, listening to the creak of the kettle arm swinging out from the fireplace, to the splash of pouring water, and the scrape of the deep, wooden tub being dragged closer to the fire.

Fear and desire mixed uneasily in his veins. If he stayed, just long enough to discover—

The third step squeaked.

He turned. As if in his dreams, she stood before him, the wimple, her armour, gone. Her hair, unbound and unbraided, tumbled around her like a silken cloak.

'Come.' She stretched out her arm. 'Your bath awaits.'

Chapter Fifteen

Renard stared at Katrine's red-silk hair spilling over her creamy white tunic. The trust she showed by baring it stopped his heart.

But could he believe even that? All the pain he had seen, her protestations, her insistence on hiding it. Was that, too, a lie?

He hesitated.

Her smile disappeared. She dropped her arm and looked at the floor. 'I do not please you. I've been told I am not attractive as a woman should be.'

He felt a surge of dislike for her absent father. If those were his words, better he rot in an English cell. 'You please me too much.'

She shook her head, and turned to flee up the stairs. He reached for her arm and she paused, one foot on the tread, without meeting his eyes.

'Look at me, *ma petite*,' he said.

She did. Hurt, wanting and something secret warred in her gaze. Whatever words he planned melted away. His tongue refused to move.

She gathered her hair in both hands, bunching it as if trying to hide it. The timid mouse he had seen at the loom had returned. 'You said it was beautiful. Another lie.'

'No.' The rough words seemed pulled from his throat. 'It *is* beautiful.' He wanted to weave his fingers through its fire, fill his hands with the wondrous weight of it until it overspilled his grasp and the silken strands tumbled across his naked belly.

'Yet you do not want me.'

He wanted her. Desperately. Wildly. He wanted to inhale her—breath, lips, tongue, ears, eyes, fingers, skin. He wanted to plunge into her secret self over and over, with no mind, no reason, no control, nothing but giving and taking.

Like a dive in a winter stream, the vision chilled him.

He had spent his life with a drawn sword, guarding the cave where his passion lurked. Now, one slender woman had unleashed the dragon he had kept safely at bay.

It could destroy him.

But his eyes were full of her sunset hair and her huge brown eyes with the too-thick lashes and the slender hips just beneath the wool and he wanted to find a way.

Just for tonight.

Once she was delirious, in a frenzy, then he could make her confess all. That was reason enough to stay.

'I want you.' He engulfed her in his arms. Her head snuggled over his heart and her breath seared his skin through the wool.

Her left hand, hidden in the folds of her skirt, played with the fabric. He plucked her fingers away from their secret ritual and kissed each one in turn. Her breath stumbled as his lips touched her fingers. His heart skipped in answer.

Bending, he traced the lines on her palm with his tongue. Her even breathing dissolved.

Steadied to feel her mastery slip as his held firm, he trailed his fingers across the blue veins of her wrist, pushing back the sleeve to reveal the sensitive skin of her inner elbow. She gasped, a little, uncontrolled cry. He felt sudden power and sharp joy at her response.

Katrine took his hand, turned it over and kissed his palm with closed lips. Then, her timid tongue tickled the crease, as if she were trying to make him cry out as she had done.

He battled for restraint, but her lips curved in a smile. She was not fooled. 'Come. Your bath awaits.'

He tucked her hand in the crook of his arm and they climbed to her bedchamber. Sunset had cooled the evening air and the steaming kettle of water was welcome. Winding sheets were stacked near the fire to catch the heat and the scent of rosemary floated from the water.

He paused, wary. 'You have produced all the pleasures of the bath house.'

She blushed until her ears, fiery red, matched her hair. 'Your water grows cold,' she mumbled.

Cold water, he thought, might be a good thing.

He forced himself to let her remove his garments as if she really were the lady of a castle and he a returning knight. She lifted his tunic over his head. Her fingers flickered like fire over his skin, tangling in the hair on his chest.

He closed his eyes, but that was worse. There was nothing to distract him from her touch.

'I will undress myself,' he said through clenched teeth, tearing her hands away.

She stepped away. 'Do you wish me to leave?'

'On the contrary. I want to be close to you.'

'I want to be…close to you, too.'

He turned his back and stripped off his shirt. Behind him, he felt her fingers trace his spine.

'Katrine.' He choked out the word and turned to look at her.

'What is it? Are you hurt?'

'Katrine,' he said again, softly this time, 'have you ever been with a man?'

She jerked as if he had slapped her. 'No.'

Was this, too, a lie? He searched her eyes. Against judgement, against reason, he believed her.

And that made his decision easy.

He must stay in control.

He would unleash her feelings—touch her, arouse her, take her to the heights and depths while he stayed safe. She would not be able to trick him because he would not lose control.

But *she* would. Then he would make her confess her lies. It would be a fitting revenge. And when he left, she would regret their meeting as much as he did.

But he would leave no seed in her to create a bastard.

His own desire was beating to escape. Eager to put the barrier of the tub between them, he stripped off his braies and chausses quickly until he stood naked, his desire evident.

She stepped back, her eyes cast to the floor in maidenly shyness, but he could see her peeking through her lashes with frank curiosity. The realisation that he was naked before her brought the impatient throb of blood to his staff.

He retreated to the tub. His knees nearly met his ears and the water, still warm, barely covered his hips. Floating rosemary leaves shielded him little better than a fig leaf.

Wood and water safely between them, Katrine stepped closer. Turning back her sleeves, she laid warm fingers on the curve between his neck and shoulder and rubbed his knotted muscles. He arched to meet her fingers, as they rippled through his hair.

The water and her touch relaxed him. Desire remained,

warm, not hot, but satisfied for the moment by her fingers on his shoulders, her breath in his ear. But when she started to reach lower, he caught her hand and placed it safely on the side of the tub.

'Hand me a winding sheet. I am ready to get out.'

'But I have not yet washed you.'

'The road dust is gone. That is enough.'

She held up the sheet, mercifully protecting both of them. He wrapped himself in the linen armour, but the cloth moulded to his damp skin. He looked down to see a body beyond his control.

But she touched his cheek, turning his eyes to hers. 'This will be the last night of our world, Renard. Let us make it like the first. Let me be your Eve.'

He felt a tug of something stronger than passion, something that made the passion deeper, beyond denial. It was too late to deny, too late to resist this tenderness he had never felt for another woman. Never felt for anyone.

Fighting himself, he tensed every muscle. He could not touch her yet. His body, his spirit, were too willing.

He stroked her hair gently, cherishing the feel of it. 'I want you like the sun, *ma petite*,' he said, in the language that had become their own. 'I want you as I want the warmth of the fire, but fire is powerful. And dangerous.'

She met his eyes. 'I am prepared to burn.'

Her words spoke not of love, but of the fires of Hell.

He reached for her. The linen fell away and her dress pressed against his damp thighs and knees and chest. His fingers ran riot through her hair, grabbing it in handfuls, letting just this much of his vision come true.

She closed her eyes and let him cradle her head in his hands, turning to press her lips to his palm again.

He rained kisses from her ear to her neck, then buried his face in the firefall of her hair. The scent of her, clove and cinnamon, permeated his veins. Sweeping his hands down her arms, feeling the heat of her skin through the wool, he was acutely aware that he was naked and she was not. She had bared her hair for him—surely bare skin would take less courage?

He drew her to the bed and settled her in front of him, at the mercy of his hands, ignoring the throbbing between his legs. It would be safer to keep her tucked in his lap.

Taking a skein of hair in each hand, he uncovered the nape of her neck and kissed the place where the shortest, reddest hairs grew.

The back of her dress was not fully laced and she wore no chemise, testament that she had dressed herself and hurried. He would not hurry. He would take slow, excruciating time until she was breathless and mindless with wanting.

He unlaced each hole, rubbing every sweet bump in her spine with wonder, and slid his hands under the cloth, teasing the edge of her soft breasts. The wool slipped off her shoulders. Her breasts, small and hot, seemed to swell in his hands. He stroked her linen bandage and the curve of her waist and hips. She arched, shuddering, with a purity of untutored desire he had never seen in the practised women of the court.

Her head lay against his shoulder, her lips parted, hungry. A kiss would be dangerous. Instead, he traced her mouth with his finger, teasing her tongue until she pulled his finger into her mouth. The stiffness between his legs swelled in response.

With a damp finger, he circled her nipples, feeling them harden, until her struggling body's reaction told him she had no thoughts except what his hands were doing to her.

'Are you burning yet, *ma petite*?' he whispered.

Eyes closed, she wriggled, each word a triumph of mind over body. 'Please…I didn't know…what…'

Suddenly, he did feel like Adam, confronted for the first time with an irresistible force of nature, strong as the wind, hot as the sun. For the first time, he feared she was stronger than he, that her passion would overcome his control.

No. He would make her mad with it. That was enough. That was everything.

His lips found the curve of her neck laid bare. Muscles curved her shoulders and her upper back, a wonderful secret, a contrast to everything soft and slender about her.

He wanted her secrets. All of them.

Her breasts were stiff with the desire he had awakened. Instinctively, she raised her left arm to cover them, fingers cupping her right breast. She gasped at her own touch. He lifted her hand to his lips.

'Eve had no secrets,' he said. 'Surrender yours, Katrine.'

He trailed his finger, warm and wet from her mouth, down to her sweet centre, where it slipped inside to a place that was soft, slick and wet with wanting. 'Open for me.'

And he felt himself the greatest of villains when, her moment of clarity gone, she did.

He teased her and himself, stroking her, looking for the cadence that was hers, seeking to understand her with his fingers as he did with his eyes and ears. Faster, slower, seeking the steady rhythm which, like the flight of the shuttle, would mean he had mastered her.

He wanted her to forget time and place and even her name. He wanted her to feel everything he longed to feel and would never allow himself.

Her hips thrust against him, her body seeking his, moving

in response to the fires he lit inside her. 'Please…I want… I don't know…'

Her innocence was no lie. Her body could tell only the truth.

He bent his head to feel her breath, matching his strokes to it. Her gasps became moans.

When he found her rhythm, his body matched it and heat engulfed him until his hips and fingers moved together and when she laid her head back on his shoulder his tongue plundered her mouth, as deeply as he wished to enter the rest of her. He echoed her thrust for thrust, until her rhythm turned to stiffness and then shattered and he matched it with his own, damp release.

And for a moment, he thought his soul had slipped through his fingers.

The weight of her head on his shoulder was sweet. He gloried in her dazed smile. She searched his eyes and then reached down, lacing her fingers with his, tangled in the dampness between her legs. 'I didn't… I didn't know.'

Neither did I.

Somehow the passion had escaped his control and it was more terrifying than he had ever believed.

Much more.

Chapter Sixteen

When the neigh of his horse in the shed finally penetrated Renard's senses, he felt as if he had awakened from a dream to find himself in the midst of battle.

Attuned to lovemaking, he had been dulled to danger, forgetting to force the truth about her father, even forgetting to stable the dray horse. Rolling off the bed and into his chausses, he grabbed his dagger.

'Stay here.' He filled his eyes with her slender, flushed body. Her silken hair mixed wildly with the rumpled white wool and linen, as dishevelled as his discipline. Yet a satisfied smile, matching hers, crept over his lips.

Outside, a half-moon lurked in a clouded sky. The horse moved, restless, as if sensing something. Renard calmed him with a touch.

The smell of hay and manure wafted from the shed on a storm-sent wind. Maybe the horse had sensed the threat of rain.

But with the thought, Renard sensed something different. He clenched his dagger more tightly just before something, someone, slammed into his stomach.

They both went down behind the horse's hooves. The animal neighed and reared. A knife slashed Renard's right arm.

Left-handed, he thought, lunging back at the moving shadow, knocking his attacker flat. There was just enough moonlight to see the man's open mouth before Renard slit his throat, turning the cry of alarm into a death rattle.

The horse, smelling blood, pawed the dirt. On his knees, right arm weak and bleeding, Renard searched the darkness for another assassin, listening for a sound that the man was not alone.

The silence of death settled over the shed.

One more sin to atone for. Was there dispensation for killing a man who attacked you first? He would have to learn the canon.

He flexed weak fingers around his silver dagger. In his useless fighting arm, the blade was nothing more than a talisman.

Eyes now accustomed to the dark, Renard looked at the face of the man he had killed.

It was the one he'd seen watching the house.

Who wanted him dead.

Who must know who he was.

Because Katrine must have told him.

Leaning heavily on his left arm, he lifted himself from his knees, sagging against the horse as he led the frantic animal from the shed, upwind of the scent of blood. Leaving the horse to forage in the garden, Renard wiped his bloody hands on the grass and staggered to the back door, every muscle tense.

Lust had wiped his mind clean. He had forgotten the danger and this was the consequence. No, worse. He had ignored the danger, knowing he was watched, knowing she lied, yet letting desire make excuses.

Inside, he sagged against the wall, cursing his carelessness. Katrine appeared at the top of the stairs, kirtle loose over her shoulders, laces still undone.

'Sweet Saint Catherine,' she whispered, eyes wide.

Dizzy, he felt his heart pounding inside the wound. He groped for the bottom stair, trying to sit before he fell.

She was beside him then, eyes dark and troubled in her pale face. 'What happened?'

'In the shed.' Each word was an effort. 'A man with a knife. Dead now.'

The fire's ruddy glow polished shining copper threads in hair that, minutes before, had rippled across his chest. Now, instead of clinging to his, her eyes flickered from front to back doors, as if trying to see beyond the walls.

'What are you looking for, Katrine?'

'You are in danger.' Without questions, she collected cloth and water to clean and bind the wound, never meeting his eyes.

As she wrapped his cut, he choked back a howl of pain at her betrayal and his folly. He had accepted her innocence and flattered himself into thinking he possessed her. All the while, she was leading him towards death by his own stiff, stupid staff.

He grabbed her arm, careless of the soggy, bloodstained cloth trailing from her fingers. Dragging her along, he barred the back door, checked the street shutters, and listened for a clank of iron on chainmail.

And every time she stumbled beside him, her soft breast brushed his arm.

When the doors were secure, he turned on her. Towering

over her, he let his dagger hover at the hollow of her throat, hoping she would not see it shake. Her scent still clung to his fingers, stronger than reason.

'Danger from whom?' The Flemish syllables were as harsh as his mood.

The pulse in her throat beat faster and she pursed her lips, as if to keep the words inside.

He trailed the dagger lightly from her throat down the gentle curve of her breast. 'You can keep no secrets from me now, Katrine.' He let the blade graze gently across her breasts until her chest rose and fell so fast he knew she wanted him again. 'I know things about you no man should know.'

Fear bleached her face. She would crack soon. He pushed on, reckless of her feelings. And his own.

'I touched you where you've never been touched and you revelled in it. What secret can be more terrible than that?'

She ripped herself from his fingers. 'Your globe of glass is faulty, Renard. You see the truth in nothing.' She shouted now, backing away from the temptation of his touch, arms crossed over her slender chest to ward him off. The wool had fallen off her shoulders and she tugged at each side, trying to cover herself. 'You have never told me the truth. Maybe you cannot even tell it to yourself.'

Wary, silent, he watched her pluck the bitter orange from the table and spin it between her thumb and middle finger. When, finally, she held it out to him, the pain in her eyes had become the disgust he had told himself he wanted to see. 'Now, it is time for you to give me *your* secrets, Englishman.'

Englishman.

Numb, he stared at the small, round dimpled fruit until it lost all meaning. 'Englishman?' He kept his words soft and slow. 'Why do you call me that?'

'You do not deny it?'

'I was born in Brabant, not across the channel.' That, at least, was true.

She blinked, absorbing his words. Maybe they would satisfy. But Katrine was not a stupid woman. And she had learned to watch for the small shiver of his lazy eyelid.

'A clever answer, worthy of a fox, but this tells me a different story.' She set down the orange and pulled a scrap of red silk from inside the ledger book. It dangled from her finger, that toy for foolish boys who knew only the romance of war instead of the reality. 'You left it behind.'

'You searched my things?' he snapped, angry at himself for keeping the scarlet Judas. Such a small thing.

'It wasn't like that,' she said, abashed with some embarrassment he could not decipher.

'What was it like?' Where had he put the wretched thing? Paying attention to her, he had become careless of too much else.

'Just give me one word.' She shook the red silk in front of his face as if it were a lady's favour she was about to bestow, but she was braced for a blow. 'Is it yours? Yes or no?'

The air, ripe with raw wool and leftover lovemaking, shimmered with the echo of her question. Calm, a patient half-smile on her lips, she let the red silk flutter.

She was his personal angel of death and she had destroyed him with what he had most denied.

And just for a moment, he felt her trembling beneath his fingers again and thought it was all worth it.

'Yes,' he answered. He had thought that lovemaking would force the truth from her. Instead, he could no longer hide his own.

Her shoulders sagged. 'Why are you here?'

He was expendable. The future of Edward's alliances was not. 'You asked for one word. You have it.'

She dropped the eyepatch into his hand as if she could no longer bear to touch it. He stuffed it in his tunic with his aching right arm. He would keep it now. A reminder never to trust a woman.

Or his feelings for her.

She knelt beside the rough bags of wool stacked in the corner, stroking each one, reciting the familiar words of Renard's story.

'"There's no truth to the lies you tell, yet I was captured by your spell."'

'Lies? What of the lies you told me?' His hands found her shoulders in a grip too close to a caress. 'You have no husband. Your father is not a dead weaver. He's alive in an English prison.' Gratified, he felt her jump beneath his hands. 'Be careful when you demand the truth, mistress.'

She withdrew from his hands and stood beyond reach. 'You heard what you wanted to hear.'

'Who is he? Who is your father?'

'Sir Denys de Gravere.'

A noble, then. Worse. 'And what is his crime against Edward?'

'Nothing! He was in London for trade, to negotiate our next wool shipment.'

Could he believe even that? 'Why did you lie?'

'If you had known, would you have brought me the wool?'

He had no answer. But this, this seemed to be truth. The wool was all she had ever cared about. The shadowed loom towered behind her shoulder and he grieved for the loss of shared moments.

But as he looked at the loom, something was wrong. Warp

threads dangled from it and dragged on the dusty floor. Katrine would have taken a blow herself before she'd damage the cloth.

His fingers tangled in her hair, forcing her to face him. 'Katrine, what—?'

Pounding at the front door cut him off.

'Katrine. Open up. Have you got him?'

Too late.

Tricked. Taken. Trapped by a woman as if he were a squire in heat. 'You played the strumpet to keep me here.'

She shook her head, still cradled in his fingers. Grief shot through her eyes, so deep that he was relieved when she shut them.

Reckless with the pain of her betrayal, he subdued her with a brutal kiss. Her breath broke into pieces beneath his lips. 'This is our truth, Katrine. The truth of the body.'

Nothing more.

She pulled away, looking wildly towards the door. 'Just a minute, Uncle.'

Uncle. The house had been watched for weeks. She must have betrayed him from the very first day.

She turned to Renard, whispering low and fast. 'To the top floor. Quickly. Out the window and down the cherry tree. I'll keep him down here as long as I can.'

'Why? So I can be taken by men waiting behind the house?'

The pounding came again, mixed with the crack of thunder. She straightened the loose gown on her shoulders. 'I'm coming.'

Anger gave him the strength to sprint for the stairs. He hoped it would give him strength to grip the tree branches.

'Ah, Uncle.' Her words floated up to him as he reached the top floor. 'What brings you here so late at night?'

* * *

When Katrine opened the door, the wind laced through her hair and cooled her burning cheeks. Knees weak, she gripped the frame, trying to block her uncle's entry until she could no longer hear Renard's footsteps.

Rain plopped out of the clouds, running in rivulets down her uncle's hair and into his eyes. He pushed her aside, shaking off the water.

'Where is he?' Sputtering, he grabbed her arm, splattering raindrops on her wool. 'What have you been doing? Why did you leave me standing here?'

She had made the mistake of believing her uncle would wait for her word, but he had not trusted her to betray Renard. In that, he was right.

She inhaled, shaking, each breath full of love's perfume, stronger than the smell of the fleece.

Surely, my uncle can see, nay, smell my sin.

But even as she thought it, she could not call their loving sin.

She strained to hear any sound of Renard. Outside, men trampled her garden, shouting at each other, capturing the neighing horse. Inside, her uncle searched every corner of the ground floor. Merkin howled, roused from sleep.

'Let the child be. As you can tell, the household was abed.' A raindrop splattered on her white wool skirt and trickled red from a spot of Renard's blood.

'Where is he? Ranf sent Will to tell me. I know he's here.' He grabbed her arm, desecrating the skin Renard had touched. 'Look at you,' he said. 'You're barely dressed.'

She tugged the back of her dress together, stepping out of his reach. 'I told you, the household was abed.'

His leer became a roar. 'You've bedded him!' He grabbed her hair, jerking her head back.

She laughed. 'Wasn't that what you ordered me to do?'

'That's where he is! Still in your bed.' He headed for the stairs.

Her cheeks burned. One look at the linen rumpled in ecstasy and he would be able to see her sin as clearly as if he had watched her commit it.

'No, wait…' she called to his back. But he did not.

Had Renard escaped? *Saint Catherine, please deliver him.* But no virgin saint would understand the blinding rush of sensation, the glimpse of paradise, the total oneness she had felt with him, nor her desolation at his scorn.

She had only wanted one night.

She should have remembered. After only one taste, Eve was thrown out of the Garden.

When her uncle came downstairs empty-handed, Katrine sagged in relief.

One of his retainers called from outside, 'Ranf's dead.'

She felt a moment's peace. Renard had avenged her after all.

And how painful did you make his death?

'If Ranf is dead,' she began, 'maybe the smuggler found him before he came in, killed him, and then escaped. That would mean he had never been in the house.'

'Then who brought this foul-smelling fleece?'

No, she was no good at lies.

'I should have known,' her uncle said, pounding his fist on the wounded loom. 'Let a man reach beneath your skirts and you can't be trusted. Get your things. You're coming home.'

She left with little more than she had brought. The mirror. The triptych. A heart even emptier than her hands.

The Baron marched Katrine back to the town house

through the pouring rain, his hand never leaving her arm. But Merkin, wriggling away from her guard's grasp, disappeared into the dark streets, choosing cold and hunger over the Baron's vengeance.

Katrine envied her.

Chapter Seventeen

Renard's slowly healing arm ached in the damp air of the bath house as he listened for a shift in his companion's voice that would tell him the burgher was ready to say 'yes'.

He did not hear it.

Dark, stolid, big-boned, and deliberate of speech, Jacob van Artevelde held firm. 'If I do as you say, my Catherine could lose a husband.'

Renard's heart lurched unexpectedly. It had been weeks since he had seen Katrine, yet the name caught him off guard. Van Artevelde's wife was a Catherine, too.

'Already,' the man continued, 'she has lost a father.'

Renard heard the accusation in the words. He deserved it. Van Artevelde's father-in-law, the Lord of Dronghen, the man Renard had persuaded to support Edward, had been killed by the Count for 'treasonable intercourse with envoys of the English King'.

For the thousandth time, Renard berated himself for his failings. Blinded by his lust for Katrine, he had missed the danger not only to himself, but to his allies. He'd escaped, but the Lord of Dronghen had been arrested and killed. Since then, the surrounding duchies had joined Edward's coalition and been rewarded with free-flowing fleece. Flanders alone refused.

All because Renard had been fooled by a treacherous woman.

Diplomacy defeated, the Bishop sailed back across the channel with his forty-nine knights, trailing their red silk eye-patches.

Renard refused to leave.

Alone and deeply disguised, he continued to work in secret, trying to fulfil his mission. Now Jacob van Artevelde was Renard's last hope.

He could not blame the man for his reluctance. To confront the Count directly, demanding allegiance to Edward could lead him to Dronghen's fate. But there might be a different way.

He must risk it. 'Perhaps if Flanders remained neutral instead of declaring for Philip, the King would lift the embargo.'

Van Artevelde's stolid face lit with hope. 'Can you assure me that King Edward would do that?'

He could not. Trapped in Flanders, he could only guess what his changeable monarch might do. Neutrality would threaten the coalition that had taken the spring and summer and a considerable amount of English gold to build.

But neutrality was better than opposition.

He took a deep breath and looked squarely into the man's hooded eyes. 'Flanders's neutrality will take a sword from Philip's hand. Can you assure me of the Council's agreement?'

Van Artevelde spoke, finally. 'The Count can return to his castle. His serfs will work his land and he and his will eat.

But without the blood of English wool in its veins, the city dies. The Council knows that.'

The decision was in his eyes, strong as a handshake.

Renard left first. He took a winding sheet from the sloe-eyed, buxom blonde, gratified that she aroused no feelings for him to deny. The brief madness he had felt with Katrine was over.

Those feelings only visited him in dreams, now, when he could feel Katrine tremble beneath his fingers, hear her un-tutored whimpers, and see her scarlet hair wrapped around his wrist. She haunted him like a succubus, that evil spirit who lays carnal hands on a man in his sleep and steals his soul.

He always woke to the reality of her betrayal. It was only a fantasy to think her passion had been genuine. Only wishful thinking to imagine she had given him those few extra breaths to escape. Just a dream, like that of being born of love and not lust.

Reality was that she had lied from the first. Reality was the men at her door. Reality fueled his anger. It was the only thing that protected him from the pain.

Night after night, as summer faded into autumn, Renard came to her in dreams. Then, Katrine would wake, warm and restless, skin tingling as if he had just touched her.

In waking, she faced the searing hatred of his last kiss.

I didn't tell him. You must believe me. I never wanted to hurt you.

She had only wanted one night. In the morning, she had planned to send Merkin to fetch her uncle, who would arrive to find Renard gone, the trap empty.

Instead, Renard had nearly been captured, the Lord of

Dronghen killed, and she now lived as a prisoner in her uncle's house.

But she had had one night.

If one night had not taught her everything, she had learned more than enough.

It was hard to remember what she had expected just a few weeks ago when she was curious as a child might be. The giggles of the ladies and their suitors had made lovemaking seem like stealing a sweetmeat before supper. A small, guilty pleasure.

She had not expected peace woven inseparably with yearning. Or this ethereal bond, stout as chainmail. She did not regret that night, more was her sin. She regretted only its end.

Her uncle, knowing she had shared the man's bed, expected she would do the same with any man. He kept her captive, never allowed outside without an escort. Trapped in the house again, she was careful to stay close to her aunt and never, never be alone with him. There was madness in the man's eye.

She wanted to pray, but she was sure Saint Catherine did not want to hear about Renard. So she prayed for her father's release from prison and for her release from the prison her life had become. As All Saints Day came and went, the Saint delivered neither.

So finally, she came back to the answer that had always saved her.

The work.

In the early days of autumn, Katrine stood before the house on High Gate Street, flanked by two of her uncle's retainers.

Her uncle had resisted until she explained that the three sacks of Cistercian wool gathering dust on High Gate Street could be spun into sixty times sixty sacks of gold.

So she had agreed to all his conditions, the guards, all of it, to touch the fleece again.

But when she opened the door, the familiar house had changed.

He was everywhere.

He had sat at the loom. He had piled the bags of wool on the floor. He had danced with her.

Leaving her guards to their dice, she climbed the stairs with leaden legs, and paused at the door to her bedchamber.

Crushed linens still covered the bed, tangled in ecstatic disarray. At the sight, she felt stones pressing her chest and honey flowing between her legs.

She gulped for air and instead caught the scent of her body on his fingers. She grabbed the door frame to hold her upright because her knees would not.

And it took all her strength to walk to the bed, rip off the linens, and throw them to the floor. The faint scent of love drifted up from the pile. She sank to her knees and stuffed the coarse cloth against her lips to stifle her sobs.

A cold drizzle hung in the air, but Renard's anger warmed him. For the hundredth time, he wondered whether she was still on High Gate Street and what she had made with her wool.

He had brought her fine fleece. It would be a pleasure to weave.

He forced his feet in the opposite direction. Van Artevelde was ready to make a public declaration as soon as Renard could foment a mass meeting. And he must do it without attracting the Count's attention.

As he passed an alley near the canal, he heard an insistent whisper.

'You. You there.'

Uneasy, he looked around.

'Renard.'

He froze at the word. Who knew his real name? Had the Count discovered him already?

From the shadowed alley, a ragged figure jerked her head at him.

Merkin.

He ducked into the alley beside her. 'Quiet. I'm not Renard now.'

She gave him a hard glance. 'You don't look much like him either.'

She no longer looked like Merkin. Her wooden shoes were stuffed with fabric scraps for warmth. Matted curls drooped. Freckles and dirt were indistinguishable.

'What happened to you? Where's your mistress?'

'Locked up with that lunatic, still. I got myself away. Even the streets are better than him.'

'Who?'

'Her uncle, of course. I'm as good as dead if I ever go back to that house.'

Merkin's Flemish had become more guttural and he was having trouble understanding words that made little sense. He must have misheard. The man wouldn't lock up his own niece. He could still hear Katrine's sweet words of welcome to the man.

He would ask no more. Katrine could be dead and he wouldn't care except that her death would rob him of revenge. 'How do you live, then?'

She swept him with her eyes. 'Same as you, looks like.'

His beard and rags were only partially a disguise. There had been no place to rest since that night.

He nodded, for a moment her companion. 'It's been hard.'

She sighed. 'No wool, no money. No money, no food. No food, it ain't the Count who goes without.' She pulled the ragged shawl closer. 'Though even the rich have empty bellies these days.'

Was Katrine cold and hungry? He stifled a pang at the vision.

'You brought us wool before. Can't you get any more?'

Without the blood of wool, the city dies.

Here was the spark to ignite the tinder. 'Not right now, but there's something you can do. Pass this word to everyone you meet. You may have food in your belly before Yuletide.'

He stooped to whisper in her ear.

A few days later, Katrine looked out of the window to see a street flooded with a rushing current of people: tanners from their stinking pits across the Scheldt River, weavers leaving idle looms and spinsters whose fingers were empty of thread.

'What's happened?' she called out. 'Where are you going?'

No one stopped to answer, but she heard phrases float on the wind.

'To the Abbey.'

'Van Artevelde will speak.'

'He has an answer.'

Running out of the door too quickly for her guards to follow, she stepped into the mass of people, hardly knowing why.

'Milady! Over here.'

Merkin waved, standing at the edge of the crowd like a stick beaten against the riverbank.

When they met, Katrine hugged her and wrinkled her nose at the smell of the girl's rags. 'Where have you been? How have you fared?'

Life had carved hungry hollows into Merkin's cheeks. 'I couldn't stay with you, milady. He'd have beaten me.'

'I know.' Katrine laced her fingers with Merkin's and squeezed. 'What's happening, Merkin?'

'Jacob van Artevelde has a plan to bring us wool again.'

She shook her head as if to clear her ears. The Van Artevelde family, clothmakers like Giles, lived in a large family complex a few streets away. What could they possibly have to do with this moving mass of humanity?

They let the crowd carry them along. As they crossed the river, it looked as if the whole city had gathered outside the Abbey, but this was no spontaneous event. Someone had built a rude, wooden platform.

Van Artevelde, a tall, big-boned man with broad shoulders, stepped on to the platform, resting his large hands on the wooden railing as if it were a pulpit. A large, bumpy nose, prominent bones circling sunken eyes under bushy brows, broad hands with large thumbs—these gave him the rough look of a peasant. But his aura of calm power gave him a dignity that was somehow noble.

What had Giles said of him? *Strong to support, perilous to cross.*

'My name is Jacob van Artevelde,' he began, 'and I speak to you today as a fellow citizen.'

The crowd roared its approval. 'Citizen' was a sacred word in Ghent. The Bell Tower guarded the documents that guaranteed their liberties.

'We stand now between two giants who would seek to force our loyalty to their needs instead of our own.'

In a rough, deliberate voice, he spoke first of Philip of Valois and told familiar tales of old battles and old betrayals. Katrine knew the stories. France was no friend of the citizens of Ghent.

'And now, when we are in need, does Philip send food to feed our hunger?'

Beside her, Merkin answered, 'No.' Behind her, a baby's cry was muffled by its mother.

'And what does Edward the Plantagenet offer? Does he send us the wool that is our blood of life?'

The crowd called out, 'No!'

'Our looms are idle. Our children go hungry because the Count persists in loyalty to Philip while we cannot live without Edward's wool.'

The crowd roared approval again.

'Both want our fealty. Which liege should we choose?'

Fealty to Renard's king. She turned the strange idea around in her mind. What difference did it make which cousin sat on the throne as long as there was peace?

'Philip or Edward. Either choice means hardship. But we have another choice.'

The damp wind whipped through Katrine's cloak, blowing his words away. She turned her ear towards the chill breeze, straining to hear.

'Let us stand for our own needs. Let Philip and Edward resolve their feud while we remain neutral. Then wool and wine will flow again.'

Clapping with the rest, Katrine felt a rush of relief. Could it be so easy?

A tall man had joined Van Artevelde on the platform. She

couldn't see his face, but she knew the easy grace of his stance, the way he held his head, the curl of his chestnut hair.

And now she knew why Renard had come to Ghent.

Chapter Eighteen

The summons came to Katrine in the afternoon, just after midday.

'You are to come with us,' said the tallest soldier of the three who crowded her shop. 'To the Hooftman's house.'

No hint of a reason. No time to change. No understanding that her brown skirt with the three-corner tear was not appropriate garb for presentation to Jacob van Artevelde, the new ruler of Ghent.

No way to ask whether she would see Renard. He was still in the city. It was even said that when King Edward left, Renard would stay behind as his representative.

She hugged Merkin and left with the men to walk the few short streets to the Van Artevelde family complex and seat of government. Three guards—did she need so many? The streets were safer now.

The city had changed since Van Artevelde's dramatic speech. Once Edward had allowed the wool to flow again, neutrality became allegiance. Edward had come to the city and been acknowledged King of France, forcing the Count and his supporters to flee so quickly that her uncle had left without her.

She had a perfect world in her beloved shop as long as she didn't think about her father. Or Renard.

At Van Artevelde's house, an officious clerk, a Van Artevelde cousin by the look of him, sent them up the stairs immediately. She felt a chill as she climbed. What could she have done to bring herself to the man's attention?

Above the ground floor, thick tapestries covered the stone walls and quieted the bustle. The twang of a lute floated down the corridor, followed by a woman's laugh, an odd contrast to the governmental commotion below.

In a corner of the top floor, they stopped before a ladder propped up against a hole in the ceiling, the entrance to the house's tower room.

'Up there.' The guard pointed.

'Why? Why am I here?'

He shook his head and motioned her on.

She protested, but they were doing as they'd been told. She started the climb, afraid to imagine what awaited her at the top.

Halfway up, the ladder swayed with the weight of a second body. 'Stop,' she said. 'The ladder won't hold two.'

'Yes. It will.'

The ice-edged words made her heart beat in her throat.

Renard.

His arms, firm on either side of the ladder, surrounded her, making her vulnerable to him and protected from the rest of the world.

It was a contradiction she didn't care to ponder.

She looked over her shoulder.

He was so close that, if he chose, he could enfold her, caress her until she was lost again. She climbed away from that dangerous closeness, telling herself it was the ladder's sway that caused the flutter in her stomach. At the top, she stepped quickly into the room, away from his reach.

By the time she turned around, he was there.

She rubbed damp palms on her skirt and swallowed, her tongue suddenly thick and dry. His eyes were as blue as she remembered and they held hers for a long time.

Is this why I'm here? Did he want to see me as much as I wanted to see him?

Neither spoke.

'I was expecting to see the Hooftman,' she said, finally.

'The summons was mine.'

Nothing more.

She let go of a breath she didn't know she'd been holding.

Though she had known he was in the city, she had not seen him since the speech. He had become more dream than real to her. Each night, she had explained it to him. *I did not mean for them to take you.* In her dreams, he understood and gazed at her with tenderness.

His face held no tenderness now. The pretence of politeness couldn't hide the angry set of his jaw. The cold, blue glitter of a winter sky lit his eyes and his left eyelid hovered on the edge of a dangerous wink.

'You betrayed me to the Count,' he said, finally.

'That's not true!'

He hates me still. How could she have foolishly hoped otherwise?

'You would have me believe the Baron appeared by chance?'

'I didn't send for him. I told you to go.' Told him after such ecstasy she could not even speak of it.

'The Lord of Dronghen was not so lucky.'

She heard the pain in his voice and her throat went dry. 'His death was not my doing.'

'How can I believe you? You lied about everything. Even about your father.' As if that were some special insult.

'I did not owe a nameless smuggler a description of my family tree. I owed you nothing but sixty gold livres.'

'Which you never paid.'

Her stomach twisted as with a blow. Never paid because she had not thought of money when he touched her. With clumsy fingers, she fumbled for a handful of coins in the pouch hanging from her girdle. Without stopping to feel their weight, she flung them at his face.

He didn't flinch as one grazed his forehead. The rest splattered harmlessly on the wood floor except for one, which sailed past the ladder, hitting the floor below with a lonely chink. 'I never conspired against you or your precious king.'

'And you will have no further opportunity. I'm keeping you here, where you won't be free to send information to your uncle and the Count in exile.'

Here. Where she might see him again.

'But I can't leave my work.' She raised her voice to him, but she argued with herself.

'You'll be escorted to and from the shop. Merkin will be allowed to attend you.'

'I run a cloth-making business. I know no military secrets and I would not pass them on if I did.'

'Why else would your uncle leave you here except to spy?'

He had left her because she had hidden from him, no longer able to bear the salacious gleam in eyes that looked at her and saw no better than a whore. No doubt Renard thought the same. 'To run the business, as I've always done. Let me talk to the Hooftman. He knows my father.'

'Van Artevelde does not rule alone. I represent the King's interests.'

She looked around her. The tower room was designed to be the last retreat if a family was attacked. It could be a haven. Or a prison. 'But I'm telling the truth!'

'The only truth you told was with your body.'

Her body had told the truth to his. But it could not just have been hers.

She took a calming breath, then spoke each French syllable clearly. 'Your body was the only part of you that could not lie.'

He never moved, but each muscle beneath his skin stiffened and his eyes darkened to indigo. *He remembers. And he doesn't want to.* Surprised, she realised she had glimpsed his feelings, as if they were the moon revealed for a moment by drifting clouds.

Then slowly, deliberately, he pulled her hands into his and, between each caressing French word, kissed one of her fingers. 'Is this a lie or the truth?'

He nibbled lower, tongue tracing the lines of her palm and then the blue pulse beating inside her white wrist.

Sweet Saint Catherine, deliver me from temptation.

The saint didn't answer. The rush of hot longing that swept through her could only have come from Eve.

'And this?' he whispered, his lips close to hers. 'What truth does it tell?'

His kiss was soft and seductive and she opened to him. Not satisfied with her lips, he touched her cheek, lingered on her temple, nibbled her ear, and drank of her throat.

Her arms answered him, stroking, caressing, yearning to feel that combination of vulnerability and safety she only knew with him. As if her dream had come to life, he took her lips again, then broke off the kiss to tickle the corner of her mouth with his tongue. Delirious, she teased his tongue with hers between each word, hearing, but not understanding his meaning until the end.

'The truth is that you would give yourself to any man.'

All the warm, loving desire turned to ash.

She ripped herself away from his arms, his lips, his fingers, away from everything he could use to lure her. Once again she had given him her trust and he had trampled it.

'That is not true.' Such feeble words.

But what if it *were* true?

Her uncle, the Church, they all said the same. Women were base, weak, lustful creatures. Renard knew her shame, exposed it, played with it, and used it against her. Why had she let herself dream that he could see her hot hunger for him and think her worthy of love?

Yet as she watched him, wordless, he clenched his fists, as if fighting something within himself. And losing. 'I know the truth of a woman's ardour. I know what it will do to her.'

'What?' She was terrified of his answer.

'Make her abandon her life in the pleasure of the moment.'

She couldn't protest. She had done exactly that, but as she watched him, she realised he was barely aware of her. Eyes closed, he was gripped by an agony old and deep.

Who was she, this woman who caused him so much pain?

'And this passion,' she said, softly, not wanting to disturb the memory, 'what does it do to you?'

She saw the answer flash across his eyes as he opened them. 'Nothing. It does nothing to me.'

'Your body cannot lie about that.'

But the past was behind him and he was in the room with her again. 'Ah, so you *are* experienced with men's bodies.'

'Only with yours.'

She saw in his eyes his desire to believe and his struggle to deny.

'Then you have much to look forward to,' he said. 'You will feel the same for the next man.'

'And you for the next woman?'

'I told you. I feel nothing.'

'Now who lies?' A lightness floated up her body. He felt something he did not want to feel. For her. 'I see something else in your eyes.'

He blinked. 'You see what you want to see.' He turned, abruptly, and climbed down the ladder.

Scrambling to pick up the loose coins she had flung about the tower, she hurled them down at him. 'Don't forget your thirty pieces of silver.'

He pulled down the ladder, leaving her in a prison.

He had been a fool to see her again. For the first moment, all he could do was stare.

Her eyelashes were as thick as he remembered, her hair, like so much about her, still carefully hidden, and yet he had nearly bedded her, despite her betrayal.

He clenched both fists as he descended the stairs. His mother's weakness, so long denied, lived in him still. Like a reflection in a mirror, it lived even when he could not see it. No matter how many times defeated, it was never vanquished.

He told her it was her fault. Perhaps that was the biggest lie of all.

He wiped his face of emotion and went to bid his king farewell.

'An excellent design, isn't it?' Edward said. The room was almost empty, packed for the return trip to England.

When next he crossed the channel, it would be at the head of an army, headed for Paris. Decorating the one remaining trunk was the coat of arms of the new King of France, paint barely dry: gold lilies of France on azure quartered with gold lions of England on gules.

'A masterful design, your Grace,' said Renard. Edward's own, of course.

Edward peered more closely at the gold smudges on the blue field. 'He needs practice on the lilies.'

He let Edward admire it a little longer before he spoke. 'Your Grace, once you return to England, I suggest you consider releasing the remaining Flemish prisoners. It would bolster the alliance.'

Edward cocked his head and gave Renard a boyish grin. 'What's his name?'

'Who?'

'The father of your weaving woman.'

'What do you mean?'

'I can think of no other Flemish prisoner who would interest you.'

Heat flashed in Renard's cheeks. He hoped it did not show. 'Sir Denys de Gravere.' He spoke the name carefully, as if it belonged to a stranger. 'But that is not why I suggested it.'

Edward's smile softened. 'Of course not. But you did bring her here to be with you.'

The thought of a night alone there with her came unbidden, as it had in his dreams. Eyes half-closed. Lips parted for his.

Remember. She only used her body to tempt you.

'I brought her here only to protect your interests, your Grace. Now that we are making war plans, she could be dangerous.'

'Ah, yes. So you said.' Edward turned back to the trunk and ran his fingers under the motto beneath the lilies and lions. '*Dieu* and *Mon Droit*. God and My Right. A fitting motto, isn't it?'

'Very fitting, your Grace.'

Edward's mood shifted, suddenly. 'Watch over my lady, Renard.' Even after twelve years, the King's marriage brought him joy. Renard doubted that he himself would find similar satisfaction in the Church.

'Of course.'

Edward clasped him by the shoulder and met his eyes. 'Surely my son will wait to enter the world until I return, but if he doesn't…'

Queen Philippa, carrying Edward's child, could not tolerate the trip back across the channel. At least that was the ostensible reason she remained an honoured hostage of Edward's allies. She had been given a suite of rooms on Van Artevelde's upper floor.

'All will be well, your Grace.'

'Perhaps she would enjoy talking to your weaving woman.'

'She's not my weaving woman and I hardly think they have anything to discuss.'

'Philippa wants to know more about cloth making. She doesn't understand why we can't make a wearable ellsworth of wool in England.'

He had saved Flanders for the King despite her treachery. He could not let her interfere with the coming war. 'Your Grace, I don't think the Queen and a spy—'

'Do you know for certain she spied?'

Did he? It could not be otherwise. If she was telling the truth, if she was innocent, he would lose his biggest reason to resist her. 'I am convinced of it.'

'Well, what harm can it do? Philippa can keep state secrets.'

'I would never suggest otherwise, your Grace.' What would it be like, Renard thought, with envy, to trust a woman so completely?

'Besides, she will soon be unable to leave the house. A new face will amuse her while I am away.'

He sighed. The King's whim was as strong as an order. 'As you wish, your Grace.'

'Too bad you are staying here, Renard. I like crossing the channel with you. Your stomach likes the sea no better than mine.'

'Who would keep an eye on the Bishop of Clare if I left?' Van Artevelde, Renard and Clare would rule as a triumvirate until the King's return. Renard hoped it would be swift. Sharing a ruling chair with Clare would make an uneasy seat.

'I've told him to write to the Pope. You should be a bishop within the year.'

'I am honoured, your Grace.' Renard looked into Edward's blue eyes, so like his own. 'Before you go, let me drink to the rightful King of France.'

Edward inclined his head, regally, but couldn't hide a grin. 'And to his duly appointed representative in Flanders.'

The words stirred Renard's blood. This was the first step. He had earned this position, this power, the place in Edward's court. And soon, he would have a bishop's ring to go with it.

Nothing must interfere with that. Especially a little weaving woman with big brown eyes.

Chapter Nineteen

Standing next to Renard on the threshold of the Queen's chamber, Katrine knew that neither of them wanted to be here.

Her Grace, apparently, had other ideas.

Katrine smoothed her gold surcoat with nervous fingers. No matter that the wool was Flanders's finest. She was a peahen trespassing in a garden of peacocks. Always more comfortable in her weaving world than in the noble one, she did not know how to make conversation with a queen under the best of circumstances.

And these were not the best. Renard would watch every gesture and listen to every word, ready to pounce if he heard anything he deemed suspicious. The most innocent talk would be misunderstood.

The Queen's solar was crammed with luxuries culled from the rest of the house. Mismatched tapestries hung on all four walls and embroidered linen hung above the bed. Instead of plain pewter, the wine goblets were silver. A chessboard in mid-game waited for the players to return.

Two ladies giggled as a curly-haired knight wearing a red

silk eyepatch dropped the soft balls he was juggling. In the
centre of it all, the dark-eyed mother of four and Queen of
England perched in the middle of a high bed, among a nest
of feather pillows.

Katrine raised her eyebrows, wide-eyed. She had not
realised the Queen was so near her time. The brocaded gowns
she wore for public ceremonies hid her condition well.

Draped across the bedclothes were the most expensive
woolens and laces in Ghent, including the indigo cloth with
the Mark of the Daisy.

She glanced at Renard's eyes to see how close her match
had been.

'Renard, join us,' the Queen said, waving at him with
ring-encrusted fingers. 'It comforts me to have you here.'

One of the ladies-in-waiting, round and blonde, looked at
Renard as if she, too, were comforted by his presence. The
wool of her tunic was poorly woven, Katrine noted with pro-
fessional interest, a fact that most would overlook, blinded
by the aggressive blood-red colour.

Renard bowed to the Queen with offhand grace that
bespoke familiarity. 'I am always ready to serve the King and
your Grace,' he said, in courtly French. 'Allow me to present
Lady Catherine de Gravere, or Lady Katrine, as she prefers.'
He had agreed to introduce her without calling her a Francophile. 'She is here to answer your questions about cloth
making.'

Heat rose in her cheeks as well as more hidden places
when he spoke the language they had shared only in private.
Katrine felt as if this room full of strangers had discovered
them naked together, yet Renard's smile was bland.

She dipped in a curtsy. Did he feel nothing for her at all?
She looked up at the Queen, whose smile was cosy and

welcoming. 'Ah, finally. I've asked Renard to bring you to us more than once. Lady Katrine, these are Ladies Elizabeth and Johanna.'

Lady Elizabeth, in blue, was tall and slender, with tapering, white fingers that sparked a moment's envy. Her broad smile showed two front teeth with a slight gap.

The blonde Lady Johanna, the one in red, did not show her teeth when she smiled, possibly to avoid cracking the white lead paste deftly patched over her pox-marked cheeks.

Katrine's smile of acknowledgement broadened.

'And this merry scamp is Sir Jack de Beauchance,' the Queen said.

As Katrine turned to greet him, her stomach flopped. It was the knight who had tossed her a kiss the night she'd been attacked.

He put a finger to his lips.

'He takes his vow of silence very seriously,' Lady Elizabeth said. 'We have a wager that no one will be able to make him speak before he has earned the right in battle.'

Jack winked as he bowed over Katrine's hand. Beside her, Renard moved closer.

'Mind yourself, Sir Jack.' Lady Elizabeth tossed a leftover ball to him. 'Can't you see she is a married woman?'

She pulled her hand away and touched her wimple. 'I am afraid, Lady Elizabeth, that my wimple deceives you. Times have been unsettled. I wear it for protection on the street.' She drew a breath, thinking how little protection it had been. 'I have no husband.'

'Pity,' said Lady Johanna, 'since only a married woman can receive true chivalric devotion. Or perhaps you pretend to be married so that you are free to accept a knight's attentions, Lady Katrine.'

'No, of course not!' Her body flamed, thinking of what she and Renard had done together. She glanced at his impassive face. She had come to talk of wool, not banter of love. How could they take it so lightly?

Lady Johanna smiled. 'Perhaps Lady Katrine is not familiar with the laws of chivalry. I understand, Lady Katrine, that you are in trade.'

Katrine hid her callused fingers. She could bargain with a weaver or a spinster, but she could not trade barbs with ladies of the court.

'Lady Johanna's family raises sheep on their lands and sells the fleece for cloth-making,' Renard said. 'Would that put your family in trade, Lady Johanna?'

Katrine looked down at the wood-planked floor quickly enough to stifle her laugh with a cough. Lady Elizabeth had not been so swift. Her giggle hung in the silence.

'Then we all have much in common,' the Queen said, smoothly. 'Lady Johanna raises sheep. Lady Katrine makes beautiful cloth. Lady Elizabeth and I love to wear it. We are fortunate that you can spare time from your important work to be with us.'

In that moment, Philippa became her queen, too.

She smiled again. 'My father has for many years held an interest in a wool-making house.'

'I wish England had such talented clothmakers on our own shores,' the Queen said. 'Edward left me with money to spend. As you can see, I've found many ways to spend it.'

'This is ours, with the Mark of the Daisy.' She reached out to stroke the smoky indigo cloth. The feel of the wool, alive beneath her fingers, steadied her. 'This is our cloth.'

'It would look good on you, Renard.'

Katrine kept her eyes fixed on the Queen. 'We are always

fortunate, your Grace, when we can obtain English fleece. The quality of the cloth begins with the quality of the wool.'

'Cistercian wool was the best, I believe you said, Lady Katrine.' Renard's voice held no echo of the night he brought it to her. She wondered again why he had done so. It could have only hurt his cause.

'Leave us to women's talk.' The Queen dismissed Renard and Jack with a wave. 'I want some lessons in the cloth trade.'

Renard hesitated. 'But, your Grace, I think it would be wise for me to stay.'

'How kind of you,' she answered, 'but I'm sure Edward had more important duties in mind for you as his representative.'

Renard bowed and turned, slowly. 'Be sure the cloth is all you speak of,' he muttered to Katrine before leaving.

Lady Johanna's gaze followed the men out of the room as the ladies rustled into their chairs and started stitching.

'Have you no needlework, Lady Katrine?' It was Lady Elizabeth, trying to be kind.

Needlework. She wondered how shocked they would be if she brought in fleece to be carded. That, at least, would be productive. 'I have little time for needlework.' She bit her tongue to keep from telling them she was doing her father's work since he languished in an English prison.

The Queen settled into her bedding like a hen preening its feathers and turned to Katrine. 'You are already acquainted with our dear friend Renard?'

'I do not know him well.' She did not know whether that was true or a lie.

'No one does except Jack and the King,' Lady Elizabeth said.

'He has been a boon companion to my Edward since they

were young. We owe him much for his loyalty.' An edge of warning touched the Queen's gracious voice.

'Oh, yes, your Grace, but he's so dark and mysterious.' Lady Johanna's eyes gleamed.

'He speaks Flemish well for an Englishman,' Katrine said, wondering whether any of them could tell her why.

'Really?' Lady Johanna looked at her with arched eyebrows.

'And the way he seems to wink at you,' Lady Elizabeth prattled. 'My mother saw the first King Edward when she was a girl. She said he had the same lazy way of winking at you.'

Silence crackled.

The Queen coughed. 'What an interesting observation. Now, tell us one thing at a time, Lady Katrine. What happens to our fleece once it reaches you?'

Renard was not spoken of again.

Later, when the Queen tired of the details of warp and weft, the Ladies Elizabeth and Johanna took over the talk.

Katrine soon realised that their job was to divert the Queen's attention from the threat of war. King Philip was rumoured to be on the march already, while King Edward was still in England gathering his own men.

Renard needn't have worried about military secrets. Ladies Johanna and Elizabeth had only one topic—love. They sang of it, they talked of it, they giggled and whispered of it. In their chivalric world, woman was not a sinful Eve, but an unattainable lady on a pedestal, revered and honoured.

Of course, a chivalric knight would never, ever expect anything more than a chaste kiss from his lady.

Perhaps if she played more the lady and less the weaver,

she could learn the ways of courtly love. The curly-headed Jack had winked at her. Could his kiss make her forget Renard?

You will feel the same for the next man, Renard had said. If that were true, if this dizzy longing could be transferred to another man, what a relief it would be.

How wonderful if the feelings her uncle had called shameful were simply a game, able to be played with any one of a number of partners.

It was time she found out.

Her opportunity came within the week. The late winter day had been mild and a whiff of spring warmed the frosty earth. After supper, as she strolled the small garden behind the house, Sir Jack joined her, smiling, but silent, his red silk eyepatch a perpetual wink.

She tried a sly smile, as she'd seen Lady Johanna give, and looked up through her lashes.

With a mischievous grin, he sank to one knee, blocking her path, and grabbed her right hand.

'Please, sir,' she said, warily. 'Let me pass.'

He held her hand to his lips.

Katrine shifted uneasily. Lady Johanna was right. She was not versed in playing games with love. Renard's intensity called to her. It matched her own. But Jack's lighthearted admiration could have been directed to any maid.

At his touch, she felt no more excitement than if he were Old Jan, her master weaver. 'Sir, I realise you cannot speak, but please let me go.'

His crushed expression coaxed her smile back. Still clasping her fingers with his left hand, he gestured wildly with his right, pantomiming a dagger through his heart.

Laughter bubbled past her lips. Jack's boyish charm was a

relief after Renard's fierce intensity, but she found no passion in it. 'Release my hand and I'll applaud, sir. You are mute, but say more than many who speak. I will give you a small reward, then, pray go bother some young lady who might be interested.'

She leaned over, intending to kiss his forehead, but he rose from his knees, enveloped her in his arms, and took her lips.

She was aware of the tension in her back as she bent over his arm, of the night breeze from the river on her cheek, of the thinness of his lips on hers, and of the twang of Lady Elizabeth's lute on her nightly rendition of 'My love is gone from me'.

She was aware of all these things outside of her body. And of nothing within.

No racing heart. No pounding blood. No melting sense of oneness.

Renard is wrong. I will not feel the same with the next man. Or with any other man.

And that realisation was even more fearful.

In the next moment, Jack's arms were gone and she stumbled back against the garden wall.

Renard held her silent suitor by the scruff of his tunic. 'I warned you.'

Katrine pushed herself away from the wall and swatted the dirt off the back of her surcoat. 'He won't answer while he's wearing the eyepatch.' Strange. The same red silk had condemned Renard, yet she had never seen him wear it. 'Perhaps you should don yours and stop your accusing tongue.'

Renard snorted. 'Children's games.'

Grinning, Jack shrugged. 'I was just practising.'

'You *will* talk!' Irritation sharpened her words. 'What were you practising?'

'Wooing the ladies.'

'Ladies in general? Not me in particular?'

Jack looked at Renard. 'Not if I value my life.'

Renard shoved him towards the house. 'Practise on Lady Johanna. If I ever see you so close to Katrine again—'

'I know, I know.' Jack flashed a wicked grin. 'Take pity on him, Lady Katrine.'

Take pity. As if Renard cared that Jack had kissed her.

Renard scowled at her as Jack disappeared into the house. 'Are you now trying to pry secrets from him?'

'Don't be foolish. He just wanted to see if he could win a kiss by wooing without words.'

'And you let him.' It was an accusation, not a question.

'Why should I not? The other ladies do. And you assured me I would feel the same for any man.' She met his eyes defiantly. 'Besides, he made me laugh.'

'Then perhaps I should play the jester.'

She searched his eyes, afraid to hope at his meaning. There was an edge in his voice. Jealousy?

'Perhaps,' she began, 'you should try wooing, with or without words.' She bit her tongue too late. Her bold words were an invitation. He did not need a reminder of how little it would take for her to melt into his arms.

He towered over her, backing her against the garden wall. The earth was soft and uncertain beneath her feet and the stone wall carried cold dampness into her spine.

'Wooing?' he repeated. 'If I were wooing without words, I would not make you laugh.' He cupped her chin in his hand to force her eyes to his. 'I would make you ache.'

He trailed his finger down to the slender mound of her left breast, covered all too lightly by the wool. Against her will, her hips pushed against him.

'If I were wooing without words…' His voice had grown husky. He seemed as helpless against the feeling as she.

His tongue traced her ear with a touch as delicate as his breath. All the fire she had missed with Jack ignited deep within her, curling like hot smoke from smouldering coals.

He pressed his knee between her legs, lifting her until she was riding him. She kissed his lips, his nose, his ear, hungry to taste any part of him. His hands were in her hair, down her back, lifting her astride his thigh. She stroked his back, trying to hold on to him as she felt herself slipping away.

This, this was what she felt for him, him and no other.

The warmth disappeared and she stood exposed to the chill air, panting, wanting, bereft. Aching, just as he had wanted.

'You see, milady,' he said slowly, and she heard the effort in his words, 'you are as powerless against temptation as the rest of your gender.'

Fool. She had been a fool to think she could play games with this feeling that bound them.

His words terrified her. He was right, but not in the way he meant. He saw her as just another fruit to taste. But she was losing herself to a deceiver who hated her, who would leave her and laugh as her need for him brought her to her knees, helpless.

He must not know. She must not let him see her weakness and trample her again. 'You flatter yourself.' She rushed to lie before the tears choked her. 'You were right. I feel no more for you than I would feel for any man.'

She took small comfort from the ragged rise and fall of his chest. He could mask his face, but not the testimony of his body. He could say he felt nothing, but it was a lie. She was sure of that now.

He grabbed her chin, refusing to let her turn away. 'It is your eyes that are a globe of glass, Katrine. You want me.'

Lies had failed her. 'The truth is that you want me as much as I want you and our wanting goes deeper than the flesh. That's the truth you cannot face, Renard.'

And neither can I, for my wanting goes as deep as my soul.

Shaking, she tore herself away and hurried to the house without looking back.

Chapter Twenty

Renard was silent the next day as he escorted her to the wool house, shortening his stride to match her swinging walk.

Wanting deeper than the flesh.

She had said the words, but he denied them.

The rage he had felt when he saw her with Jack still rolled through his body. He wanted her, true, but only in the flesh. Flesh could be controlled. He only came with her to be sure she passed no secrets to the French.

Yet when she opened the shop's door, the air trembled with memories. Bread and cheese in front of the fire. Dancing with her in his arms.

Feeling her shake beneath his fingers.

That is the truth you cannot face.

He must not let her body distract him. She only wanted to divert him so that she could pass information to the French unfettered.

That he could not allow. He would watch her every move.

Yet now that the draper business was running, her opportunities were endless. What had been a woman and a loom had become an empire. Apprentices, spinners, weavers, journeymen, fullers, and dyers came and went. He could hardly keep them straight. Any one of them could carry a message.

That was why he kept close to her. Not because he craved everything about her.

He stayed close enough to hear a round-faced woman with uncovered hair and a covered basket call a cheery 'good day' from the counter facing the street.

'We have spun your fleece into a score of skeins,' she said, hoisting her basket on to the counter. 'I'm here for payment.'

'Who is that?' he whispered near Katrine's ear, shaking off the scent of her before it fogged his brain.

'The oldest de Coster spinster,' she hissed at him over her shoulder. 'They do good work, but they can be lazy about it.' Katrine rose to let her in. 'Good morning, Mergriet,' she called. 'How nice, but I sold you enough wool for another five skeins. Where are they?'

'Well, my one sister had the stomach pain and my other sister cut her finger.'

Katrine clucked in sympathy. 'I'm so sorry to hear that. Why don't you return with all twenty-five skeins tomorrow and I'll pay you the full amount then? Wait here and I'll give you something for your sister's stomach.'

Renard followed her to the cupboard. 'What are you giving her?'

'Hops and peppermint. Does this look like a secret message to Philip of Valois? The spinster sisters don't know ten words of French between the three of them.'

Next came the dyer, with his stack of cloth. Only because Katrine examined every piece did she discover the two bolts of faded yellow buried under those of sturdy gold. She adjusted his pay accordingly while Renard turned over every piece to make sure no notes had been slipped within the folds.

Then a young man, barely in beard, banged on the door, exchanging a grin with a suddenly shy Merkin before he ducked his head to Katrine. 'Milady, I must talk with you about my journeyman piece. Old Jan says—'

'Who is this?' Renard asked, gruffly.

'This is Young Jan, an apprentice weaver. Good morning, Jan,' she said sweetly. 'Merkin will get you some ale and then we'll discuss it.'

Her work was as complex as running an army on the move and she did it with unflagging energy and a deft touch. She was patient and firm and stubborn and flexible and something about her glowed as she worked. Just as he would have been able to ignore her in the midst of battle, she paid him little more notice than a stick of wood while she lavished her attention on a lump of fleece and a bolt of cloth.

He didn't mind that she ignored him, of course. It was only that he needed to know what she did so he could be sure she did not attempt to contact the enemy.

At the end of the day, when the shop was quiet again, he peered over her shoulder at the account book.

She slammed down her quill, splattering the page. 'Look!' She shook the page so close to his nose that he could smell the wet ink. 'This is the account of what I've bought and sold today. Nothing more. No secret messages. Now stop interfering and leave me to conduct my business.'

He frowned. 'Not when you may endanger the King's peace.'

'I am flattered that you find the Mark of the Daisy crucial to King Edward's crown.' The woman who had trembled beneath his hands was a warrior again, eyes blazing with anger. 'If what I am doing is so important, then stay out of my way.'

'I must be sure what you do is work and not treachery.'

'I don't have time for treachery! There was work enough when my father, Giles and I were together. Now, I must do it all myself while you question my every move. I barely have time to sleep. I don't have time to answer your suspicions twenty times a day. If you insist on being here, at least stay out from underfoot.'

He stepped back from the blast of her temper, bumping into the long-neglected loom in the shadowed corner. Caught up in the business, he had barely glanced at it all day.

Now, it was covered by a length of cloth and he saw beneath the loom warp threads trailing in months of dust. He had opened his mouth to ask her about them just before her uncle had arrived, all those months ago.

He threw back the length of cast-off cloth covering the loom.

Someone had slashed the warp.

The sight felt like a knife in his belly. He stroked the cloth, his fingers feeling the difference between his weave and hers. 'You would have cut your heart out before you destroyed your work. Was mine so despised that you had to ruin it?'

She blinked, yet he could see the pain. 'Of course not. I did not cut it.'

'Who, then?'

'You won't believe me if I tell you.'

'How do you know?' He could hear truth in any opponent's voice, yet he was never certain of hers. Was it because she told truths he did not want to hear? Or because she told falsehoods he wanted to believe?

'Because you have questioned every truth I have told.' Her words were calm, resigned.

It might have been her voice, or her eyes, or his wanting. He wasn't sure. But this time, something made him trust. 'Tell me. I will believe you.'

She gazed at him for a long moment before she spoke. 'My uncle.'

The man Merkin had called mad. 'When? Why?'

She measured him with her eyes before she spoke. 'That night. To force me to do as he wished.' Fear, loathing and disgust echoed in her voice.

She despises her uncle. How did I miss that? What else did I miss? 'What did he want you to do?'

'He told me to offer you my body so you would stay until he arrived.'

Grim, cold anger seized him. The passion that had trapped him was even more feigned than he had thought. Not even her own idea, but her uncle's. 'And so you did.'

'Not because of him, more's my shame.' She turned away. 'I did it because I wanted you. Wanted you enough to risk my soul.'

He swallowed, speechless, trying to force back the craving coursing through his veins. It stunned him, that she could accept the desire he had always despised. How would it feel to embrace it instead of loathe it?

'I believe you,' he said, though he did not want to, for it meant facing what he most feared.

Deeper than the flesh. Worth risking all.

She faced him again, blinking back tears. 'He told me to send word when you arrived. I did not.'

'But…' His protest died. He had heard her send Merkin to bed. Had he misjudged her? 'Then how did your uncle know?'

'He did not trust me, so he had two men watching the house. One went to tell him when you came. The other, you killed.' She smiled, wistful. 'And that one? He was the man who attacked me in the street, so you avenged me after all.'

'Your uncle had you beaten?' He shook his head, trying to absorb it all. 'I thought you were in league with him.'

'And wanted you dead? How you must hate me.'

'Not hate,' he whispered, realising it was true. 'Never hate. But how could there be trust? I had just discovered that you lied about your father.'

'Because I trusted you no more than you trusted me.'

He had no answer for that. She had been right not to.

She joined him at the loom, caressing the dead cloth until her fingers tangled in the threads. 'But it was not a large lie to let you think I was Giles's daughter. He was like a second father to me. Did I tell you? This is the last thing he ever made.'

'I thought it was yours.'

'Only part of it. This is a "home-piece". That's the only reason I had the courage to touch it after he died.'

'A home-piece?'

'It can't be sold, only used in this household, because it was not woven according to guild regulations. Giles was always experimenting.' She smoothed out the sagging cloth. 'See the difference in the weave? Mine starts here.'

He followed her fingers, then found his own section. 'Yours is more even, but my weave is tighter.'

She sighed. 'I don't have the strength that Giles did.'

'Did Giles teach you how to weave?' He said the words softly, realising how little he really understood her.

She nodded. 'He would hold me on his lap and show me how to thread the warp and how tight to tamp the weave. He taught me even though I was a girl and could never join the guild.'

'What about his own children?'

'He had none. That's why he left his share to me.'

Renard felt a pang for the dead man. A man without a son. And he a son with no father.

'His home-piece deserves a decent burial.' He drew his dagger, looking to her for permission. 'Let's cut it free and lay it to rest.'

She nodded.

He plunged the dagger cleanly, slashing the final threads. Wordless, they gathered the wounded cloth. She walked towards him with the two ends folded to meet the ones he held, until she stood so close he could feel her heart beat.

Her fingers brushed his as they folded the cloth.

He handed it to her and she laid it reverently on the loom's bench, patting a farewell.

'Katrine, let me weave a new piece.' The words escaped before he wondered why he wanted to. Something in his hands, his shoulders, his legs cried out to the loom. 'I think you have more to teach me.'

She hesitated and he hoped she would not ask him why he wanted to learn. He would not know what to say.

'All right,' she answered finally, 'but I won't waste my good Cistercian wool on you.'

He put on a mock frown. 'I did not risk my neck and the King's wrath to see it mangled by a novice. Have you some leftover French swill?'

'Yes.' She smiled. 'Mangle that to your heart's content.'

He laughed at her stubborn, practical, lovable words, then lifted her off her feet, whirling her around, still laughing—

when had he last laughed?—until they both staggered to stand, out of breath. Her wimple was askew and the riotous red hairs ran to freedom close, too close, to his fingers.

And his heart knew a moment of contentment as it beat next to hers. How could he have believed her a spy?

One night, a few days later, with Queen Philippa's kind permission, Katrine withdrew from her solar before Lady Elizabeth's nightly concert descended into giddy silliness. She had taken to joining them at day's end, enjoying the female companionship.

Renard, busy with the war council, did not hover outside the chamber this evening. They seemed to have reached a fragile peace and their closeness at the loom gave her hope for something more.

Overtaken by a yawn, she bumped into the Bishop of Clare in an empty passageway. Steadying her, his hands lingered too long on her arms.

'Good evening, Lady Katrine. I see you've been talking of mortal sin with the Queen's ladies again.'

The candle she held cast a feeble glow, but the hard light in his eyes did not become a man of God. She stepped beyond his reach.

'I think they were only amused over Lady Elizabeth's playing of the lute.' Despite her uncle's slurs, and the Church's disapproval, she could no longer think of their banter as sinful. 'For all her practice, the tune sounds the same.'

She started to walk on, but he blocked her path.

'It is past time for you to confess your sins.'

Startled, she wondered what he knew. His words resurrected buried guilt, a sharp contrast to her moment of hope.

She had not even gone to annual confession, afraid to confess her night with Renard. God, the priest would say, demanded true repentance.

She felt none.

'I make my confessions in church, your Excellency.'

He leaned closer, his hand cold on her arm. 'Perhaps you are thinking of sin right now.' His breath hugged her cheek. 'Come with me. Confess your sins.'

She struggled to swallow. Her uncle had told her the priest would enjoy hearing her confession. Was this what he meant?

Not waiting for her answer, he moved forwards, backing into a shadowed alcove. 'You dress as a married woman. You must do what married women do,' he whispered, too close to her ear. 'I've seen you smile at Renard. Do you let him kiss you? Do you let him touch you? Tell me. Show me. Show me what you do with him.'

He groped for her breast and pressed his mouth to hers.

She tried to pull away, but he was immovable. Desperate, she thrust the candle towards his cheek. With a howl, he freed her and struck out against the flame.

Gripping the wavering candle like a talisman, she stumbled back into the still blessedly empty corridor. How had she inflamed a man of God with such thoughts? Did she exude lust, simply by walking down the hall?

No. As he stood in the darkness beyond the candle's glow, clutching his cheek, she could see the Bishop was a temptation of Eve in every woman and believed her imagined sins excused their own.

'I am going to my room now, your Excellency,' she said, battling the fear clutching her throat, 'and I will pretend I never saw you this evening.' No one must know. Not even Renard. 'If you ever approach me like this again, I *shall* confess. I shall confess it all, including your name, at St John's the following day.'

His eyes burned with banked rage. 'You will regret your threat.'

'I only regret being forced to make it.' She stepped by him quickly, praying he would not touch her while her back was turned.

But his insinuations were a stark reminder. The ladies sang of chivalrous love, but that was love of the spirit, not of the flesh. Her world was no longer private, as it had been when Renard slept unseen beneath her roof. If she brushed too close to him, if someone saw her smile and understood it, no one would doubt that she had sinned. As a noblewoman who worked, she lived close to the edge of respectability. It would be easy for someone to accuse her of something less.

She must be on guard.

Renard set aside his responsibilities a few days later and began his lessons as the room glowed with morning light. Katrine had flung the shutters open and a river-scented wind played with the threads still clinging to the loom.

Instead of the intimacy of their nights together, these lessons would be practised in the glare of sunlight, witnessed by every spinster, weaver and dyer.

All the more reason to keep his mind on the loom. He would soon be its master.

'First,' she began, 'take off all the old threads.'

Her voice, sweet and firm as her body, tickled the top of his head as he sat on the bench. She reached over him, picking at the leftover yarn clinging to the loom. Distracted by her nearness, he tried to follow her deft fingers, only to scrape his knuckles on a splinter. He stifled a curse.

'As you can see,' she said, 'your next task is to rub the wood and oil it again, inspecting every inch for rough places.'

The small loom suddenly seemed an endless collection of parts and pieces. 'Is this task meant to demean me?'

She stared as if he were demented. 'Is it demeaning to make sure your battle horse is properly cared for?'

'Of course not.'

'Don't you run your hands over his legs and inspect his hooves for stones?' She didn't wait for him to reply. The answer was obvious. 'Then don't you inspect your sword for nicks? And don't you then repair them?'

He waved his hand in surrender. He had learned those things as a squire. To learn weaving, he would again have to begin at the lowest rank.

'"A *chevalier* who rides the loom must know his tools as well as the *chevalier* of the battlefield knows his weapons."' She smiled. 'Giles always said that.'

Chagrined, he picked at the threads waving from the upright, determined to learn the loom as intimately as she knew it.

As intimately as he wanted to know her.

But the loom was baffling and the cleaning tedious. By midday, he had barely completed rubbing all four legs. The frame, pedals, the uprights still awaited.

He rose, throwing down the cloth in disgust. Young Jan looked up from his conversation with Merkin and smirked. 'It's not so easy, is it?'

Renard grumbled an answer and returned to the loom. He would not be bested by a boy. Katrine and a city full of men had mastered the work. So would he.

Gradually, he became absorbed, inspecting, rubbing, memorising every inch of the loom. It intrigued him in a way the workings of the Bishop's office never had. As he made progress, he would look over, hoping she was watching, seeking a smile. Instead, she nodded, curtly, never speaking to him.

It was only late in the day, when they were alone, that she came to inspect his work. Her fingers caressed every beam and he held his breath in fear she might find a rough edge or a splinter.

Her fingers escaped unscathed.

His chest swelled like a squire who had unseated his first opponent. 'Now, how do I string the loom?'

She handed him a basket of washed wool and a wooden comb. 'Next, you must comb the wool.'

He stared at the mountain of fleece. He could sit patiently through hours of negotiation, waiting for the perfect moment, but days spent wrestling with another inanimate object seemed impossible. 'Isn't this a job for the spinster sisters?'

'Yes, but "the weaver who does not know his craft will be cheated in his trade".'

He reached for the basket and sighed. 'Giles said that, too?'

She smiled, with a nod.

He eyed a square paddle with metal teeth, surely an instrument from the torture chamber. 'What about that?' He nodded at it. 'Wouldn't it be faster to card it instead of comb it?'

'Of course, but it breaks the fibres. You can card the weft threads, but not the warp threads.'

Stifling a harsh answer, he plunged his hands into the fleece. It felt soft, springy and familiar on his fingers.

'What wool is this?' His words were sharper than he intended.

She walked back for another stack of fabric, seemingly deaf.

A warm tingle began in his fingers and travelled up his arms. 'Let me see if I can guess, for how can I be a weaver if I do not know my materials?'

She paused before lifting the stack of madder-dyed scarlet and pursed her lips, suppressing a smile.

'Let's see,' he began. 'It is very soft.' He tugged at the ends. 'But very strong.'

Her smile escaped.

'Something soft and strong, tangled,' he said, 'yet it will unravel beautifully at my touch.'

She blushed.

'Cistercian.' His word was an astonished whisper.

'You are an apt apprentice,' she said briskly.

He cleared his throat, grateful that they were, for the moment, alone. He was as flustered that his fingers recognised it as he was with her gift. 'Then show me how to coax this tangled pile into the obedient strands I need.'

She returned to his side, so close that her skirt brushed his ankle. He gritted his teeth.

'Hold the comb so.' Her small fingers touched his. Her breast nearly brushed his arm.

He jerked the comb through the soft creamy cloud with a trembling hand. He could make a loom gallop, but he was clumsy with the comb. Or was it just her nearness that made him awkward?

'Gently,' she said. 'If you break the strands, I'll give you the French fleece.'

Growling an answer, he struggled in silence, seeking a rhythm. Looking at the comb in his hand, he wondered how it would feel gliding through Katrine's hair. He gentled his stroke.

'That's better,' she said.

'I imagine it is your hair I am combing instead of the wool.'

Her blush pleased him, but she frowned, looking around as if to be sure no one was near. 'Hush, or there will be no more lessons.'

He grinned. Her words sounded harsh, but her voice sounded soft as Cistercian wool.

Chapter Twenty-One

❦❧

In the weeks that followed, Renard seemed to trust her more and see her less. He no longer escorted her to and from work each day, but came when he could for lessons at the loom. Even the ladder to the tower room was hers to command.

Yet questions still nagged at her heart.

Seeking a measure of peace, Katrine stopped at the church one morning before reaching the shop. Unwilling to confess her wantonness to a priest, she knelt on the cool stones, trying to pray.

I want you, she had said, no longer able to lie. And with every day by his side, she wanted him more. Now, her body not only ached for him in dreams, she craved that closeness in daylight. She wanted his touch that said *I care for you* as clearly as words.

Cared for a red-haired tradeswoman no one else would have. Despite everything, she was sure he felt that way still.

She wanted to believe her feelings, but her encounter with the Bishop was a painful reminder. Lust was a sin, a temptation from Satan, not to be trusted.

She searched the statues, seeking one who would listen to

what was in her heart. The saints offered little comfort. Carved with human features, but without human feelings, they stood ready to judge, not to console.

Peering between her fingers, she sought the images of women. Every one, even the Mother of God, was a virgin. Every one, like Saint Catherine, had not only never fallen, but never even been tempted.

Except Eve.

She gazed at the stained-glass window. Light shimmered through the blue sky and unearthly green of the Garden of Eden. On the left of the tree stood Adam. On the right, Eve.

Definitely not a saint, Eve knew the price of paradise lost and paid it. Any influence she had with God was highly uncertain, but at least she could understand a woman's weakness.

In the changeable light, the snake seemed to slither up the Tree of Knowledge and offer Eve an apple. At that moment, Eve, frightened, but curious, could still say no.

Katrine knew that moment. She had been at the top of the stairs, hair flowing, lips dry, pinching her white wool, knowing that if she held out her hand to Renard, she could not turn back.

A cloud blocked the sun, sending ripples through the light streaming through the stained-glass sky. The pool of cobalt on the stone floor shimmered a darker blue, the shade of Renard's eyes.

Was she a sinner? Or something else?

In the silence that followed, a startling thought blossomed. What would have happened if Eve had said no?

Adam and Eve each would have stood alone for ever, one on either side of the tree. In ignorance, they would have been separated for eternity. It was knowledge that joined them.

Knowledge answered 'yes' to the mystery. Knowledge meant union of the two halves of the universe. How could such knowledge be shameful?

On her knees, head buried in her hands, she glanced left and right to make sure no one was near enough to hear her heretical thought.

Yet as she rose and crossed herself, the idea wove itself slowly into stubborn conviction. Physical union opened a spiritual window. Renard had touched her body, but he had reached her soul. A wanting deeper than the flesh. In that, they were joined already.

She stumbled out of the church and into the soft light, hugging Eve's wisdom close to her heart. Man and woman belonged together. So did she and Renard. If she was patient, he would come to her in time.

Time that felt like eternity.

No longer able to distinguish his threads in the soft shadows, Renard watched Katrine, head bent gracefully over the ledger, entering the day's accounts.

Over weeks, the patience Renard had long used in negotiation came to his work with the wool. As he had learned to listen for his adversary's silences and hesitations, he learned to gauge the tightness or looseness in the threads, to know when to pull and when to slacken his stroke.

Some days, he neglected his other duties, not wanting to question whether it was to be with her or with the loom. He had seen nothing that would lead him to suspect her of spying.

Gradually, he stopped watching for it.

Tonight was the first time in weeks he had let himself be alone with her. It was safer not to be tempted. Safer to speak only of the wool and the work.

Safer not to face the questions still hanging between them.

But when his eyes met hers, it was easy to forget the bishop's mitre waiting for him in England. Easy to live for today and her smile.

She was not smiling now. She had been up since daybreak and weariness weighed on her.

He rose, stretched, then stood behind her, his hands on her shoulders.

Oblivious to him until then, she straightened with a start, parting her lips to warn him off.

He shushed her with a word and, holding her against him, worked his fingers like a caress over her tight muscles. The warmth of her skin seeped through her tunic and the faint scent of rosemary tickled his memory. 'You must rest.'

'Just a few more—'

'No. No more. Neither of us has eaten since midday. There are guild regulations against such working conditions, I understand.'

'Yes, but you are not a guild weaver.' She leaned against him, belying her sharp words.

'Close your book. We are going back to Van Artevelde's and hope someone has left an uneaten morsel in the kitchen.'

She sagged with fatigue, no longer fighting him. He had a terrible sense of rightness and inevitability with her beneath his hands.

The last time he had touched her like this, he had pulled off her wimple.

Perhaps that is because you are the Devil.

Then perhaps it means you belong to me.

A pounding on the wooden door jarred his thoughts. 'Lady Katrine. Lady Katrine. The Queen—'

He lifted his hands from her shoulders as if they had burned him. There was no place for a red-haired draper at the right hand of a bishop. No way to have her without destroying everything he had worked for.

He pulled open the door so suddenly the messenger stumbled into the room without stopping his blabber.

'She asks for you,' he said. 'The babe comes…'

Katrine grabbed her cloak, blew out the candle and questioned the messenger all at once. 'Has the midwife been sent for? Tell me about the Queen. Does she have sharp pains? How often?'

He looked at her blankly. 'I don't know, lady, they just said fetch you quickly.'

They followed the messenger's lantern through the black streets. Take care of my lady, Edward had asked. He understood so much better now what that meant. 'What do you know of childbirth, Katrine?'

She gripped his left hand. 'Not as much as the midwife.'

Van Artevelde himself greeted them at the door. The house was aflood with candlelight so that the midwife would be able to find it in the dark.

Katrine wasted no time. 'Has the midwife come?'

He shook his head.

She swirled out of her cloak. One of the servants whisked it away. 'Stay. Watch for her,' she ordered Ghent's most powerful leader and started up the stairs.

Renard followed, oddly awkward as she took charge. That brief moment that was their own had vanished.

At the door to the Queen's solar, she paused.

'If you would stay,' she said, not turning, words almost too soft to hear. 'I might—that is, the Queen might need you.'

She disappeared into the solar before he could say yes.

And it was not his promise to Edward that kept him there.

Chapter Twenty-Two

Renard paced outside the door, hearing little, seeing less. He heard the Queen's voice, gracious, but cracked with pain. 'Ah, you have come, my dear. I am sorry to disturb you so late.'

A soft, female moan floated off the stone wall, the echo muffled by the tapestry.

Suddenly, he hoped his mother had not been alone when her time had come.

He staggered at the unfamiliar thought and leaned against the stone wall, trying to think.

Instead of being surrounded by her ladies, she must have given birth in secret. Bearing a child so many months after the Duke's death, anyone would have known the child was not his, but the fruit of her lust.

What if he had been something else?

What if he had been a child of love?

He could imagine such a thing now, something he could never have dreamed before.

'Renard?' Katrine stood at the door, fatigue shading her eyes.

He pulled her to him, wanting to shelter her against all life's hurts, and she leaned into him.

'The midwife,' she said, words muffled in his shoulder. 'Is she here?'

'I haven't seen her.'

'Then get the priest.'

His fingers tightened and he stood back to see her face. 'Is the Queen near death?'

She shook her head. 'She seeks spiritual comfort…and a touch of home. I wish for her sake that the King were here.'

Alone. His mother must have been so alone.

'Lady Katrine, she asks for you.' Lady Johanna stood at the door, eyes wide at the sight of Katrine in his arms. Her tone became arch. 'If you have time.'

Katrine pulled away with a start, as if they had been caught abed. 'Of course.' She turned back, so tired that she seemed uncertain where she was.

He let her go, fighting the urge to give her an encouraging kiss.

Finding the Bishop was harder than he expected. Despite the bustle around the Queen, most of the household still slept. They crowded into beds and stretched out on pallets in every nook and corner. Even the Bishop's exalted rank did not earn him a private room. But as Renard tiptoed around sleeping figures, none carried the Bishop's sloped shoulders.

In the kitchen, Renard's stomach reminded him that neither he nor Katrine had eaten. He grabbed a loaf of bread and had paused to look for cheese when he heard a scuffle. In the alcove beside the fireplace, he saw the Bishop's skinny flanks, naked as Adam, humping a struggling wench.

A struggling wench with Merkin's terrified eyes.

Visceral anger swept him. He tore the man away, ready to plunge his dagger directly into the hypocrite's heart.

Gasping for an even breath, the Bishop shrugged off Merkin as if she were a discarded orange peel. She closed her eyes and curled away in shame, a smothered epithet the only remnant of the plucky girl Renard knew.

The Bishop retied his *robe de chambre*. 'Would you like a taste of her, Renard? Or have you already sampled her wares as well as those of the weaving woman?'

Years of control snapped. Renard's fist flew into the Bishop's stomach. The man doubled over, groaning, and Merkin scrambled away, disappearing into the corridor.

Renard took a steadying gulp of air, unable to regret letting his emotions free. It was as if a wind had swept him clean inside.

Clare staggered back against the wall, cupping himself. 'You bastard,' he spat. 'If I can make you a bishop, I can unmake you as well.'

Renard straightened. He had never considered that when he swung. And now, only the thought of the Queen stopped him from striking again.

'Queen Philippa's time is here,' he said. 'She has expressed a desire for spiritual support. God help us, you are officially empowered to give it.' He picked up the fallen loaf. 'I will tell her you are coming.'

'Childbirth,' Clare muttered, shaking his head. 'God's punishment of women for Eve's sin.'

Renard backed away as if the man were a snake. 'One more thing, your Excellency.' He nearly spat the title. 'If you try to deny my appointment, I will be forced to explain this entire incident to his Holiness. Right after I tell the King.'

He wrestled with his anger all the way back to the Queen's

solar, but his unruly emotions were getting harder to conquer. Little wonder so few ordinary mortals obeyed the commandments when so many of their leaders flouted them.

He never would, Renard vowed again. He had had too much of lies.

He paused outside the solar, struggling to regain control. The activity around the Queen had quieted, and Katrine's calm voice murmured soothing words.

'So the gifts streamed in, tribute to her beauty, wisdom and wise rule. But as the Queen surveyed her treasures, she saw nothing from Renard the Fox, and she wondered at it.'

Her voice. His words.

He had never been sure she had heard them, lying so still and unmoving while he tried to coax her back to the world. But now, she recreated their comfort.

'But the Queen still saw nothing from Renard. "Do you not honour me?" she asked.

'"Oh, most perfect Queen, I have sent a gift beyond price. One that will put all the wonders of the world in your hand and give you power beyond measure," he answered.'

The Bishop, walking as if he had sat too long on a horse, stumbled past Renard without a word and entered the chamber. 'Your Grace, I was on my knees in prayer. I came as soon as I heard.'

Katrine stepped into the hall, draped in weariness, her wimple discarded. An auburn braid caressed her breast.

Renard held his tongue about Merkin, reluctant to add to Katrine's burdens yet. Instead, he waved the bread at her. 'I could find no cheese.'

'Bread will serve. I'm so hungry the Queen heard my belly growl.'

He broke a hunk of bread and held it out. She reached for

it and then hesitated as her fingers came close enough to touch his, shy as the first time they had broken bread together.

'You remembered the story,' he said.

Her cheeks turned pink and he knew she remembered more, remembered her body beneath his eyes and all that came after. 'I never heard the end. Where did they find the globe of glass that would allow her to see the truth?'

The fox lied. All I ever told you was a lie. And it was a lie to let her hope, to let them both hope. 'Katrine—'

The Queen's voice interrupted, her pain more commanding than her words. 'Lady Katrine.'

She rose, shedding her weariness, and disappeared into the room.

The bustle increased. Lady Elizabeth darted out and came back with more cloths. Someone moaned. He heard flat, Flemish tones that must belong to the midwife. The Bishop droned on in Latin.

But the voice he heard most clearly was Katrine's. Soothing, coaching. She must be holding the Queen's hand now, or stroking her brow.

He felt a fierce pride in her, a woman who had never had a child. She somehow found the right words, the right touch to comfort the Queen.

He was not comforted. The Bishop's sins, Merkin's frightened eyes, questions about his own birth and his feelings for Katrine tumbled together like a ship on rough seas.

A lusty cry split the cool March night.

A few minutes later, Katrine appeared, glowing auburn braids tumbled untidily down her back, stray hairs curling free. She wore a weary smile and carried a small, swaddled bundle.

'I thought you would want to see the new prince,' she whispered.

His chest twisted with emotion. 'The King will be pleased.' He couldn't look away from her tired, triumphant eyes. Silently, they drew closer and he raised his arms to create a cradle for the child. She slipped her arms away and left the baby snugly in his.

His warring emotions stilled. He wanted this. Her. Their child. In a way he had never wanted the bishop's seat. In a way he had never allowed himself to want anything.

His denial appeared like a soldier for a battle that was long over. And long lost.

She gazed at the baby, cradled in Renard's arms, and stroked his tiny red cheek. 'I'm so tired I may not be able to climb the ladder. If Merkin were not long abed, I would ask her to help me undress.'

Her name brought back all the pain of the evening. Katrine had to know now. He had to tell her. 'Katrine, if you can leave the Queen, Merkin needs you.'

She retrieved the baby and cuddled him, jiggling him in an instinctive rhythm. 'Is she not asleep?'

'When I found Clare he was…with Merkin.'

Swinging to meet his eyes, she clutched the child, who squealed in protest. 'With her? Do you mean—?'

He nodded.

With a cry, she turned back to the solar to leave the babe, then ran towards the stairs.

He let her go. A man could offer little solace now.

Frantic, Katrine searched for Merkin near her kitchen pallet, in the garden and in the attic rooms. There were few places for privacy in Van Artevelde's home, and Katrine tried each one.

Finally, legs shaking, she took each rung of the ladder to

the tower. It would take this disaster to force Merkin up the wobbly ladder, but she had looked everywhere else.

The bells of St John's pealed for prime and she looked towards the window, surprised her eyes had not closed from sun to sun. Dawn still carried the blue cast of winter, but the rising sun blushed orange. She caught the sharp, spring scent of moving water and well-stocked boats. The city was casting off the hungry months of the wool-starved winter to embrace a new season.

A new life.

Her bones ached. She longed for rest. Longed, she realised, to rest in Renard's arms.

All night, although birthing was woman's work, he had been there, waiting. She wanted that, wanted to know he would be there tomorrow and tomorrow and for ever.

Thumb nestled in the indent below her waist, Katrine cradled her womb with outstretched fingers, thinking of a child she could place in Renard's cradling arms.

Their child.

Katrine pushed herself away from the window and shook her head to clear her tired thoughts, startled to feel her braids swing freely across her breasts. When had she lost the wimple?

She must find Merkin. What if the Bishop had planted a seed in her belly?

'Milady?'

Merkin's curls peeked over the edge of the bed. Pain dulled her eyes. Katrine swept the girl into a hug, cooing senseless words as the girl cried with her whole body.

How could the same act which brought such joy to the Queen create such agony?

It is not the same act, she heard Eve answer. *One was an act of love.*

Arms full of Merkin's shaking shoulders, Katrine felt older and wiser than she wanted to be.

'I must tell you…' Merkin choked on the words. 'The Bishop, Renard…'

'Shhhh,' Katrine answered, grateful to Renard. 'I know. I already know.'

'You'll dismiss me.' It was as much a howl as a sentence.

Katrine leaned away, looking into the girl's tears. 'I won't. I promise.'

'What shall I do?' Merkin gulped, dragging her sleeve across her eyes. 'I can't…ever…face anyone. Everyone will know.'

'No one else will know.' Katrine gripped Merkin's shoulders with a little shake and then poised her finger on the girl's chin, emphasising each word with a tap. 'We will not tell them.' Telling would bring no justice. If they accused the Bishop, he would blame Merkin for it all.

With wide eyes, Merkin held out her arms, searching her skin as if she expected black blotches to break out. 'Won't it show?'

Katrine's body burned with the remembrance of Renard's touch. 'It is hard to believe, but there are things that can change your heart for ever that do not show outwardly.'

'But I'll have to go to confession.'

'No,' she answered sharply, thinking of her own sins. 'The sin is the Bishop's, not yours.' But Merkin needed a future. And hope. 'Tomorrow, you shall begin to learn the distaff. You'll have a trade, like the de Coster sisters so you can start a life with some bright young apprentice.' She and Young Jan had been eyeing each other. Perhaps it was time.

Merkin smiled and blushed, then her forehead furrowed. 'Won't the Bishop condemn me?'

'The Bishop said he was at prayer.' Katrine wrapped her arms around Merkin again. 'And who will dispute a bishop's word? Not even a king!'

Katrine rocked Merkin until they both fell asleep, tired enough to filter out the daytime sounds of the busy household that floated up to the tower refuge.

Later, halfway between dream and waking, she saw Renard, still wearing yesterday's rumpled indigo-dyed tunic.

'What are you doing here?' she asked.

'I could stay away no longer.'

Chapter Twenty-Three

Sleep gone, Katrine struggled to sit up, still unsure what brought him to her bedside. 'What is the hour? Where is Merkin?'

He smoothed an unruly strand of hair away from her temple. For the first time, she saw no barriers behind his tired eyes. 'After midday. She's gone to find her dinner.'

'The Queen?'

'Resting.' He pressed a finger to her lips before she could ask. 'And the shop can stay closed for one day.' His hands pushed her gently back onto the pillow. 'I've pulled up the ladder, *ma petite*. There is no one else in our world.'

She traced his eyebrows and eyelids, trying to read his heart by touch. Had he finally come to her? 'What do you see in your globe of glass, Renard?'

'You.'

His word stole her speech.

'You said once that we were Adam and Eve on the last night of our world,' he said. 'Can this be, instead, our first?'

The rush of *yes* that swept through her body scarcely left her with breath to say it.

He stretched out beside her, pillowing her head on his arm while his hand spanned the space below her waist as if it were sacred. He worshipped her with his fingers, caressing her through the wool, friction kindling fire in her veins.

She stroked his tunic with impatient fingers, trying to re-discover every long-remembered inch of him. 'Please. Let me feel you.'

He discarded his tunic and shirt and she let her gaze linger on the smooth heat of his shoulders and the muscles of his arms now shaped by shuttle as well as sword.

Her fingers followed her eyes, ready now to reach out for what she wanted. Delighted, she watched him lose himself in her touch.

'Do I please you?' she whispered.

He stifled a groan.

She tangled her fingers in the curly chestnut hair of his chest, tugging on it, glorying in its texture.

He opened one eye. 'Cistercian?' he asked, with a lop-sided smile.

'Better,' she whispered through a kiss. 'The finest merino.'

He held her as if they could merge into each other, skin to skin. Face burrowed in his neck, she filled her lips and tongue with his taste.

His lips moved against her hair. 'Give me your back.'

Cool air and warm fingers trailed her spine. She shrugged the dress off her shoulders, baring her breasts to the breeze. Suddenly shy, she crossed her arms in front of her.

A warm, nuzzling kiss began at the nape of her neck, then wandered down her shoulder, meandered up to her ear. Hugging her against his chest, he cupped a breast in each palm. A feeling, like Gascon wine, flowed directly from his fingers through her skin. The hot touch on her breast became a slow circle until she panted in rhythm, each breath shorter than the last. Finally, she pulled away, wanting to see him face to face, trembling from the feel of his eyes on her, hot and tender as his fingers.

The first time he had touched her, she had waited, unsure. Now, she let her fingers run riot down his arms, across his chest, down his belly, up his backbone, through his chestnut curls, discovering the mole behind his shoulder, the old wound on his right forearm, the bump at the crown of his head.

She gasped now, unravelled, aching to feel him everywhere. Tangled in her skirt, her legs opened to him.

He felt her move, and helped sweep her clothes off and on to the floor. His chausses and braies followed.

Easing her back on to the bed, he hovered over her. She opened her legs and her hips strained closer, remembering ecstasy, seeking his touch again at her sweet centre.

Urgency vied with tenderness. She reached for him, strong and straight as a dagger, in a sheath as soft as fleece. He jumped in her hand like a live thing.

She wanted him, but the feeling was too new, too wonderful, and she let her fingers run over his shaft, through the tangle of curls at its base. Every touch sent fresh quivers through him. She revelled in the life she brought to his body.

He answered her fingers with his, stroking her to madness. All the humours in her body ran towards her core. She was a tickle, an itch, an open, empty hand that only he could fill. He moved over her, teasing her slick opening at the nub of all her feeling.

She wanted too much. She wanted everything.

He took her chin, forcing her to look at him.

'There will be no going back this time.' His voice was husky.

She gave herself to him through her eyes, transparent glass to wherever it was that God hides the soul. 'Be my Adam.'

Spreading her legs, she shifted, grabbing him inside of her, gasping at the sense of completion when he entered. They began to rock as one. Every stroke, like the flight of the shuttle, wove them closer, as if she were the warp and he the weft. Pushing, pulling, pounding until her world was only him and this dark, light, wonderful feeling; she had only enough presence of mind to smother her cries against his neck when the rush came.

She could think of no words to thank Eve.

Nestled in the crook of his arm in the sweet aftermath, she felt them united like cloth tightly woven, individual threads indistinguishable, threads that could only be separated if cut apart.

Only when he moved did Katrine realise how long they had lain tangled. Full of the feel of his skin, warm and smooth against hers, her world and time had shrunk to a bed within round stone walls.

He muttered a few words, lips pressed against the part between her braids.

She pulled her head away, leaning back to see his eyes, now the clear blue of a summer sky. Feeling bold, she nibbled his lower lip and it was many moments until she remembered with a sigh and a smile that he had mumbled something. 'Now, what did you say?'

'I want to comb your hair,' he said, separating the skeins of her right braid. 'As you taught me to comb the fleece.'

She did not want to think of wool and fleece and cloth. 'I would have to find the comb,' she said, burying her nose in the sweet crook of his armpit, and delighting in her lazy mood. 'And I am much too comfortable to move.'

'Then by all means,' he said, with a teasing lilt she had never heard before, 'stay comfortable in my arms and I will take you to find it.' Standing, he scooped her up, nearly tossing her into the air.

Arms locked around his neck, she felt light, beautiful, happy. No man would ever want you, her uncle had said. But this one, this most wonderful of all men, did. 'Over there,' she said. 'On the trunk.'

In two strides, he reached it, smiling with delight she had never seen in all the months together, until he turned his laughing face from her and towards the trunk.

His arms and legs went rigid. He stared at the comb, next to her small silver mirror.

'What is it?' she asked. 'What do you see?'

'The mirror.' A stranger would call him calm, but she heard the tremor in his voice. 'Where did you get it?'

'From Giles. Why?'

He set her down gently, but as if he were no longer aware of her. Outside the circle of his arms, her skin missed his warmth.

'Where did *he* get it?' His eyes, never leaving the mirror, had turned smoky.

'He had it as long as I can remember.' She picked up the mirror, comforted by the familiar feel of it nestled in her palm. It helped her stand steady, outside the protection of his arms. 'He used to hold it up to my face to show me "how special Katrine is".'

She held it up to her face as if she were still a child with nothing to fear.

The mirror reflected the love-warmed eyes and well-kissed lips of a wanton, contented face that had never felt so special.

'Look.' Teasing, she thrust the glass in his face, seeking to reflect her laughing lover again. 'See? Renard is special, too.'

No smile touched the mirror. It reflected, instead, his broad, muscled back.

When he faced her again, naked, powerful, towering over her, he clutched a silver-handled dagger like an avenging sword.

She gasped, heart pounding, certain a madness had taken him and he was going to kill her for their sin. Instead, he plucked the mirror from her fingers, laid it face down on the trunk, and set his dagger beside it.

A silver-handled dagger engraved with a four-petalled daisy.

Finger on the dagger, she traced the pattern she had learned from the mirror.

The match was perfect.

She stared at them, uneasy. 'What does this mean?'

'You are looking at a matched set. It was a wedding gift from Edward, King of England, grandfather of the current king, to his daughter, Margaret Plantagenet, on the occasion of her marriage to the Duke of Brabant.'

His words were French, but she did not understand their meaning. A chill crept up her legs and shivered on her cheeks. 'But why do you have the dagger?'

'Because Margaret was my mother.'

She tried to trace the connection. That would make him King Edward's cousin. 'Then you are the son of the late Duke of Brabant and brother of Duke John.' Even as she said it, she knew it was not true.

The bitterness of years etched his face as deeply as his dagger. 'My mother was a widow for a twelvemonth when I was born.'

Not the Duke's son, then. But whose?

Moving back to his side, she wove her fingers with his. His hand lay in hers like a stone. She formed the next words slowly, as if she would not have to face the truth if she did not finish the question. 'But why would Giles have the Duchess's wedding present? And why do you?'

'Because he was her lover. And my father.'

Chapter Twenty-Four

She gazed at the mirror and dagger. Hers. His. 'Your mother gave the mirror to Giles.'

The mirror engraved with the four-petalled daisy. The one Giles had adapted for the trademark on the cloth.

'Daisy,' she whispered, trying to make sense of it. 'He named the mark for her.'

For Renard's mother, who had loved a weaver and had borne him a son. If anyone had ever known her shame, she would have been cast away for ever.

The warm comfort of Renard's arms faded. She suddenly realised she was naked. The amber puddle of her garments lay out of reach. She needed the armour of clothes to ward off the chill of the room.

The chill in Renard's eyes.

The love-stretched muscles in her thighs trembled. He did not turn to watch her, gaze fixed on the matched silver set as if expecting it to speak. Shaking her surcoat free, she slipped it over bare skin, then stared at Renard with new eyes.

Now, he seemed all Giles, except for the height and the

blue eyes he shared with his royal cousin. The chestnut curls. Familiar. His long, strong hands in Giles's shape.

He fingered the dagger, then the mirror, as if expecting them to disappear.

'Your mother must have loved Giles very much.' She felt a kinship with this woman who had also loved where she shouldn't.

A ripple of surprise creased his brow. 'She should have controlled her lust.'

His voice was as cold as the silver, his eyes drained of the joy of their union. Renard's seed lay heavy inside her. 'And should your babe grow in my womb, will you blame me as well?'

His eyes burned, not with love now, but with the fires of hell. 'I shall blame myself.'

She wanted to wrap her arms, her legs, her love around him, but his wound was too fresh. Instead, she reached for his hands, rubbing them between hers as if the friction could rekindle his fire.

He endured her touch silently.

'You cannot blame yourself,' she said. 'And you cannot blame her.'

He did not shrug her off and she held his hand in hers, tracing the lines that formed a crossroads on his palm, trying to grasp this final thread of connection as he slipped away.

Panic fluttered in her throat. He must believe in what they had shared to forgive himself. And her. 'I think love was their truth,' she said, in a whisper that was almost a kiss. 'I think that is our truth as well.'

Teeth chattering as if she stood in snow, she hugged him, wanting his warmth, hoping touch would reach him since words did not.

Neither his eyes, nor his lips, nor his arms responded at first. Then, moaning like an animal wounded, he crushed her to his chest and kissed her, a kiss as long and deep and hard as joining.

And she kissed him as if there would be no tomorrow and she wanted all of today she could taste.

As the vesper bell faded, flickering candlelight and fading sunlight fought the darkness in Van Artevelde's private solar, but as Renard looked at the faces of the men gathered for the war council, he felt lost in shadows the light could not touch.

Just as he had always feared, he was no different from his mother.

The weakness he had battled for a lifetime had slipped under his guard and felled him like a squire at his first tournament.

Maybe it was a night without sleep or an attempt to wipe out the sick sight of the Bishop with Merkin. Maybe it was the sight of Katrine with a babe in her arms, making him believe for a moment he might have a life like other men. Whatever the excuse, the passion he had always feared had finally shattered a lifetime of control. The madness that had spawned him still lived in his veins.

He could think of no redemption.

What better reminder did he need than to discover, at that moment, the father he had never known? The irrevocable loss of a royal birthright.

Despite everything, the rightness of it rushed upon him again. Had he, without knowing, connected the Mark of the Daisy with the one on his dagger? All this time, he had lived in his father's house, learned his father's work. Something hot stung his eyes. Tears? But he did not know how to name them. He had found a father after a lifetime of nameless years. Surely that was joy.

But what was the truth of that union, the mirror and the dagger reunited? Had the Duchess's gift been one to cherish or a hasty guarantee of silence that became an embarrassing reminder?

Yet despite it all, he would have joined with Katrine again if the page had not called him to the war council. His palm ached with the remembered feel of her fingers. Her scent still clung to his hands and, when he spoke, he felt her lips on his again.

Each moment with her had made him less sure he could take a bishop's vows. He could not even keep the vows he made to himself.

He clenched his fist as if to hold on to the bishop's ring that was almost within his grasp. *Get Flanders for me and I'll make you a bishop.* A bishop who need not bow to the King. A bishop who would be strong enough to resist temptation.

If he could not be all that, what could a weaver's bastard be? Nothing. Certainly, he had nothing to offer Katrine. No land. No title. No life.

Trying to concentrate, he looked around the table, pondering opponents and allies. Philip and Edward's war was close at hand. The purpose of the meeting was to assess the situation. Assessment was beginning to sound like panic.

'King Philip has ten thousand men.'

'We can raise barely half so many.'

Ignoring the rest of the table, Van Artevelde spoke to Renard. The spring evening was too cool, Renard thought, to cause the trickle of sweat that threatened the Hooftman's eyebrow. The man had taken Renard at his word and delivered Flanders's future into Edward's now curiously absent hands. Renard had to answer for it.

'Philip's troops burned a fief of the Queen's own brother,' Van Artevelde said. 'Everything is gone—the village, castle, fields, even the abbey. The sisters barely escaped the flames. Now they march this way.' His words were a personal plea. 'We need King Edward's troops.'

Renard looked squarely into the man's eyes, hiding his personal unease with the pace of Edward's progress. 'He must assemble an army—men, horses, equipment, and cogs to carry them across the channel,' he said, with a steady voice. Strangely, his empty hands ached for the shuttle's rhythm. 'It takes time.'

'We have no time,' Van Artevelde said. 'Philip's men are directly south of the city. If any of the castles between us falls, they could reach Ghent's gates.'

Renard turned to the Queen's brother, a veteran of many battles. 'Are the rest of your castles prepared for defence?' Practice kept his voice calm.

'All except for Douvre. The vassal has not yet pledged his allegiance to Edward. I am not certain of his loyalty.'

Silence ringed the table. How many of them could trust every vassal?

They could spare no men to fortify a castle against the French. 'Take our troops and pursue them. Keep them away from Ghent until Edward returns.'

He prayed that would be quickly.

But mixed with his prayer were thoughts of Katrine. She knew his worst secret and accepted him still.

No. Not the worst.

The worst was that he had not told her he was to be a bishop.

And unless he had something else, something that would allow him to offer for her, he must keep dreams of babes further away than ever.

He must not touch her again.

He did not touch her again. And she could not form the words to ask why.

When he did come to the shop, seldom now, he retreated to the loom, throwing himself into each stroke as if Giles guided his arms. He barely spoke and rarely looked at her and even when he did, she was not sure that he could see.

She thought at first he was wrestling with his demons. The shame of his mother. The sudden discovery of his father. How had he borne the secret alone all these years?

So she tried to tell him, in stolen moments, how wonderful Giles was and how brave Renard's mother was, but he turned away, silent, even when she squeezed his hand and pressed her cheek to his shoulder while Merkin and Young Jan whispered in the corner and did not notice what she did.

After a while, she spoke no more of Giles and Margaret.

And he did not touch her again.

Then, she decided, it must be the war. The Council met into the night. Armies marched. The King, who was Renard's cousin, she had realised, had left the defence of Flanders in his hands. An honour and a responsibility. He must have many cares.

So she stayed awake, waiting for the meetings to be over, staring at the ladder still propped up against the tower room floor, mocking her to come and go as she pleased.

And he did not come.

And then, finally, she came to what she should have known all along.

It was not his parentage or the war or any of the other excuses she had tried.

It was her.

She had asked for one night in Eden, but when he finally came to her, she had dreamed of a lifetime. One in which he could look at the colour of her hair, her rough hands, her unmaidenly urges and love her still.

How foolish she had been.

Once he had seen her, wild with wanting, he must have been disgusted.

But she could not accept that, either. The love in his eyes had been real. Until he saw the mirror and everything changed.

And there were no answers.

So as winter turned to spring, she took comfort in teaching Merkin to comb, card and spin. The de Coster sisters looked askance at first, but she engaged them in Merkin's training, and when they took her home to show her their spinning wheel, Katrine smiled. At least Merkin had a future. And hope.

And despite it all, despite everything, she cherished a hope of her own.

Late one spring day, Renard entered the shop, wordless, and retreated to the loom, pounding the heddle against the long-neglected cloth.

Katrine put aside her inspection of Merkin's latest work.

'I sold several ells today,' she said, talking to herself as much as to him. 'The sun made people ready to buy.'

He nodded, but did not answer. New lines shadowed his eyes and weariness weighed his eyelids. She could not resist touching his cheek, the day's-end stubble rough against her fingers.

He jerked his head away.

Gently, she slipped her fingers up to his shoulders, rubbing the knotted muscles, hoping to smooth the tangled threads. 'Something troubles you.'

'*Ce n'est rien,*' he muttered, never looking at her.

'You say it is "nothing", but my globe of glass tells me it is "something".'

The pounding paused. She held her breath.

'You read me too well.'

Because you let me, she thought, frightened to realise it was true. He who let no man see beyond the mask had given her a glimpse. *And because I love you enough to recognise what you let me see.*

He tugged her fingers away from his shoulders and his lips hovered above them for a moment before he let them go. 'I hope I never face you across a negotiating table.'

She wrapped both arms around his neck and whispered in his ear. 'You already did. I got wool for twenty gold livres per sack.'

What might have been a chuckle rumbled in his chest.

Vesper bells rang. She stood, knowing she should bring in the unsold cloth and close the shutters. But she did not want to move, savouring the first private moment they had shared in weeks. 'You are worried and tired,' she said.

Defeated, he dropped his head back against her shoulder. 'Yes, I am worried. Yes, I am tired.' He sighed. Then the words marched forth, as if he no longer had the strength to hold them back. 'There are thousands of French troops moving towards us. We have only half their number. The nearest castle to their path now is Douvre, where the vassal is less than trustworthy. The allies grow nervous that Edward does not return and I cannot promise them when that will be.' He turned and met her eyes. 'Now, how many more burdens do you wish to share?'

His precious gift of trust lay shimmering in her heart next to her unspoken joy. 'All of them.'

It is the war, then. Not me. Now, surely, he would speak of tomorrow.

Instead, he closed his eyes and rose abruptly, the moment gone. 'We should go.'

Silent, she brought in the unsold cloth and lowered the shutters, asking Eve for patience.

When the war was over. Then, surely, he would talk of their future.

Chapter Twenty-Five

Elbow to elbow with the dyers, the fullers and the spinsters of Ghent, Katrine stood well back and at the edge of the nave on a glorious summer morning, as the Bishop of Clare baptised Philippa's Prince John.

The crowd welcomed the diversion. The French king's army hovered within a few days' march of Ghent's gates.

Renard stood with easy grace near the Queen. Katrine caressed his broad back with her eyes, wishing she and Renard could be rebaptised and reborn into another time and place. One without worry. One without war.

Merkin, next to Mergriet de Coster, waved at her. Katrine waved back, gratified. Even here, with the Bishop standing at the font, Merkin could smile. The girl and Young Jan stood close enough to see each other, always. Soon, she was sure, they would stand together. For them, at least, there would be happiness.

All eyes turned to the altar, where the Bishop, his thumb moist with holy water, made the sign of the cross on the babe's soft, round, hairless head and washed away Adam's sin.

A bruising grip jolted her arm. Gasping, she turned to see her uncle's red-veined eyes staring into hers.

Her cheeks turned to fire, her fingers to ice and her stomach to a tangled skein.

'Uncle,' she whispered, twisting against his hold, 'what madness makes you walk amidst the common folk of Ghent?'

He had cast his lot with the Count and fled the city to fight with Philip's men against the citizens of Ghent. If he were recognised, he'd be taken prisoner. But disguised in a hooded cloak, he was unremarkable and the crowd was focused on the ceremony.

'Why, I come to talk to you, Mary,' he whispered. Without loosening his grip, he pulled her away from the nave.

He thinks I'm my mother. Has he gone mad?

Yet she stifled her scream. Even now, she could not condemn her father's brother to death. Surely if she spoke to him calmly, he would leave. Or when they went outside, she could run.

But instead of leaving the cathedral, he pulled her down a flight of steps into the crypt beneath the church where the bishops of Flanders lay in cold, dank eternity. No sounds penetrated the stone room. Now, if she screamed, no one would hear.

Candlelight wavered over the fresco of St John holding his chalice with the emerging serpent. In the uncertain light, the snake seemed to writhe.

Her uncle pressed her against a stone pillar. She wrinkled her nose against the smell of day-old wine and tried to see his eyes in the dim light. 'Please, Uncle. It's Katrine. We are in a house of God.'

'And God will punish you for breaking our family's oath to serve King Philip.'

Breathing slowly, she flexed her cold fingers and tried to

think over her pounding heart. At least he seemed to know who she was.

She had thought herself free from her uncle when he left the city. Now, seeing him again, her body told her how much terror she had carried. 'Ghent recognises Edward as the rightful King of France before God.'

'Heresy.'

She would not argue. He would not listen.

'But you can redeem yourself,' he said, leaning closer. She pressed herself against the stone, as far away from him as she could. 'Tell me his plans. How many men are there? When do they march? Where? Tell me everything you know.'

Never.

Her loyalty had been cast. Once, she cared naught for kings, but now, she cared for one king's family. For Queen Philippa, who called her countrywoman. For baby John, slippery from the womb.

For Renard.

Her uncle thought her a stupid woman. She would let him. 'I am a woman.' She shrugged, palms open, hoping he would not see them tremble. 'I know nothing of war.'

'But you live in the house with their leaders. Go to one of their beds. You did it before. Do it now and you can find out everything we need to know.'

'No.' She tried to twist away, but his hold was too strong. At least, thankfully, he did not know that she still shared a roof with Renard.

'Do it or I will tell them that you did.'

Her mouth was so dry she could barely move her tongue. 'Who can you tell? You are a traitor in exile.'

He scoffed, as if she were indeed an idiot woman. 'I don't have to appear for a missive to reach the right hands.'

She pinched her surcoat so tightly the weave imprinted itself on her fingers. 'No one would believe you.'

'They will when I tell them about the last time. When you trapped the Englishman.'

She felt frozen to the cold stone floor. Renard believed her innocence now, but if someone else accused her, would he believe her still?

'Decide. Now.'

She shook her head. What little Renard had shared of castles and marching would surely be of no value to him. And she would not share it, regardless. 'No. I will not.'

She thought for a moment the death blow would fall, but instead, his eyes narrowed and his face took on a cunning expression. 'You have made your choice. God will punish you.' Then he turned, leaving her alone.

She sank to the floor, waiting for her thumping heart to slow, and stared at the drops of wax as they spilled over the candle. Over. It was over.

Or was it? What if he did accuse her of spying? Renard had believed her a spy before. If she told him she had seen her uncle, would he again?

No. He could not. He had been honest with her, shared his burdens. He had let her come and go without guards. He knew, now, that he could trust her.

She rose from the cold floor and started up the stairs.

She would tell Renard. He would know what to do.

Distracted, Katrine rejoined the crowd as a bubbling stream of well-wishers flowed through Van Artevelde's house to pay their respects after the christening. A few moments to greet the Queen, then she would find a quiet moment with Renard.

Round and resplendent in blue velvet trimmed with pearls, Queen Philippa received each guest tirelessly, graciously, and with just the right word. As Katrine stepped before the Queen, the warm touch of Renard's hand on her elbow guided her forwards.

Queen Philippa enfolded her hand. 'Ah, my dear, I do not know how I would have got through that night without you.'

Katrine squeezed her hand and smiled. 'I am glad I could be of service, your Grace.'

Behind the Queen, Lady Johanna held the baby John. The Queen reached back to stroke his cheek. 'All through his life this one will be called John of Ghent. I will make sure he also knows the name of the faithful friend who stood by my side at his birth.'

Her Grace turned to Renard. 'Renard, we owe this joyful day in no small measure to you.' She patted his hand and stretched to her toes to whisper in his ear, 'I had word from Edward yesterday. Edward will announce your appointment as Bishop of Norwich before Yuletide.'

Katrine turned to stone. Immobile.

Renard the deceiver had fooled her again.

She would find no respite here. No way to trust him with her secret when he had concealed one so massive that it made everything he had allowed her to foolishly hope for impossible.

She refused to meet his eyes. She had thought she could discern truth there. She had only deceived herself. Deceived herself into believing he would want her as a wife. He had wanted no more than the Bishop. And she, stupid she, had given it to him gladly.

She stared at his hands, at the fingers that had stroked the centre of her being and coaxed forth her shuddering spirit.

Hands that would hold the consecrated host as it was transformed into the body of Christ. A man who would be no better a bishop than Clare.

Renard spoke to the Queen and Katrine heard his words as if through thick, mottled glass. 'I must speak to the King on the subject when he arrives, your Grace.'

She knew she should move away as if Renard were nothing to her, but, like Lot's wife, she stood like a pillar of salt, able only to gaze fixedly at what she had lost.

The Queen looked at Katrine, still standing beside her. 'I must say, Renard, you look less like a bishop every day.'

Then, anger burned through her numbness. Anger at him because he had taken her and never told her. Anger at herself because she had let him and hoped for something more. Anger that cauterised her bloodless wound and melted her frozen tongue. 'The King is to make Renard a bishop? I thought that privilege was reserved to the Pope.'

Renard's eyes darkened in warning.

'Of course the Pope must confirm the choice,' the Queen said, 'but the King's recommendation carries the greatest weight.'

Katrine swayed and felt his arms behind her. She pulled away, certain his touch would leave large black smudges of sin on her sleeves.

Renard's tongue was as smooth as ever. 'In her rush to congratulate you, Lady Katrine has not eaten today.' He gave a short bow to the Queen. 'With your permission.'

Renard gripped her shoulders, steering her towards the tower instead of the kitchen. 'This is a conversation for a private place.'

She jerked away. 'Why would we need privacy for you to receive my congratulations on your forthcoming appointment to so public a position?' Each word must be as sharp as shears. 'This calls for celebration in the Market Square!'

'You forget yourself.'

'No, it seems you are the one who forgot. Though it is such a large thing, I wonder that you could forget it. Perhaps you only forgot to tell me.' She climbed the ladder, each rung a memory she had to fight. He followed her, so close that his scent touched her.

At the top, she faltered at the sight of the rumpled bed.

He touched her shoulder, too close to a caress, and she struck his hand away, fury taking her. 'Do not touch me.'

Hands clenched, Renard took her with a look. 'To look at you is to touch you.'

The fire in his eyes seared her breasts and heated her blood. Her hands craved the smooth skin of his shoulders, the rough scars of his back.

She squashed the desire. She had trusted her feelings and they had played her false. Shame claimed her again. Shame she had almost forgotten in becoming gloriously herself. She hated him for that, for ripping away the silken coverings she had wrapped around their joining.

Oh, Eve, is this what it felt like to be thrown out of paradise for something you did not know was wrong?

She groped for words light, bitter, stinging. 'Strange words from a prospective bishop. I must disagree with the Queen, however. I think you look very much like a bishop. The Bishop of Clare, for example.'

Lines of pain deepened around his lips, but she plunged on. Each syllable must slash the feelings weaving them together until they were destroyed as completely as the walnut-dyed wool. 'Part of an English bishop's service to God appears to require carnal knowledge of Flemish women.'

His voice was dark and hot. 'It is not like that with us.'

'So say you now. No, you were quite right. I was the only one who prattled of the truth of love.' Her throat closed over the bitter words. 'What we did was only the lustful coupling of animals.'

He stepped towards her. 'That is not our truth.'

'Truth?' Laughter flowed out of her, bitter as an orange on her tongue. 'You are too late for truth, my friend Renard. I asked you for it too many times.' She stopped him with her eyes. 'We have no truth.'

Her words raced her breath now, raced the tears searing her eyes. She must speak quickly or words would not come at all. She wanted to wound him. She wanted his pain to match hers. She wanted him to regret sharing his secrets as much as she regretted sharing herself. 'It is a high honour for a bastard to be made a bishop. I am sure your mother would be so glad that coupling with a weaver did not interfere.'

His control shattered like glass.

Rage, shame, guilt, and a hundred other emotions she could not name, chased each other across his face. No negotiator's skills protected him. A raw cry, the howl of an animal in pain, tore from his throat.

He lunged towards her.

She ran, but not fast enough. They fell together on to the bed, strands of hair spilling free of her wimple, and over the linens like blood.

He surrounded her, arms like an iron band around her ribs. His warm breath trembled in her ear. She swallowed, feeling the daisy-patterned dagger against her throat and, for a moment, she did not know whether he meant to kill her or love her.

And she could not bear it if he loved her.

She swallowed, teasing the dagger's edge. 'Now that you have so clearly shown me how to sin, please instruct me in proper church penance.'

Chapter Twenty-Six

It was not her words that brought Renard to himself. It was the sensation of her hair spilling over his fingers.

And over the sharp edge of the dagger he pressed against her throat.

His arms were filled with her, as if in an embrace. Her chest rose and fell calmly, as if he held her in sleep. As if she were not afraid of death.

Or not afraid of him.

He was afraid.

Katrine had shredded his restraint, allowing emotion to wash away reason and sweep him to the edge of madness.

He might have killed her.

He looked less like a bishop because she had made him more a man. Weak. Mortal. A glorious sinner who had used the sins of the flesh to succour the soul.

Deeper than the flesh. That is our truth.

And it had brought all the unbearable pain he had always feared.

Shaking, he lifted his head away from the soft, addicting

scent of her. He had trusted her with his deepest secret and she had skewered him with it.

And despite it all, the skin below her ear was sweet and tender and hot and he wanted to press his lips against the vein where her heart beat fast as spring rain.

Slowly, he eased the dagger away from her throat. But the blade snagged in her wimple's folds, ripping a jagged wound in the soft, white wool.

The frayed edge gaped in mute accusation, as if it were a larger transgression than his dagger at her throat.

'The wool…I couldn't…I'm sorry,' he said, his voice as unsteady as his muscles.

She sat up, leaving him sprawled in the bed linens. At the edge of the bed, she turned back, chin up, a few strands of her hair tangled in the torn white wool like blood in a fresh wound.

He struggled to sit up, gathering every bit of his courage to face her. Her eyes, huge and dark and surrounded by that impossible thicket of lashes, were full of tears. And self-loathing.

That emotion, at least, they could share.

'Which of us bears the greatest sin?' She pursed her lips against the tears, but they fell anyway and she let them. 'Is it you, for breaking vows of celibacy you have not yet taken?' The clear bell of her voice rang again, as cruel to herself as to him. 'Or perhaps my sin is worse, for tempting you beyond even a bishop's endurance?'

Too late. Too late to explain he had planned to ask Edward to release him from the vow. Even his tongue, that had negotiated with kings, could never convince her.

Silent, he gripped the silver handle, feeling the imprint of the daisy on his palm. He wanted to hold her, but he had forfeited the right. How could he have thought to marry like an ordinary man? He was worthy of being neither a bishop nor a husband.

She left the bed and circled the round room, dragging wool in her wake. 'Maybe it was the sight of my hair that tempted you beyond endurance. I tried to keep it covered, you remember I tried.' Her voice broke and she cleared her throat, laying mocking anger over her pain. 'And what penance must I pay the Church for the sin of being seduced by one of its own? Will the Bishop of Clare hear my confession and set my punishment? Or perhaps he will want to sample the sin personally in order to judge.'

'Stop.' He flung the word and the dagger together. The dagger clattered against the stone wall, then dropped to the floor, dented.

He dragged himself to his feet. 'The penance is not yours to pay.'

Empty, black cold seized his stomach, as it had gripped him when he looked over the side of the boat taking him away from home over a deep, icy sea. Slipping into those waters meant oblivion with no hope and no reprieve.

He did not call the black feeling fear. Fear was about death of the body. This feeling, this glimpse into a world without her, was about the death of the soul.

A cheerless laugh hovered in her voice. 'If the penance is not mine, then whose? Yours? What penance will you pay?'

Filling his eyes with the sight of her, brave, passionate, reckless, he sentenced himself. 'To live in the hell of a world without you, knowing what I have lost.'

He picked up the dagger and turned away, plunging into the cold, dark waters of a world without Katrine.

At the bottom of the ladder, Renard reached for the wall to steady his step, but instead of hard stone, he grabbed a handful of tapestry. Ripping the wool from its moorings, he crushed it, yet another thing he had destroyed this night.

'Where is the Hooftman?' The tapestry fell to the floor as the young page hurtled into him. Renard grabbed him by the shoulders. 'Control yourself, boy. What has happened?'

'The castle at Douvre has fallen.' He thrust a sealed parchment at Renard.

Douvre. Where the Queen's brother had not trusted his vassal.

No signet marked the sealing wax. He scanned the lines. The vassal had left unseen in the middle of the night, no doubt with a pocket of gold for his pains. At dawn, the ramparts were deserted. Philip's men had simply marched in.

Who could have known? Who but the Council knew the weakness in our defences?

He read the final line with the cold shiver of certainty. 'Look for your traitor in a woman's form. The woman whose family abides in Philip's court.'

Unsigned.

'Who gave you this, boy?'

The boy's eyes were round and blue and frightened. 'I know not, my lord. A man. I assumed he came from Douvre. He said to get it here as soon as possible.'

A terrible certainty gripped him. *Katrine. Katrine knew because I told her.*

He had trusted her. Let her come and go. Told her his secrets. And she had betrayed them all. Now, his weakness had created more than a private hell.

It threatened his king.

Chapter Twenty-Seven

'Renard, how can you accuse her of this?' Jack stood before the fire, bouncing on the balls of his feet. He had been badgering Renard since the evening meal.

Renard let the crumpled red silk eyepatch dangle from his finger, a wretched reminder of Katrine's treachery and his gullibility. After he had shared the letter with the war council, he had confined her to the tower, taking away the ladder and adding guards. Without the ladder, she could not leave the tower.

With the guards, he would not enter it and be tempted to believe her again.

'King Edward crosses the channel within a fortnight.' The allies' few forces were harrying the French as they traversed the countryside, slowing their progress. 'No more secrets must escape to the enemy.'

Jack snorted with disgust. 'Saying she bewitched secrets out of you is like saying she bewitched me into kissing her.'

'Maybe she did.' He had shared his guilt with no one but Jack. 'She lied to me.'

Jack shook his head. 'And you lied to her.'

'I had to.' Yet he had deserved every bitter word she had hurled at him. Lies about smuggling had served his King. Lies about being a bishop had served himself. Which of them, after all, had been the worst?

'You are blind in the brain, my friend. Why should she have trusted you?'

For no reason. No reason at all.

But Jack was right. Katrine had not bewitched him. His own weakness had betrayed him. He had let her come and go unguarded and this was the result.

And even after all this, he wanted to trust her still. Wanted her to prove against proof that she was innocent.

The Bishop of Clare swept into the room without pausing at the threshold. 'We must talk,' he said to Renard without a glance at Jack.

Jack bowed with exaggerated politeness, but slammed the door behind him as he left.

Renard forced himself to rise from his chair. His bow was stiff and he did not even pretend to kiss the Bishop's ring. 'Your Excellency.'

Standing with calculated ease in front of the fireplace, Renard watched the man's robes snap around his pacing ankles. Such agitation was uncharacteristic.

The Bishop slowed his stride. 'In the matter of the Gravere wench. Since Flanders has acknowledged King Edward as liege, we are responsible for justice.'

'Yes.' Renard shifted, uneasy.

Wadding his robes around his flabby haunches to cushion the wooden chair, the Bishop stretched his feet towards the fireplace. He did not invite Renard to sit. 'I've conferred with Van Artevelde. We will create a panel to judge the woman.'

'English justice calls for a jury.'

'We are not in England.' The Bishop pawed through the small bowl of dates beside the chair. 'Van Artevelde will represent Flanders. I will represent the Church.' Picking a date, he flung a look at Renard. 'You will represent the King.'

'What is the charge?' His voice sounded very far away.

The Bishop's eyebrows rose in mock surprise. 'Spying for the French, of course.'

The knot in his stomach tightened. 'We have only an anonymous accusation.'

'You support a traitor?'

'I am simply considering the implications of such a trial.' As long as he kept her in the tower, she could do no more damage. Surely that would be enough. 'She is a citizen of this city. A hasty conviction might turn the people against the King.'

'I doubt that. They found the vassal, you know.' The Bishop studied the sticky date carefully, as if uncertain whether it was worthy to share his tongue. 'He's been hanged. Drawn.' The Bishop's thin lips almost disappeared as he smiled. 'And quartered.'

Renard closed his eyes, only to see Katrine at the end of a rope. He opened them quickly. 'Convenient. He cannot speak of who aided him.'

'Ah, but we know that, don't we?' Warming to his subject, the Bishop waved his hand, the date on the pedestal of his thumb and two fingers. Like a cat, the man played with his food before eating it.

He had a cat's eyes, too, Renard thought. The yellow, almond-shaped eyes of a cat about to pounce. 'Do we?'

'You suspected her from the start. In fact, it might be considered suspicious. You were in charge of her. How could she have received such information and passed it on under your very nose?'

The Bishop's subtle threat chilled the back of his neck. 'I do not know.'

The Bishop twisted his hand as a woman might, admiring his sapphire in the firelight. 'It would pain me,' he said, in a voice that carried no pain at all, 'to revoke my letter to the Holy Father.'

Fists clenched behind his back, Renard tightened his grip. Tight enough for the pain to overcome the seasick feeling in his stomach. Tight enough to keep his fingers from circling the man's hypocritical throat. Tight enough to hold back his own guilty secret. Once, he would have been glad to be relieved of his promise to take the ring. Now, it was all he had left. And all he could offer his king.

'What if the evidence does not condemn her?'

'There's no question of that, is there?' He popped the date into his mouth and chewed with relish.

He didn't know. Was she the woman he had held in his arms? The one he could love and trust?

Or was she the one who had summoned her uncle to seize him? Had she lied about that night, too?

Renard could neither leave her to the Bishop's prejudice nor leave his king unprotected. 'Set a date for her trial.'

With a curious sense of detachment, Katrine watched a tear tremble on the end of Merkin's chin. Despite her heedless sobs, the girl's hands were gentle as they combed Katrine's hair, gentle as they had never been when she wrestled with the wool.

Unbound, the mantle of red strands flowed over her shoulders and down her back.

Katrine would be tried today. She would wear no wimple.

In the weeks since she had been accused, guards had hunched like gargoyles beneath her room. She had surmised that her uncle had sent a letter, as he'd threatened, but she had been told little.

She knew King Edward had landed, triumphant, after his ships had destroyed most of the French fleet. He had suffered a slight leg wound, so the Queen and her ladies had flocked to the coast to nurse him.

Did the Queen, too, believe her guilty? She did not know. She had seen no one.

Including Renard.

And why would she expect to see him? She had thrown him out of her room, out of her life, with the cruellest words possible. She had used his deepest, secret pain to attack him. He would never forgive her.

Never believe she loved him still.

The ladder rattled. It was time.

Hugging Merkin, she rose, smoothing her fingers over the bumps and nubs of her gown. The undyed, natural cloth showed the variation of each strand of wool that curled out of the sheep's skin.

Without the swaddling wimple, the unfamiliar pull of her hair held her head high.

Flanked by guards, she marched to the Council Meeting Chamber and entered. The crowd gasped. Hearing their whispers, Katrine felt like Saint Catherine on trial before the fifty pagan professors of ancient Alexandria. The saint, dazzling them with her knowledge, had converted every one to Christ.

But Saint Catherine had been a virgin. Katrine had forfeited her right to God's help.

She strode to the dais, lifted her chin, and faced her judges. 'You called me here, good sirs. What am I to answer for?'

Three sat in judgment—Van Artevelde, the Bishop and Renard.

Van Artevelde slumped in his chair, chin in hand, bushy brows furrowed. A reassuring smile tugged at his craggy face. He knew her father. He would support her.

In the centre, snarling, the Bishop looked as if she were a particularly delectable treat he was determined to devour. She had refused him. He would have his revenge.

Renard held her fate.

Renard, whose moods had become an open book to her, was unreadable. Not even the flicker of an eyelash warmed the judgement in his eyes. She had recognised the passion he had hidden so long. Recognised it, released it, and loved it.

That, in his eyes, was her real crime.

The Bishop spoke first. 'Lady Catherine de Gravere, you stand accused of spying for the French, an act of betrayal against King Edward, rightful King of France and liege lord of Flanders. The penalty is death.'

Head light and fingers numb, she struggled to stay upright. 'What is it you think I have done?'

The Bishop recited the accusations in a singsong suited to the mass. 'You had information that the vassal of Douvre was disloyal. You communicated this information to Philip's troops who turned him against his lawful liege.'

Her eyes flew to Renard. Only Renard knew he had told her that secret. 'Who accuses me?'

For a long, breathless moment, she held Renard's gaze. Something—love, vengeance, or doubt—flashed deep within his eyes.

'We have a letter,' the Bishop said. 'It says a woman was responsible.'

'Who sent the letter?'

'It doesn't matter,' the Bishop said.

'And what does the vassal say?'

Renard answered, 'The vassal is dead.'

'Why do you think I am that woman?'

The Bishop's slick smile returned. 'Your uncle even now fights with Philip. Your position with the royal guests gave you access to information. You speak with strangers every day, coming and going in a manner unseemly for a noble-woman. You had opportunities no decent woman would have.'

Renard sat too straight for ease. 'Yet we have no proof but an anonymous letter.'

'Perhaps,' the Bishop said, with a whiskered smile, 'we should ask your help on that point.'

She watched Renard for any trace of emotion. Silent, he did not even tighten his lips.

So still she did not know. Was it Renard or her uncle who sought her death? 'Would you condemn me without allowing me to speak?'

'Please, Lady Katrine.' Van Artevelde's gravelly voice held a trace of kindness. 'Tell us what you have to say.'

A ripple of agreement fluttered through the crowd. The un-familiar weight of her hair lay hot and heavy at her back. She lifted her chin.

Renard's was the only judgement that mattered now. She hoped he would hear her words and forgive the pain she had caused him, the only thing she regretted.

'I am innocent,' she began, slowly and clearly. Hidden in the folds of her surcoat, her fingers lay calm and still.

Somewhere behind her, Merkin sobbed.

'The Bishop accuses me because I walk with my head held up. Because I make cloth with the Mark of the Daisy as a man would do. That is true, but it is not treason.'

The fog surrounding her senses had cleared. All her life she had been condemned for being what she was. She would run no more. That much, her time with Renard had taught her. If she were to be condemned, let it be for the truth.

Her words rushed out now, relieved. 'You see, the business is in my hands because my father had no brother he could trust and because my father sits, even today, in an English jail.'

Behind her, the crowd murmured with the memories of months before, when the English were not allies, but adversaries.

'Then you have good reason to hate the King,' Clare said. 'And to plot his defeat.'

'I hoped to gain favour with the English so that the King might look favourably on my request and free my father. I would not jeopardise his life by such a foolish act. But my uncle sneaked into the city on the day of the Prince's christening, and—'

The Bishop did not let her finish. 'An impossible tale! Such a man would be mad.'

'Madder still,' she continued, remembering his rambling speech. 'He asked me to spy for him. I refused.'

Van Artevelde's voice was calm, but his expression was puzzled. 'Even if we believe you, we have a letter. It says a woman whose family fights for Philip caused the castle to fall. Who would have sent that if it weren't true?'

'He would. When I refused, he threatened to send an anonymous letter accusing me.'

'And you never mentioned it?' Renard's question was sharp.

'I was afraid no one would believe me.'

The panel's silence suggested she was right.

'He was your kin,' Van Artevelde said, finally. 'It would not be easy to refuse him.'

'I had to.' She drew a large breath and spoke to Renard alone. 'I have come to know the English. I have held a royal child in my arms in his hour of birth.'

Renard blinked. The sight gave her courage.

Renard shimmered before her, blurred through her tears. She forced the final words past the lump in her throat. 'There are those I love among the English. I could never betray them.'

Chapter Twenty-Eight

Renard's fingers tightened on the arm of his chair as the tears she had blinked into submission spilled down her cheeks. She had the courage to bare her true self, letting her feelings tumble forth. It had always been her failing. And what he loved most about her.

Unwelcome possessiveness tightened his loins. He gripped the chair to keep from running to her. The sight of her hair, unfurled before strangers, seemed intimate as a love letter read on a street corner. He was the only one who should have the right to see it.

'A pleasant tale, Lady Katrine.' The Bishop's whine assaulted Renard's ears. 'But hard to believe in light of the facts.'

Before a room full of enemies, she dabbed her cheeks with the trailing sleeve of her gown, then lowered her damp sleeve. 'Facts, Bishop?' Her voice, more steady than he had expected, carried the arch tone she used when she thought Renard was lying to himself. 'I hear only of an unsigned letter.'

A drop of sweat escaped from under Renard's arm, leaving

a chill trail in its race towards his waist. He leaned so hard on the arm of the chair that the wood bruised his elbow.

Casually, he shifted, draping his fingers over its round arm. His sweat must stay hidden.

Everything he felt must stay hidden.

Who was the true Katrine? He had been with her at the loom, on the streets, in her bedchamber. If she had planned to betray him, surely he would have felt it.

But hadn't she fed him, bathed him, seduced him, kept him beside her, and betrayed him once before? The thump at the door still lodged in his chest. She had blamed her uncle then, too. Lunatic, Merkin had called him. Could it be true?

'But what about last summer?' he began, duty and doubt driving the words past his tongue. 'Did you not betray the secret peace negotiations, nearly capturing a key English negotiator?'

She staggered, crushing creamy wool in white-knuckled fists.

His accusation echoed strangely in the shocked silence.

Van Artevelde grimaced and sat silent, his large, dark eyes pondering consequences.

The Bishop, on the other hand, nearly leapt from his chair with glee. 'Well, well, Lady Katrine, it seems this is not your first offence against the King.' The words were for Katrine, but his smile was aimed at Renard. A pink tongue darted out to lick his lips in anticipation. 'Indeed, it seems that you have used your female deceptions before to trap servants of the King. Speak to this new offence.'

Her shoulders drooped. Then, she lifted her head and tossed back her hair, no guilt, no shame, no surprise in her expression. She faced him as if she had known from the beginning that he would be her salvation or her death.

'Renard makes the accusation. Let him speak to it. It seems as if he cannot keep his dagger from my throat.'

Love, guilt, all the things he did not want to feel pounded him.

The Bishop looked from Renard to Katrine. His voice dropped to a coaxing whisper he might have used to elicit unwilling admissions in the confessional. 'Or perhaps, Lady Katrine, you are not the traitor. The traitor may be the person who told you about the castle's weaknesses. Tell us who told you. We may go easier with you.'

The Bishop's eyes slithered to Renard.

Katrine followed the glance. Her startled eyes met his.

Trapped.

Never underestimate an opponent, Renard reminded himself, as he looked at the Bishop. His lips tightened in what he hoped passed for a calm smile. The Bishop wanted both of them, but he would settle for either. All she had to do was tell the truth. She would be free and he would be dead.

I don't care whether she is guilty or not. I cannot let her die.

He rose. 'You are right, your Excellency. I told her that the castle was vulnerable. The fault is mine. Let her go and take me.'

The room dissolved into babble, but he could see only Katrine's eyes, full of love and anguish. And as the Bishop's ring and even his life slipped from his grasp, he felt it was all worth it.

'Well, it seems the conspiracy goes much higher,' the Bishop said, a smile carving his face. 'To the very man the King trusts most.'

'That's not true.' Katrine started towards the Bishop, but the guards grabbed her arms.

'The King will have something to say about this,' Van Artevelde said. 'We should wait until he arrives.'

'We can't wait for the King when the security of his crown is at stake,' the Bishop said, nodding towards the guards. 'Take them both. Give them a traitor's death.'

The guards started for Renard, but Katrine was quicker, rushing forward to kneel at the Bishop's feet. 'I will tell them about Merkin. I will tell them—'

Renard grabbed her. 'Katrine, don't.' No one would believe her now. 'Let her go, Clare. I'm the one you want.'

A new voice broke into the mêlée. 'You can't let her go. She is guilty!'

A stout, sweating man with wild eyes broke through the crowd.

Katrine went pale.

The Bishop squirmed in his chair. 'Who are you?'

'Charles, Baron of Gravere. I am her uncle.'

Renard hated him at first sight. And judging by the fact that he was showing up unannounced in a court of Edward's supporters, he might be capable of the things Katrine had said.

The guards, confused, hovered between Katrine and her uncle, holding no one. Even Clare seemed at a loss.

'You accuse your own niece?' Renard began. The man had never seen him, so he wouldn't know the very spy he had tried to catch now questioned him.

'Last summer, I found the red silk eyepatch and I knew right away she was harbouring an English spy.'

And Renard smiled. The man was mad. Mad enough to condemn himself. '"Harbouring" suggests aiding,' he said, rising from his chair, not bothering to disguise the joy in his voice. 'It sounds as if she has supported Edward from the start, not worked against him.' Renard nodded to the guards, who moved to either side of the Baron.

The man's eyes had clouded over. 'She wouldn't do what I wanted,' he muttered. 'She would never do what I wanted.' He no longer seemed to be capable of understanding and answering a question.

'So, it seems that you are the traitor here, not Lady Katrine.' Renard moved closer, hardly able to smother the ecstasy in his voice. 'What really happened at the castle?'

He met the man's eyes, determined to make him confess by force of will.

A moment of clarity touched his eyes. 'The vassal. He sent word himself. No one else.'

Renard turned, looking for Katrine, but speaking to the room. 'So Lady Katrine is innocent, as she has said, and the traitor has delivered himself into our hands.'

Behind him, the Baron babbled, his lucid moment gone. 'She wouldn't have me. Just like her mother. I should have killed her then.' He spoke as if he had crossed into another place where he answered only to his own judge. 'I had to kill her mother and I should have killed her, too.'

Katrine gasped and nearly fell before he caught her.

Not waiting for the King's justice, two men from the crowd lunged at the Baron, ready to rip a murderer limb from limb. With a lift of the Fleming's bushy eyebrows, the two white-shirted guards grabbed the Baron's arms, hustling him away from the mob.

'Long live Philip, the rightful King of France.' His voice, shrill, echoed behind him.

'This hearing is over,' Van Artevelde said, dismissing the crowd.

As they filed out, the Bishop did not move, except to

pound his clenched fist against his ringed hand with the inexorable rhythm of a battering ram. Hypocrite, Renard thought. He had been willing to condemn an innocent woman to attain his own ends. Not God's. Not even the King's.

He thought once more of the bishop's chair. Imagined the weight of the ring. Felt the swing of the robe. And had no desire for its power and protection. Edward would have to find another ally.

Katherine had taught him, finally, to embrace who he was. All of it.

Would she forgive him for doubting her?

Chapter Twenty-Nine

Katrine walked into the sunshine, barely aware that Renard walked beside her. She walked free and her uncle had murdered her mother. How her father would weep.

'He would have killed me, too,' she whispered. Perhaps her blood had always known.

Renard did not break stride to answer. 'You are safe now.'

Just like your mother, he had said, so many times. But she was not. She was not even like the woman she had been a year ago, hiding her hair because her uncle hated it.

When they stopped, she saw they were in front of Van Artevelde's. She looked at Renard's face, so dear, and wondered how she had let herself be in his care again. It would just be that much harder to leave him.

So many betrayals, on both sides. Could she forgive him?

He would not forgive her. She did not expect that. But still, she must try. 'What I said to you. It was wrong of me. I was cruel because I hurt.' Hurt and she wanted him to hurt just as much.

He took her hand. 'Let us talk. Alone. I, too, must…'

His eyes pleaded where his tongue would not. She let

herself drink in the sight of the twisted curl of chestnut hair around his ear, his eyes, deep blue now with emotions he no longer hid.

I will say goodbye. Just one moment of goodbye. Then let him return to England and collect his ring.

Silent, they climbed the ladder to the tower room. She walked to the window, gazing at the unfinished steeple of the weaver's church, reaching but not grasping heaven. French words in now familiar English accents drifted up from the street.

As vesper bells chimed, she heard him pull up the ladder and drop it on the floor. He spoke as the last stroke died. 'I have decided not to accept a bishopric.'

She whirled to face him. 'Because of my sins?'

'No.' The word allowed no doubt. 'You have no sins I do not share. And more you must forgive me for. For doubting you.' He came close enough to embrace her, but his arms hovered without resting. 'I cannot pledge my soul to the Church. I have already given it to you.'

All the truth she had ever wanted was in his eyes. 'You asked for the end of the story,' he said. 'Renard's globe of glass was a lie. He had nothing to offer the Queen, as I have nothing to offer you. No land, no title, nothing of my own. I serve at Edward's pleasure. The bishop's seat was to be my reward.' His empty hands hung at his side.

'Do you not yet understand? I expected nothing from you. Adam had no lands. Eve had no title. All we have to give is ourselves.'

A lopsided smile touched his lips. 'Adam and Eve were thrown out of paradise, you know.'

'Into the world in which we live.'

'Where did you get such courage?'

'From loving you.'

Passion flared in his eyes and he wrapped her in his arms, sweet, slow, loving. He slipped the wool off her shoulders slowly, letting his fingers follow her warm curves, and when she was naked, he trailed the red silk eyepatch he always carried from her forehead down every inch of her skin. It teased her breasts like his fingers, tickled her ears like his tongue, and tripped along the soles of her feet like his toes until she was writhing and laughing and moaning and reaching for him and he dropped the scrap of silk to fill his hands and his lips with her and to wed them into one flesh.

And in return, she loved him as if it were the last night of their world.

Because it would be.

Just one more night. Then I must let him go.

Afterwards, Katrine lay, dozing and waking in perfect contentment, held against the linens by his left arm. Her very skin rippled at the tolling of the morning bell, so alive to his touch that it could hear as well as feel.

She inhaled the sweet, ripe scent of their lovemaking. She wanted to remember every moment, touch, word so she could relive it later. Her hair, riotous around them, twisted, grasped, his hands, his mouth, even hers, full of it. His fingers, caressing every inch of skin, from the curve of her ear to the sweet, hot place between her legs. Coaxing her passion. Meeting it with his. The feel of him inside her, stretching. Wanting his seed to take root inside her even as she prayed to Eve it would not.

Renard shifted in his sleep, finally turning away, freeing her from his weight.

As she would free him. She would not stand in the way of the life he could have.

I have nothing, he had said, but that was not true. King Edward would not abandon the man who had given him Flanders, the man who shared his blood. If Renard refused the bishop's chair, the King could bestow a rich widow or a noble title. He would have a life at court. Any of those would fit him better than a woman with fleece under her fingernails.

He might forgive her. Love her, even. But she knew herself now. She loved the wool and her work more than the life that would be his. He needed another sort of woman. One who would not cry aloud at the sheer joy of their joining.

When he woke, he would see that, see her and lament his promises.

If I leave now, I will never have to see the regret in his eyes when he wakes.

Holding her breath, she rolled off the bed and slipped into the serviceable brown wool, not bothering to bind her hair. Fumbling for her small sack with trembling fingers, she grabbed only her mother's triptych, her comb and the daisy mirror. She would never look at it again without seeing the dagger, its mate.

She juggled her sack and her skirt in one hand, clutching the side of the ladder with the other and stopped to look at him one last time.

He never stirred.

Then, she stepped on the next rung and, at the bottom, pulled the ladder down.

Chapter Thirty

Renard knew before he opened his eyes that she had gone. The very air was empty of her.

Before he could clear his muddled thoughts, a man's voice drifted up from the floor below. 'Katrine, are you there?'

Renard knew the voice of every courtier. He did not know this one. Leaping from the bed, he reached for the chausses and tunic he had flung away in abandon. He mustn't be found naked in her room.

The voice came again. Older. Excited. Impatient. 'Katrine, it's me. Are you there?' The ladder waved into place and swayed with the weight of a climber.

Jamming his left arm into the sleeve and buckling his dagger in place, Renard reached the ladder and came face to face with a grey-haired, wiry man with deep lines framing brown eyes with lashes as thick as Katrine's.

Sir Denys de Gravere was home.

The man was staring as if he'd seen a wraith. 'Who are you?' he whispered. 'You look like my partner born again.'

Silent, Renard held out the handle of his dagger, relieved the man had not asked why he was in Katrine's room.

'Where did you get this?' The question was sharp.

'From the same woman who gave him the mirror.'

Katrine's father nodded. 'So there was a child. Giles was never certain.' His gaze never left Renard's face. 'What name did she give you?'

'Renard.'

'She could not give you his name, but she named you for him. *Renard* means fox in French. *Vos* means fox in Flemish.'

The thought pleased him, and he wondered why he had not noticed it before. His mother had laid her secret in plain sight, yet none had seen.

De Gravere finally let his gaze search the room. 'There is much I would ask, but where is Katrine?'

The vision of Katrine, naked and satisfied, flashed before him. 'I believe she has gone back to High Gate Street.' Back to the one place she had always felt safe until he had upended her world. Well, he wasn't done with that.

De Gravere paused, and Renard heard all his unasked questions in that silence.

'Let's go together,' Renard said. 'There is much you need to know of the last few months.'

While they walked, Renard told the man of how he had come to Giles's shop and of the trial and his brother's confession. He said nothing of Katrine and himself.

'All that time,' de Gravere said, regret shaking his voice. 'I should have known. If I had not been away from home so often…'

'Please,' Renard said, as they rounded the corner, 'tell me of my father.'

De Gravere took his measure with a sweeping gaze. 'Your colouring is much like his, except for the eyes. He was energetic and vigorous. An artist at the loom.' He smiled. 'They say that weavers are cleverer than other men because they have so much time to think. That was certainly true of Giles.'

'And what can you tell me of…her?' He could not call her Mother, even now.

'I only saw her through his eyes. She was a widow then, after more than twenty years of a loveless marriage. Giles was to be in Brussels a week. I did not see him for six. He never spoke of that time, but he was not the same man after.'

'Yet he did not come for me when she died.' He could not keep the bitterness from his tongue.

'He did not know, and she hid you well. A prince can scatter bastards freely, but a princess…'

He thought for the first time that his mother had needed more passion, rather than less—passion enough, courage enough, to risk filling her life instead of leaving it empty.

He had that kind of courage now.

'Did he ever speak of her?'

'Only with his work. He created the Duchess cloth and sent it to her, each year a different colour, as long as she lived. The last year it was a deep blue. The colour of her eyes. And yours.'

They had reached the Mark of the Daisy. The painted sign, petals fatter and rounder than the ones on the dagger, creaked with the wind. Through the window, he saw Katrine sweeping the hearth.

Her hair flowed down her back like silk.

De Gravere turned to him. 'You will ask her to go with you.'

After a lifetime of revealing nothing, he had shown this stranger all without saying a word. 'I will ask. I do not know what she will say.'

The man nodded. 'Let me see her first.'

Katrine's happy shriek rang against Renard's back as he walked away.

A few hours later, when Katrine was alone again, Renard entered the shop, squeezing an orange so tightly it might turn to pulp.

'I have an offer for you, *ma petite*,' he began, not giving her a chance to speak. 'If you let the opportunity pass…' He cleared his throat. 'I will offer it to no other.'

Hope flickered across her face. 'What do you propose?'

'Let us weave the home piece of our lives together.' He held his breath, trying to read her eyes in the silence.

'Are you certain? I am a not a perfect woman. I work with wool. I am outspoken.' She bit her lip but did not look away. 'And rarely in control of my passions.'

'I want no other woman. Your passion has taught me to accept my own.' He smiled. 'The dagger matches only one mirror.'

'But the King will reward you. If not with a bishopric, with a wife worthy of your birth.'

He touched her chin, holding her eyes with his, hiding nothing. 'After all this, do you not know that you are worth everything to me?'

Her smile warred with the tears. 'More than a royal birthright?'

'I have another birthright. I am the son of Giles de Vos. I want to take his place at the loom with you beside me. Come with me to England. Let us make our own Garden of Eden.'

He held out the orange to her, then held his breath, waiting to see whether she would take it. What he asked would take all her courage. And his.

A smile teased the corners of her mouth. 'An apple is the usual offering, I believe.' She reached for the orange, then pulled back her hand and let the smile free. 'If I say yes, can you get me the wool I need?'

'If you say yes, you'll have all the Cistercian-raised fleece you can weave.'

She plucked the orange from his fingers, slipped her other arm around his waist, and looked up at him, her heart in her eyes. 'How do I know I can trust you?'

His entire face ached with a smile and he wrapped her in his arms. 'Just look into the globe of glass my eyes have become. You will see the truth.'

Author's Afterword

Many of the events and the people in this story are a part of history, including King Edward's wool embargo, the Bishop's embassy—though not the name I gave him—the battle over the Flemish alliance, the murder of Sohier de Courtrai for conspiring with the English, the rise of Jacob van Artevelde, and the birth of John of Gaunt—Ghent—though later than the date I give here. The stories of Renard the Fox were well-known in France and in the Low Countries.

Students of the period will forgive me, I hope, for my artistic liberties. I streamlined and condensed the events of several years into one and chose the time and place of Queen Philippa's confinement and the baby's birth and baptism to suit my story. King Edward did once travel to France disguised as a merchant, though not—so far as we know—as I portrayed here. The word 'globe' came into use one hundred years later, but 'sphere of glass' lacked the poetry I sought.

Renard and Katrine are, of course, creations of my imagination. History does not record any illegitimate children for Margaret, Duchess of Brabant, daughter of Edward I. The

Duke's illegitimate sons, however, are documented by the chroniclers.

About the time this story takes place, a few Flemish weavers came to England. Eventually, England overtook Flanders as the world's major producer of wool cloth.

I like to think Renard and Katrine might have helped.

* * * * *

Love Inspired
HISTORICAL

*Powerful, engaging stories of romance,
adventure and faith set in the past—
when life was simpler and faith played
a major role in everyday lives*

See below for a sneak preview of
HIGH COUNTRY BRIDE
by Jillian Hart

*Love Inspired Historical—
love and faith throughout the ages*

Silence remained between them, and she felt the rake of his gaze, taking her in from the top of her wind-blown hair where escaped tendrils snapped in the wind to the toe of her scuffed, patched shoes. She watched him fist up his big, work-roughened hands and expected the worst.

"You never told me, Miz Nelson. Where are you going to go?" His tone was flat, his jaw tensed as if he were still fighting his temper. His blue gaze shot past her to watch the children going about their picking up.

"I don't know." Her throat went dry. Her tongue felt thick as she answered. "When I find employment, I could wire a payment to you. Rent. Y-you aren't think-ing of bringing the sher-rif in?"

"You think I want *payment?*" He boomed like winter thunder. *"You think I want rent money?"*

"Frankly, I don't know what you want."

"I'll tell you what I don't want. I don't want—" His words cannoned in the silence as he paused, and a passing pair of geese overhead honked in flat-noted tones. He grimaced, and it was impossible to know what he would say or do.

She trembled, not from fear of him—she truly didn't believe he would strike her—but from the unknown. Of being forced to take the frightening step off the only safe spot she'd known since she'd lost Pa's house.

When you were homeless, everything seemed so fragile, so easily off balance, for it was a big, unkind world for a woman alone with her children. She had no one to protect her. No one to care. The truth was, she'd never had those things in her husband. How could she expect them from any stranger? Especially this man she hardly knew, who was harsh and cold and hardhearted.

And, worse, what if he brought in the law?

"You can't keep living out of a wagon," he said, still angry, the cords still straining in his neck. "Animals have enough sense to keep their young cared for and safe."

Yes, it was as she'd thought. He intended to be as cruel about this as he could be. She spun on her heel, pulling up all her defenses, and was determined to let his upcoming hurtful words roll off her like rainwater on an oiled tarp. She grabbed the towel the children had neatly folded and tossed it into the laundry box in the back of the wagon.

"Miz Nelson. I'm talking to you."

"Yes, I know. If you expect me to stand there while you tongue lash me, you're mistaken. I have packing to get to." Her fingers were clumsy as she hefted the bucket of water she'd brought for washing—she wouldn't need that now—and heaved.

His hand clasped on the handle beside hers, and she could feel the life and power of him vibrate along the thin metal. "Give it to me."

Her fingers let go. She felt stunned as he walked away, easily carrying the bucket that had been so heavy to her, and quietly, methodically, put out the small cooking fire. He did not seem as ominous or as intimidating—somehow—as he stood in the shadows, bent to his task, although she couldn't say why that was. Perhaps it was because he wasn't acting the way she was used to men acting. She was quite used to doing all the work.

Jamie scurried over, juggling his wooden horses, to watch. Daisy hung back, eyes wide and still, taking in the mysterious goings-on.

He is different when he's near to them, she realized. He didn't seem harsh, and there was no hint of anger—or, come to think of it, any other emotion—as he shook out the empty bucket, nodded once to the children and then retraced his path to her.

"Let me guess." He dropped the bucket onto the tailgate, and his anger appeared to be back. Cords strained in his neck and jaw as he growled at her. "If you leave here, you don't know where you're going and you have no money to get there with?"

She nodded. "Yes, sir."

"Then get you and your kids into the wagon. I'll hitch up your horses for you." His eyes were cold and yet they were not unfeeling as he fastened his gaze on hers. "I have an empty shanty out back of my house that no one's living in. You can stay there for the night."

"What?" She stumbled back, and the solid wood of the tailgate bit into the small of her back. "But—"

"There will be no argument," he bit out, interrupting her. "None at all. I buried a wife and son years ago, what was most precious to me, and to see you and them neglected like this—with no one to care—" His jaw ground again and his eyes were no longer cold.

Joanna didn't think she'd ever seen anything sadder than Aiden McKaslin as the sun went down on him.

* * * * *

Don't miss this deeply moving story
HIGH COUNTRY BRIDE
Available July 2008
From the new Love Inspired Historical line

Also look for
SEASIDE CINDERELLA
by Anna Schmidt,
where a poor servant girl and
a wealthy merchant prince
might somehow make a life together.

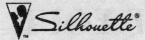

Silhouette®

Romantic
SUSPENSE

**Sparked by Danger,
Fueled by Passion.**

Conard County: The Next Generation

When he learns the truth about his father, military man Ethan Parish is determined to reunite with his long-lost family in Wyoming. On his way into town, he clashes with policewoman Connie Halloran, whose captivating beauty entices him. When Connie's daughter is threatened, Ethan must use his military skills to keep her safe. Together they race against time to find the little girl and confront the dangers inherent in family secrets.

Look for

A Soldier's Homecoming

by *New York Times*
bestselling author
Rachel Lee

Available in July wherever you buy books.

REQUEST YOUR FREE BOOKS!

 Harlequin® Historical
Historical Romantic Adventure!

2 FREE NOVELS PLUS 2 FREE GIFTS!

YES! Please send me 2 FREE Harlequin® Historical novels and my 2 FREE gifts (gifts are worth about $10). After receiving them, if I don't wish to receive any more books, I can return the shipping statement marked "cancel". If I don't cancel, I will receive 6 brand-new novels every month and be billed just $4.94 per book in the U.S. or $5.49 per book in Canada, plus 25¢ shipping and handling per book and applicable taxes, if any*. That's a savings of 20% off the cover price! I understand that accepting the 2 free books and gifts places me under no obligation to buy anything. I can always return a shipment and cancel at any time. Even if I never buy another book, the two free books and gifts are mine to keep forever.

246 HDN ERUM   349 HDN ERUA

Name	(PLEASE PRINT)

Address	Apt. #

City	State/Prov.	Zip/Postal Code

Signature (if under 18, a parent or guardian must sign)

Mail to the **Harlequin Reader Service:**
IN U.S.A.: P.O. Box 1867, Buffalo, NY 14240-1867
IN CANADA: P.O. Box 609, Fort Erie, Ontario L2A 5X3

Not valid to current subscribers of Harlequin Historical books.

Want to try two free books from another line?
Call 1-800-873-8635 or visit www.morefreebooks.com.

* Terms and prices subject to change without notice. N.Y. residents add applicable sales tax. Canadian residents will be charged applicable provincial taxes and GST. Offer not valid in Quebec. This offer is limited to one order per household. All orders subject to approval. Credit or debit balances in a customer's account(s) may be offset by any other outstanding balance owed by or to the customer. Please allow 4 to 6 weeks for delivery. Offer available while quantities last.

Your Privacy: Harlequin Books is committed to protecting your privacy. Our Privacy Policy is available online at www.eHarlequin.com or upon request from the Reader Service. From time to time we make our lists of customers available to reputable third parties who may have a product or service of interest to you. If you would prefer we not share your name and address, please check here. ☐

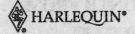

HARLEQUIN®

American ★ Romance®

MADE IN TEXAS

It's the happiest day of Hannah Callahan's life
when she brings her new daughter home to Texas.
And Joe Daugherty would make a perfect father
to complete their unconventional family. But the
world-hopping writer never stays in one place
long enough. Can Joe trust in love enough to
finally get the family he's always wanted?

LOOK FOR

Hannah's Baby

BY

CATHY GILLEN THACKER

*Available July
wherever you buy books.*

LOVE, HOME & HAPPINESS

COMING NEXT MONTH FROM

HARLEQUIN®
HISTORICAL

- **THE DANGEROUS MR. RYDER**
  by **Louise Allen**
  (Regency)
  Those Scandalous Ravenhursts!
  He knows that escorting the haughty Grand Duchess of Maubourg to
  England will not be an easy task. But Jack Ryder, spy and adventurer,
  believes he is more than capable of managing Her Serene Highness.
  *Join Louise Allen as she explores the tangled love-lives of this
  scandalous family in her miniseries.*

- **THE GUNSLINGER'S UNTAMED BRIDE**
  by **Stacey Kayne**
  (Western)
  Juniper Barns sought a secluded life as a lumber camp sheriff to escape
  the ghosts of his past. He doesn't need a woman sneaking into camp
  and causing turmoil....
  Watch sparks fly as Juniper seeks to protect this vengeful beauty.

- **A MOST UNCONVENTIONAL MATCH**
  by **Julia Justiss**
  (Regency)
  Initially, Hal Waterman calling on the newly widowed Elizabeth
  Lowery is just an act of gentlemanly gallantry. Hal is enchanted by the
  beautiful Elizabeth and her little son—but it is a family he knows he
  can never be a part of....
  *Follow Hal's quest to win over Elizabeth's heart—and the approval of
  the ton—so he can take her as his bride....*

- **THE KING'S CHAMPION**
  by **Catherine March**
  (Medieval)
  Troye de Valois, one of the king's own élite guard, has long lived in her
  heart and dreams. Dreams that are shattered when he reveals his anger
  at their forced marriage and the emotions Eleanor is reawakening in
  him....
  *Drama and passion collide in this stirring Medieval tale of a forced
  marriage.*

HHCNM0608